Writ of N

D0630453

By

Rick Robinson

Publisher Page
an Imprint of Headline Books, Inc.
Terra Alta, WV

Large Print Edition

Writ of Mandamus

By Rick Robinson

Publisher Page
an imprint of Headline Books, Inc.
P.O. Box 52, Terra Alta, WV 26764
www.PublisherPage.com
www.AuthorRickRobinson.com

Tel/Fax: 800-570-5951
Email: mybook@headlinebooks.com
www.HeadlineBooks.com

CoverDesign by Kevin T. Kelly www.kevintkelly.com
Author Photo by Sheri Besso

ISBN 0-938467-35-9 / ISBN 13 978-0-938467-35-9 Hard Cover
ISBN 0-938467-42-7 / ISBN 13 978-0-938467-42-7 Paperback

Library of Congress Control Number: 2012935059

Robinson, Rick, 1958-
  Writ of Mandamus / by Rick Robinson.
    p. cm.
  ISBN 978-0-929915-96-8
  1. Ireland--Fiction. 2. United States. Congress.--Officials and employees--Fiction. 3. CIA--Fiction 4. Kentucky—Fiction 5. Political fiction.

PRINTED IN THE UNITED STATES OF AMERICA

To Dr. Tom Myers

Vice President of Student Affairs, Eastern Kentucky University who passed away in 2002... on behalf of all the men and women he mentored and inspired during his tenure at EKU.

The turn will come when we entrust the conduct of our affairs to men and women who understand that their first duty as public officials is to divest themselves of the power they have been given.

Barry Goldwater, *The Conscience of a Conservative* (1960)

Keep your friends close, but keep your enemies closer.

Michael Corleone, *The Godfather: Part II* (1974)

Prologue

Jane Kline reveled in the winter drive along the George Washington Parkway from her small townhouse in Old Towne Alexandria. It was one of those rare, early winter mornings where a coastal warming front caused the morning air to be just warm enough to put the top down on her old red Miata convertible, and the wind whipped through her dishwater blond hair whenever she was able to get a break in the stop-and-go DC traffic long enough to inch her speedometer above 20 m.p.h.

Stoic buildings defining the harsh borders of civilization were to her left, but the peaceful Potomac River was to her right. As she drove, Kline looked out at the morning sun trying to cut through the light fog covering the water and let her mind wander. As she shoved the car up into third gear, she saw a lone fly fisherman standing along the shore tossing his line into the river. The barren trees were a perfect frame to the angler who was quietly stalking his prey. The air smelled fresh and moist. She dreamed she was there with the fisherman, but she knew she could not be late for her daily morning briefing with CIA boss, Ellsworth Steele.

It had been several years since Kline left the operative side of the Central Intelligence Agency and joined the policy wing of the Company. Kline jokingly liked to describe herself as being one of the many "desk jockeys," but her past work in the field earned her a reputation for being something much more. Policy analysts with counter-intelligence field experience were hard to come by and, since her arrival at the CIA main office, she had risen quickly in the ranks. In just over three years, she became the deputy director of the Central Intelligence Agency—No. 2 behind Director Steele.

At first, Kline was upset with the move to headquarters. She had been a field operative and she liked working away from Washington. The further she was away from DC, the better she felt she could do her job without interference. Moreover, everyone at the Company knew her heart was in the covert side of the business. So when Ellsworth Steele called her home, she was quite simply pissed. In their first meeting following the move, Steele explained to Kline that, being a political appointee, he needed her as a part of his inner-inner circle. Many political appointees do not comprehend the importance of having career operatives at their side, and the fact Steele understood this eased the pain a bit. Then Kline got to the desk and began to enjoy her work, especially the authority she was able to exert at the Company. She knew the field, and that experience allowed her to influence decisions at the highest levels.

Anyway, Kline quickly realized she came home at the right time. Although she stayed in shape and could outwork most of the new recruits, she knew there was a natural life span to her activities in the field. Running around in a foreign countryside looking for bad guys was, in the end, a young person's job.

President Jack Mocker was gone. The American people had seen through the thin veneer of his political smile and un-elected him a year earlier. His replacement was President Nathan McKinney. An unknown politico four years earlier, Kline considered McKinney as clueless as Mocker had been evil. Unfortunately for her, she could not figure out which attribute was worse for the country. Ellsworth Steele was one of just three appointees McKinney kept from Mocker's administration.

The move to the policy side of the CIA changed Kline's personal life as much as her business life. The desk job offered her some much needed stability. She owned her own home for the first time, and a male, black Labrador retriever named Hoover now accompanied her each morning on her predawn five-mile run.

And Hoover wasn't the only new man in Kline's life. She was now seeing someone on a regular basis. On one of her last assignments in the field, she got to know FBI Agent Leo Argo. On a long flight home from Romania, they had become friends. Shortly thereafter, they had become something more—casual lovers. Their devotion to their jobs kept the relationship from getting really serious. But, occasional casual sex led to real dates and sleepovers. Over time, Leo Argo and Jane Kline became something more than friends with benefits, but something less than committed lovers.

Once past the bottleneck near Arlington National Cemetery, the road opened up and Kline pushed the accelerator of the Miata down a bit harder, weaving in and out of cars as if she was driving a cross-country race for a million-dollar prize. The Miata slowed as she approached the traffic light at the entrance to CIA Headquarters, and she silently cursed when the light turned red before she could make a right onto the access road. The oncoming left-turn lane had the green arrow, and she waved at CIA Director Ellsworth Steele as his black sedan made the turn across the GW Parkway onto the access road into headquarters.

Steele looked over from the back seat of his chauffeured ride and smiled at Kline. She nodded in return, watching somewhat impatiently as the Director's car slowly glided onto the narrow road.

When the large flash of light first ignited the morning sky, Jane Kline's field training instinctively kicked in. She quickly ducked her head onto the passenger seat as a wave of fire, debris, and sound ripped past her car. Shrapnel shattered the windshield of the Miata. The sound waves had a similar effect on Kline's left eardrum.

For a few seconds after the initial reverberations rolled past her car, Kline was too stunned to do anything, or think anything. Then, as her mind cleared, she mumbled to herself, "Holy shit, Steele's under attack."

Kline ignored the pain in her ear as her blood began to race. Adrenalin shot through her body as she reached into the glove box. She pushed aside an R.E.M. CD and she grabbed her revolver. When she realized the engine of the Miata was still running, Kline turned off the starter and raised herself cautiously out of the vehicle. Glancing rapidly in each direction, Kline recognized one of the guys from the IT Department who sat shocked and motionless in the car behind her, his face covered with blood from the shards of glass that flew into his face after his windshield exploded.

Weapon drawn and pointed at the ground, Kline ran forward toward the Director's car, which was rolled onto its side by the explosion. Flames shot out from the engine area and smoke from the explosion rose in a small mushroom plume above the car. She was about twenty-five feet away from the vehicle when the second explosion hit. The man from IT watched as Jane Kline was thrown backward by the blast. Debris flew in all directions. A large piece of metal from the Director's car ripped through her right leg as she flew.

Kline hit the ground and her body did an involuntary backward roll from the momentum, finally landing her on her stomach on the grassy bank running beside the road. As she opened her eyes, she was dizzy and disoriented, but she could see the IT guy in the car behind her own. The second explosion sent a piece of metal through his windshield which was now lodged in his forehead. He had a surprised look on his lifeless face.

Kline tried to lift herself up, but failed. She knew she was badly hurt, however, she was unable to focus her mind long enough to determine where. She tried to slow her rapid breathing as she laid her head down on the grass and closed her eyes.

A lifetime in the field and I am going to die on the lawn of the Company, were Jane Kline's final thoughts before everything went dark.

Five days later Jane Kline opened her eyes again in a private room at Walter Reed Medical Center. The reflection of the fluorescent light on the white ceiling tiles made her squint her eyes. She tried to speak, but something was in her throat. A bandage covered her left ear. There were several people standing around the room talking in low whispers. Some she recognized from the agency, some she did not. Her eyes darted around the sterile room. The light from the window cast menacing shadows across several machines on her left that were beeping out her life status. Fox News was on the television, but as with the whispers from the people in the room, Kline was unable to make out the words being said. Everything sounded muffled. She started to move in quick frantic movements.

"She's awake," said one of the nurses, who immediately moved to the side of the bed. In turn, Kline struggled to get up. "Stay down, honey," instructed the nurse sternly. "You've been in a bad accident."

Inaudible noises came out of the tube taped to Kline's mouth. Confusion was overwhelming her instinct to remain calm. She weakly pulled at the tube in her mouth as she glanced at the wires hooked to her body.

"Please, honey," the nurse repeated, looking at Kline's heart monitor as her pulse and blood pressure increased. "Calm down."

Instead of following the nurse's instructions, Jane Kline's actions became more deliberate. Her face tightened as her eyes moved wildly about the room. People were closing in around her. She pulled at a wire attached to her chest. The nurse called for a doctor by pushing a button on the remote attached to Kline's bed and then started shooing people away with her hands. "Everyone please leave the room. We're going to need to sedate Ms. Kline."

While she continued to struggle, Kline heard a calming familiar voice. Even though the voice sounded muffled in her ears, she recognized it enough to focus on it as a lifeline. "Jane, calm down. It's me. It's Leo." Leo Argo positioned his burly Cuban-American frame so Kline could see him hovering over her right side. He put his hand on her shoulder, grabbed her hand and leaned forward so he could whisper in her ear. "You need to calm down. Okay? Otherwise, they're going to shoot you full of drugs. Trust me. You don't want that right now. Calm down. Okay?"

Eyes anchored to Argo's, Kline nodded as her mind struggled to swim through the foggy layers of drugs to a clearer reality. Unable to speak because of the tube taped to her mouth, she looked wide-eyed at Argo and tried to calm her heavy breathing. The sanitary smell of the hospital suddenly sunk into her nose and she knew where she was. The beeps from the medical equipment around her seemed to intensify as she focused on Argo's eyes. She did not have to speak. Argo knew what Kline was asking.

"You've been here for a few days—almost a week, I think. They've had you in a drug-induced coma. There was a bad accident and you were in the middle of it. You've got a concussion and a serious injury to your leg. Understand?"

Closing her eyes, she nodded again. Kline took a deep breath to steady her breathing and glanced down her body at the empty space where her leg used to be. Her eyes shot back to Leo's, wide and wild.

"Yeah," said Argo, his grip tightening on her shoulders. "There was an explosion and it tore through your leg pretty badly. They had to amputate it, Jane, just below the knee." Jane closed her eyes in silent acknowledgement of the grim news.

The doctor walked in with a nurse who was carrying a sedative-filled syringe as Kline raised her eyes upwards, fighting back tears. Argo looked up and waved the doctor and nurse off. "She's fine now, Doc." The doctor looked at Kline, whose eyes shifted towards him bleakly. Nodding was her primary mode of communication, so she did so at the doctor. He moved back while Argo leaned back down even closer. "Jane, do you remember anything that happened?"

Frowning, Kline struggled to remember. She remembered driving down the parkway and seeing a guy fly fishing, but nothing afterwards. She shook her head no to Argo.

"We need to get the breathing tube out," the doctor said, hinting that Argo should relinquish his position.

"Just a minute, Doc," Argo replied, holding his finger up to indicate that he needed some time first. "I need to talk with her before you do anything."

The doctor stepped back.

Argo knew from Kline's blank look she had no recollection of the explosion. He stayed close to her ear so no one else could hear. "Listen up, babe. This is real important. There was an attempt on Steele's life. A real professional hit. Someone blew up his car at the entrance to the agency. You had the misfortune of being in the wrong place at the wrong time."

Kline shifted her eyes around the room at the other men and women looking at her as Argo continued to speak softly in her ear. He put his hand on Kline's arm. "Steele is dead." Her eyes shot to Leo's and she stiffened under his grip. "These are your bodyguards, Jane. As Steele's top deputy, you are now the acting interim Director of the Central Intelligence Agency."

ONE

"Hey, everybody," Jordan Hehman greeted the group of lawyers and title examiners. The young attorney was clearly excited as he burst into the real estate record room of the county courthouse. His brown eyes danced with anticipation under his shaggy blond hair. "The old man's trying a case upstairs. They're getting ready for closing arguments."

Another young lawyer, Tyler Wallace, squinted at the computer the title examiners use to search real estate records online. "No shit," he replied, looking up from the computer screen at Hehman, adjusting his eyes as he spoke. "The old man's here today? What's he wearing?"

"You'll love it, Tyler," Hehman snorted with laughter. "He's wearing a black, pin-striped suit, red power tie, and fuzzy pink slippers."

"Beautiful," replied Wallace, wiping his hand through his tight-cropped red hair as he spoke. "Absolutely, fucking beautiful." The strapping young man was beaming with excitement at the prospect of seeing Sean Sullivan in front of a jury. Sullivan was a courthouse celebrity. A big, old ruddy-cheeked Irishman, with long white hair and beard, Sullivan was part brilliant trial attorney and part nutty old man. Which side of the brain he used on any given day was always up in the air. His antics in front of a jury were legendary.

"Laundromat client or random perp?" Wallace knew that Sullivan ran his law practice out of a store-front laundromat in the roughest section of town. When he ran short of clients, he would simply hang out in the courtrooms and randomly pick out indigent-looking locals whom he would offer to represent for free.

"Soap and Suds Special," Hehman shot back, laughing at his own witty title for one of Sullivan's clients from the laundromat.

A buzz began around those assembled. Even the "dirt lawyers" who hung out in the real estate record room got excited upon hearing Sullivan was going to be arguing in front of a jury.

"Felony or misdemeanor?" Wallace continued his lively interrogation. Viewing a trial orchestrated by the legendary Sean Sullivan was starting to get his blood racing.

"Felony possession and it's a state third-strike charge. The defendant is a young black kid from the projects who's looking at serious time." Hehman clapped his hands in quick succession making believe everyone was not already looking at him. "Who's with me?"

Wallace was not going to miss the show. "I'm out of here," he said as he started tossing his personal belongings into a blue cloth, soft-shell briefcase.

The real estate record room of the courthouse is a dirty place occupied by lawyers and title examiners who can withstand the onslaught of dust that fills the air from the opening and closing of old books that contain the deeds and mortgages of the county residents. Those who survive the allergic conditions spend their days plodding through the computer indexes, yellowing books, and equally antiquated microfiche to insure their clients have proper titles to the soil their homes and businesses sit upon. Lawyers who spend their working days within the confines of the drab walls of the real estate record room are not normally accustomed to the excitement and flash of a trial.

"I'm sure as hell not going to pass up the chance to see Sullivan in action," Wallace declared, "This is going to be great." He looked around the grimy shelves of the record room. Several of the lawyers looked up and with shrugs indicated their willingness to join their counterparts in the courtroom upstairs. They, too, started packing their belongings.

"Come on, gang," Wallace continued to plead. "If he's anything like Tiana has described, we're in for a treat."

All eyes suddenly focused on the pretty, light-skinned African-American woman sitting near the back of the room.

"You little boys need to leave the old guy alone," warned Tiana Bolton, her voice tightening as she spoke. "He wears the slippers because he has diabetes. His feet hurt when he stands up too long."

Until she had been forced into the conversation by Wallace, Tiana tried to avoid everyone in the room. She did not want to be a part of the conversation, but Wallace calling her out forced her hand. She could feel her skin starting to heat up under the thin, black, ribbed sweater that clung to her small 5'8" frame like a second skin. She decided to hit back. "What the hell do you care anyway, Tyler? You're a real estate lawyer. You don't know a courtroom from a bathroom."

"Oooooohhhhh," laughed the other lawyers in the record room. Wallace immediately backed down at the taunts from the others in the room as his face turned almost as red as his hair. He looked down at the floor.

With laughter echoing through the small room, Tiana continued. "And in both instances you can never figure out when to stand up or sit down."

Wallace fell silent. Hehman took over the debate and decided to take another tactic. His voice went soft. "Come on, Tiana," urged Hehman over the continuing laughter. "Go upstairs with us. This is going to be fun."

Tiana was having none of it. "You want me to go upstairs and watch you guys make fun of a man who's twice as smart as you?" she asked. "I don't think so. That's too damn depressing."

"Hey, I know you like the old guy," said Wallace, trying to recover some of the dignity Tiana verbally smacked out of him only moments earlier. Like his colleague, he softened his voice, too. "I respect that. I really do. But they say he's nuts in the courtroom. I've never seen him before and I want to see him in action for myself. Come on. Go with us."

"Who's prosecuting?" asked someone from the other side of the record room who was barely visible behind the stacks of old deed books in front of her.

"The Commonwealth Attorney's taking it on herself," replied Hehman, turning his head in the direction of the hidden voice. "She heard the old man was defending the case, so she took it away from an assistant." Soft words had not worked on Tiana, so Hehman changed gears. He looked directly at Tiana and rubbed his fingers together right in front of her face while smiling. "I've got a ten-spot on the prosecution."

"You're going to bet on a trial?" Tiana exclaimed. Her eyes went cold as she smacked Hehman's fingers away from her face, her other hand on her hip. Hehman pulled his hand back quickly. "You're sick." She pointed her finger for emphasis, before repeating. "You're fucking sick."

"What's wrong, T?" The slap had caused Hehman's eyes to widen, but he continued his taunting. "You talk about the old guy all the time like he's the Clarence Darrow of the inner-city. Do you think he's lost his touch?"

Wallace jumped back in, trying to stir it up further. "Maybe he lost his Depends?" he said snidely.

"Fuck you," said Tiana, gritting her teeth over the laughter of others in the room.

Hehman felt the momentum in the room shift once again and put it all on the table. "What's wrong baybeee," said Hehman. "Are you and the old man going out on a date tonight? Oh, right, you don't want to blow the ten bucks because you'll need it to keep him in Ripple for the evening." He waggled his head back and forth with his mouth hanging open, trying to get Tiana to respond.

Tiana stared at the Hehman and the goofy face he was making at her. If Hehman wanted a bet, she'd give him a bet. "Make it fifty bucks at two-to-one and you're on."

Hehman's mouth snapped shut as he drew back in surprise, his face going blank with shock.

"What's wrong baybeee?" Tiana said, mimicking Hehman's earlier taunt. Now the aggressor, she rubbed her fingers together in front of Hehman's face. "C-note a little strong for your cheap-ass blood?"

"O-k-k-kay," Hehman stammered, nearly whispering while politely moving Tiana's fingers away from his face.

"I didn't hear that?" Tiana asked, raising her cupped hand to her ear.

"I'm in. I'm in." Hehman said, more loudly. "Fifty bucks at two-to-one."

A roar went up from those in the record room who had been following the verbal joust. "Game on!" shouted one of them as the gaggle of buzzing lawyers rushed from the record room to the elevator. Once on the fourth floor, however, they quieted themselves. Even the record room lawyers from downstairs know how to be respectful in the courtroom.

The record room in the county courthouse might have been as dull and boring as the black shoe scuffs on its old linoleum floor, but the floors of the rooms only three stories away were lined with wall-to-wall carpeting, as if to muffle the action and excitement that took place within their walls of gleaming walnut. Portraits of the many judges who served the court at one time or another during the preceding hundred years lined the walls, standing guard over several rows of church-like wooden benches that made up the gallery.

Past the gallery, in front of the low wooden railing that delineates the "bar" between the court and the spectators, is where the real action in a courtroom takes place. In the particular courtroom where Hehman, Wallace, Tiana and their colleagues entered, a podium separated the tables used by the attorneys for the defense and prosecution. The jury box was to the left of the advocates, while the courtroom staff sat to their right. In the front and middle of the courtroom, the central focus of the room, was the bench—the exact spot where the judge would sit dispensing just-above-eye-level justice.

Most of the attorneys from the record room shuffled sideways and single-file into one of the wooden pews at the back of the gallery. Tiana continued to the front row by herself, a couple of feet directly behind the defense table and Sullivan.

"All rise," shouted John Dewey, the uniformed bailiff, as he entered from a door behind the judge's desk. The elderly man was nearly as wrinkled as his tan and brown uniform. Tiana noted the man's age and wondered if he could even lift his gun if an altercation were to arise in the courtroom, let alone wrestle an errant defendant to the ground. "Oaye, Oaye, Kenton County Circuit Court is now in session. All persons having business before this court may now come forward. May God save the Commonwealth and this honorable Court." He sneered at the young attorneys in the gallery with disgusted surprise.

Judge Patricia Summer, an attractive fifty-something woman with salt and pepper hair, entered the courtroom in her black robe and looked around. She looked directly at the Tiana, Wallace, Hehmann, and the crew of lawyers in the gallery as she sat down. "Well, well," she exclaimed, smiling. "I see the young lawyers section of the real estate bar has decided to come up and join us this afternoon for closing arguments." The lawyers smiled toothsome grins as they too sat down. However, none of them dared to say anything in response to the veteran judge. Even within the dusty walls of the real estate record room, Summer's no-nonsense reputation preceded her. "Welcome to my courtroom, ladies and gentlemen," she nodded.

The Commonwealth's Attorney, Darla Andress, sat at the prosecution table with a male assistant attorney at her side. Andress was a young upstart amongst local elected officials. A former college tennis standout, the broad-shouldered, short-haired brunette had been elected to office on a law-and-order platform that played well to the conservative base of voters in the county. Both of the prosecutors wore what most lawyers would describe as their "trial garb"—dark blue suit, white shirt, and power tie.

At the table to the prosecutors' left, closest to the jury box, was the defense. A young African-American male with corn rowed hair sat in the middle chair with his head bowed, as if he were contemplating the very nature of his ill-fitting T-shirt and baggy jeans. An older woman, whom Tiana supposed was the defendant's mother or aunt, sat on one side of the young man in a tasteful blue flowered dress, suitable for a Sunday church service. A flowered, pillbox hat sat on the table in front of her.

On the left side of the defendant sat Sean Sullivan, the man who the crew in the gallery had left their title exams to come and watch in action. At 6'5" and 325 pounds, his white beard hung from a face that beamed pure Irish. What was left of the hair on the top of his head had just a hint of red remaining in it, visible only when the light hit it in a particular way. His residual hair was pulled in a ponytail that ran down his back like the mane on a white stallion. Sullivan was so large that, even sitting, he seemed to dwarf everyone else in the room. He too was wearing his "trial garb," but for Sullivan the dark suit was crumpled and the red tie was stained with coffee. And, of course, he was wearing the fuzzy pink slippers that had become his odd trademark.

"He looks like he slept in that suit," observed Hehman, leaning over to whisper in Wallace's ear with a half-smile on his face.

"He probably did," replied Wallace.

Tiana, overhearing the whispered exchange, turned halfway around in her seat and shushed them both with a laser look that could have cut through the steel bars of a jail cell.

Judge Summer cleared her throat and pounded the gavel. "We are here today for the closing arguments in the case of Commonwealth versus Mason." She looked around the room to confirm everyone was in their places. She then looked to her right at Dewey who seemed to be staring solemnly at nothing in particular. "Mr. Dewey, is the jury back from lunch?"

"They are, Your Honor." Dewey stood as tall as he possibly could at his age.

"Very well. Is the prosecution ready?" asked Summer as she thumbed nonchalantly through a binder of pleadings on her walnut wood topped desk.

"We are, Your Honor," said Andress who stood up in order to address the court properly. After speaking, she promptly sat back down. Her face was set in stern, no-nonsense lines.

"Is the defense ready?"

"We are, uh, Your, uh …," Sullivan paused for dramatic effect. He stood up in a casual fashion and scratched his head. "Well, not quite, I suppose."

"Excuse me, Mr. Sullivan?" asked Judge Summer, leaning forward in her chair in anticipation of Sullivan's next move. She cupped her chin on her right hand. "Why are you not ready for closing arguments?"

"Oh, I am ready your Honor, but I suspect I should give the prosecution one last chance to drop the charges." Sullivan looked as serious as possible as he spoke. He turned and pointed to the prosecution table. "Ms. Andress has a third-strike case that is based in large part on a very questionable search of my client by an over-aggressive police officer, who is no doubt a racial-profiling bigot. She's going to lose and I am going to be forced to bring a federal action for violation of this young man's civil rights."

"This is outlandish," Andress exclaimed as she bolted back up out of her chair. She looked alternatively at Sullivan and the judge, not knowing in which direction to telegraph her rage.

"I am just trying to save the county's taxpayers some money, Your Honor," said Sullivan, who was looking at the floor and shaking his head. He then looked directly at Andress, who had her hands firmly on her hips. "The Commonwealth's Attorney has an election coming up next year. When the jury comes back in my favor, and I win a big verdict against the county, it will look bad on her record. I'm just trying to help her out a bit."

"Your Honor," said Andress, agitation shaking her voice. "This is obviously one of Mr. Sullivan's tactics aimed at trying to get me off my game."

"Sounds like he's doing a good job of it," whispered Tiana to no one in particular.

"Sit down, Ms. Andress," instructed Judge Summer firmly, interlocking her fingers as she spoke. "You, too, Mr. Sullivan. The two of you have been at each other's throats throughout this entire trial. Quite honestly, I'm tired of it. It's closing argument time. Please, let's try to show a little decorum. Keep this tone up and I'll toss both of you in jail for contempt."

"In that case," said Sullivan, "the defense is ready." Sullivan turned and, with his back to the judge and bailiff, looked over at Tiana. He raised his eyebrows in quick succession and twinkled the trademark Irish grin which had made him one of the most likable figures in the courthouse. Sullivan had, in fact, gotten under the prosecutor's skin and was damn proud of it.

"The prosecution is also ready," said the Commonwealth's Attorney, trying to regain her dignity.

"Very well," said Judge Summer, rolling her eyes at the actions of both attorneys. "Mr. Dewey, please lead the jury back into the courtroom."

After the jury was settled in, the Commonwealth's Attorney spoke first. As if nailed to the floor behind the podium provided for the use of the advocates, she stood rigid—a foundation of law and order. Slowly she began outlining the evidence presented at the trial. Her dialogue with the twelve strangers presented a case of robbery, probable cause, arrest, and confession by a young man who had been in trouble all his life. As she detailed it, line-by-line, the case against the young man seemed airtight. Through it all, Sean Sullivan sat shaking his head, occasionally breathing a sigh just loud enough for the jury to hear.

When it came the defense counsel's turn to offer closing arguments, Sullivan did not immediately rise and head to the lectern as the prosecution had done before him. Instead, he quietly sat back in his chair at the defense table and pulled a crisp dollar bill from his pocket. He folded it in half. The jury sat up a little straighter, straining to watch Sullivan play with the dollar bill.

Sullivan's quirky personality played well to juries. "Ladies and gentlemen of the jury," he began. "Thank you for your service today. It is fine folks, like you, who keep our nation free. We all appreciate your commitment to justice and liberty."

The young lawyers assembled in the gallery shuffled in their seats, looking around and wondering what Sullivan was going to do next. Wallace bumped Hehman with his elbow in giddy anticipation.

"Now the prosecution has presented to you a case which appears to condemn this young man to a life in prison," Sullivan said. He unfolded the dollar bill and refolded it lengthwise.

"In fact, if I were you, I'm not sure how I could live with myself if I let this scoundrel walk free. Why, to listen to the Commonwealth's Attorney tell this case, this young man is the greatest scofflaw since old John Dillinger himself. Their case is airtight and was flawlessly presented." Sullivan used the fingernails of his thumb and forefinger to crease the fold in the dollar bill for dramatic effect. The eyes of the jury were fixated as they watched Sullivan fold and refold the dollar bill.

Then in a slow move of magic, Sullivan separated his open palms by about twelve inches. The folded dollar bill seemingly floated in mid-air between his big meaty hands. "But, ladies and gentlemen of the jury, things are not always as they appear."

Outraged, Andress jumped up immediately, placing the palms of her hands on the table to steady herself. "Objection, Your Honor."

The judge pounded her gavel as Sullivan quickly crumpled up the dollar bill and shoved it into his coat pocket. He knew he was about to be lectured by the judge, so he had to look remorseful before the jurors. He looked at the floor and curled his lower lip in the same direction. "Mr. Sullivan, I have warned you before about using magic tricks in this courtroom to make a point. I will not tolerate this conduct again."

Tiana put her hand over her mouth to stifle her giggle. Judge Summer saw the movement, cocked her head and frowned at the young lawyer. Tiana quickly sat up straight at the nonverbal admonition she had just received.

"My sincere apologies, Your Honor," said Sullivan as he stood up and walked to the podium. "I must have forgotten your previous admonition. You may rest assured it will not happen again."

The old Irishman then went into a fifteen-minute methodical rant as brilliant as any argument presented to the Supreme Court, only on a level the lay men and women of the jury could comprehend. You could almost see "reasonable doubt" creeping into their heads as he spoke. Their eyes spoke as loud as Sullivan's booming voice, looking repeatedly at Mason, the young defendant, who sat emotionless. The woman with Mason, however, would catch the glances, make eye contact and gently nod at each juror before they looked away.

When Sullivan finished, the Commonwealth's Attorney and her assistant looked deflated. All sat still as Judge Summer read the jury their instructions and sent them to the jury room for their deliberations.

John Dewey escorted the members of the jury through a door near the judge's bench. A deputy appeared to take the defendant to a holding area. As soon as Judge Summer left the bench to await the verdict from the comfort of her chambers, Sullivan turned his chair to the rail and then leaned towards Tiana. "I expected some of those miscreants to be here for closing arguments," he said in a low voice, pointing at Tiana's colleagues from the record room. "But I thought you stayed away from courtrooms."

"I heard you were closing today," she said, smiling as she came forward through the gate in the railing to talk to the old man. "I thought I would come up and watch."

"Good for you," Sullivan replied, patting her on the arm. "I'll make a trial attorney out of you yet."

Sullivan had been trying to get Tiana to try a case with him since she had graduated from law school. Sullivan took each rejection as a challenge to keep trying. "Not a chance," she replied, shaking her head. "How have you been doing? Are you eating well?"

"I'm doing fine, darlin'," he replied. He took his hand off her arm and moved to sit down sideways on the railing separating the court from the gallery. Sullivan pouted his lips. "And, no, I am not eating well. There is not a single establishment in town which serves their Guinness properly at room temperature. How am I supposed to eat cabbage with an ice-cold Guinness?" he asked in disgust.

Tiana tried to look out for Sullivan's health and his poor diet was always a topic of conversation. "Cabbage and beer," Tiana said, her shoulders slumping in disapproval. "That's exactly what I mean. You don't eat properly. You're probably not taking your diabetes medicine either."

"No, I am not," he replied crossing his arms, his brow furrowed. "The medicine gives me the shits."

Tiana looked around, hoping the other lawyers had not heard the comment. Fortunately, they were all too busy talking among themselves about Sullivan's closing argument, to care about his graphic description of his bathroom habits. Tiana leaned in and whispered a reply. "The beer and the cabbage give you diarrhea, not the diabetes medicine."

"What? Do you expect me to eat like you? Look at you. You're as skinny as a rail." Sullivan laughed loudly as he poked at her belly for emphasis. She pulled her body away like a baby being tickled. "I can count all your ribs through that skimpy sweater."

"I work out four times a week."

"My point exactly." Sullivan threw his hands in the air. "You could use a few extra calories with all that silly running you do. Come with me to the Pub tonight for dinner. I'll buy."

Tiana rolled her eyes at the old man. "This isn't a trial. Quit being so damn melodramatic. We'll have dinner, but not tonight. I have a date."

Sullivan gave her a dubious look. He cocked his head sideways and slyly grinned. He knew she was lying. "Very well, we'll stick with our regular Monday night dinner at Chez Nora."

"Good," Tiana replied. She lowered her voice as she glanced around the courtroom to see if their conversation was still private. "Have you made a decision?"

"Yes, I have," Sullivan said with a determined smile. He placed his hand on Tiana's arm. "And I have decided to do it."

Tiana winced. It was not the answer she wanted to hear. It was obvious to Sullivan when she pulled away from him. "I really wish you wouldn't."

"Why? What's wrong?" Sullivan asked, reaching for her.

"It will put you on the front page." There was distress clearly evident in Tiana's voice and eyes.

"And you are afraid people will make fun of me."

"No, not really," she shrugged.

"Are you afraid they will make fun of you?" he asked gently, patting her arm.

"Absolutely not." Tiana jerked back at the sting of having Sullivan think she might be opposed to his plans out of any selfish consideration of how it might indirectly impact her.

"Then what is it?" Sullivan scratched his head. "Why don't you want me to do it?"

"Because you have no chance of winning," said Tiana. She looked him squarely in the eye and spoke in a tone was low enough so no one but the old man would hear her. "There is no way on earth you can beat Richard Thompson in an election for the United States Congress. It's futile."

Sullivan's face broke out into a wide grin as he leaned backwards. "You are operating under the assumption I am doing this to win."

Tiana frowned. "You're losing me now," she said.

"I am not doing it to win," Sullivan explained, shaking his head for emphasis. "I have absolutely no expectation whatsoever of victory."

Tiana was truly confused at why the old man wanted to run a race for public office when he knew he was destined to lose. "Then why do it?" The exasperation was clear in her voice.

"I used to like Richard Thompson," said Sullivan. "I didn't agree with him on much, but when he was first elected he was principled. He used to come down to Chez Nora all the time for dinner and eat pork chops. I'd talk to him at the bar. He had some core beliefs back then, and he stuck by them come hell or high water."

"And…"

"He's fallen victim to Washington. He's become one of *them*." Sullivan's lips curled in disgust.

"And who is *them*?"

"*Them, them*," said Sullivan sternly, pointing at some imaginary demon as he spoke, his eyes focused. "The lyin' rat bastards who say one thing to get elected and then go off to Washington knowing we aren't paying attention. They go up there and they do anything they have to in order to belong to their little club. They'd sell their mother's soul to the devil himself to get something as insignificant as a ride on Air Force One with the President."

Sullivan had a way of getting fired up when he spoke on a topic on which he was passionate. It was one of the traits that made him good with a jury, but sometimes abrasive with people. Tiana rolled her eyes. "Whoa, this isn't a closing argument." Tiana cast a furtive glance around the room to make sure no one was eavesdropping on their conversation.

Sullivan knew now wasn't the time to continue with his diatribe, so he lowered his voice again. He stood up straight and his face softened. "Ah my dear, but it is a closing argument and Richard Thompson is my solo juror. Somewhere he lost his way. I don't know what he stands for anymore. And I bet he doesn't either."

"That's not exactly a real strong campaign platform."

"I don't mean it to be. He's become so politically strong in the district nobody else will run. The party, God bless 'em, can't even find anyone who is willing to appear on the ballot against him. But, no one is entitled to that office, girlie. It's up to me to remind him of that. It's up to me to remind him of who he is and why he ran in the first place."

"And just how are you going to do that?"

"I can't give up my campaign secrets." Sullivan's eyes twinkled and he silently danced a little Irish jig in his pink slippers. "I have a plan," he sing-songed with an exaggerated Irish brogue.

"Well, I just wish you'd reconsider."

"That's not going to happen, sweetie." Sullivan tapped his big index finger on Tiana's forehead with each word. Tiana swatted his hand away. "Come on. Jump on my old Irish bandwagon. It'll be fun," he said laughingly.

"You have a weird way of having fun," Tiana said, shaking her head in disapproval.

"My life is as blessed as those of the Irish saints."

Tiana huffed. "You always tell me the Irish saints were all drunks."

"Yeah, don't you love 'em?" Sullivan opened up his suit coat to show Tiana a small flask he was hiding in his inside breast suit pocket. He made his eyebrows dance up and down a couple of times. "I'm saving this for the jury verdict."

"For winning or losing?" Tiana asked laughingly.

"Does it matter?" Sullivan smiled. "Good whiskey can either be used as a toast to victory or a way to make defeat palatable. I'm ready for either."

It seemed as if the jury had been out of the courtroom barely long enough to elect a foreman when the bailiff told everyone to return to their places. Judge Summer herself was zipping up her black judicial robe as she reentered the courtroom from her chambers. The defendant was brought back in, and the attorneys for the prosecution and defense returned to their respective tables. The lawyers from the real estate record room all moved quickly back to their seats.

As quiet descended on the courtroom, Judge Summer nodded to John Dewey. With an exaggerated gravity, he turned and opened the door to let the jurors back into the jury box. When they were seated, the judge asked: "Has the jury reached a verdict?"

"We have, Your Honor," said the tall, lanky foreman in a button-down shirt with the sleeves rolled up. He handed a piece of paper to Dewey. Without reading it, the old bailiff walked over to the bench and handed the slip to the judge. Judge Summer looked at it and then asked the defendant to rise and face the jury. Sullivan and the woman who was there in support of the defendant immediately stood. The young defendant himself needed a little verbal prodding from the woman, who was more than a bit agitated at having to do so.

Judge Summer's face indicated she, too, was not at all happy at the young man's lack of respect for the court. She looked at Dewey who shrugged his shoulders. When all three at the defense table were finally properly standing, Judge Summer asked: "Ladies and gentlemen of the jury, what is your verdict?"

"In the case of Commonwealth versus Mason, we the people find the defendant Antwone Mason … not guilty on all counts."

As Judge Summer dismissed the jury, the defendant stood emotionless while the woman, dressed in her Sunday best, thrust her hands in the air. "Have mercy," she exclaimed. "Lord have mercy." Trembling with excitement, she hugged Sullivan repeatedly as the jurors filed out of the courtroom. "Thank you. Thank you for saving my boy," the woman said to the jurors as they exited. She hugged Sullivan again.

Sullivan returned the final hug with a genuine show of affection. He turned and put his giant paw on the young man's forehead. "Now, go forth and sin no more," he instructed and slapped Mason on his head for emphasis.

The kid's eyes narrowed on Sullivan. "I'll see you around," he mumbled before being led from the room by the woman who was still nearly hyperventilating with joy.

Once Judge Summer had left the chambers, the young lawyers in the gallery began to talk more audibly among themselves, sharing their opinions freely on the generous verdict. Jordan Hehman walked up to the front of the courtroom with a stony expression on his face, stopped at the front row of benches, and slapped four twenty and two ten-dollar bills on the seat of the bench before briskly turning and walking out the door.

Sullivan saw Tiana pick up the cash and walked to the rail. "What in the name of St. Patrick was that all about?" he asked.

Tiana was embarrassed Sullivan had caught her taking the money. "Nothing," she replied, averting her eyes from the white-haired giant.

"Don't try to outwit an old mick," Sullivan mocked. He pointed his finger at the pocket where Tiana had stuffed the money. "Did you have a wager on the outcome of my trial?"

Tiana knew she was busted. "A little one," she replied, smiling sheepishly at the floor.

"How little?"

"Fifty bucks," Tiana said. She looked over at Hehman leaving the courtroom and was now nearly laughing as she spoke. "But I got two-to-one odds." She glanced back at Sullivan who was smiling with approval.

"You should have held out for better odds."

"You're too much of a sure thing." Tiana leaned over the rail and gave the large Irishman a big congratulatory hug.

Sullivan reached into his pocket and pulled out a wad of bills held together with a thick rubber band. He peeled off a couple of fifties and stuffed them into Tiana's front jeans pocket. "Here," he said. "This makes up for the odds you should have gotten on that bet."

Their eyes met and both smiled. Sullivan leaned forward and hugged her again. "I'm proud of you," he whispered in her ear. "And tell your mother I said hello."

"I will," Tiana replied in a similar low whisper. "I love you, Daddy. I'll see you Monday night."

TWO

Congressman Richard Thompson sat in the front seat of his dark grey Chevrolet four-door pick-up truck waiting for the top-of-the-hour morning news. The parking lot outside his office in Kentucky's Fourth Congressional District was full, but that was not a worry for a Member of Congress with a reserved parking space. Just as he pulled into the parking lot, he heard a short tickler update on the radio about Interim CIA Director Jane Kline returning to work following a lengthy medical leave of absence for injuries she sustained during the assassination of her predecessor, Ellsworth Steele. Thompson decided to sit through the incessant chatter from several talk radio callers so he could hear the actual news story about Kline.

Thompson had met Jane Kline while in Romania. A field operative at the time, Kline was sent to Romania to effect the safe return of Josh Barkman, one of Thompson's staffers who had been kidnapped by Communist rebels living in the Carpathian Mountains. In the process, events had gone awry, and Thompson ended up saving Kline's life by shooting one of the rebels who captured her.

As Thompson sat in the truck, he fidgeted in his seat. Out of nothing more than nervous energy, he reached up and adjusted the rearview mirror, inadvertently catching his own reflection in the process. The sight on the narrow glass caused Thompson to pause. His once sandy brown hair now seemed to have a lot of gray in it, and dark rings encircled his eyes. He pulled at his cheeks and then gently brushed the ends of his fingers through the hair on his temples.

"Damn," he exclaimed to himself. "I look like shit." He shifted his head from side to side surveying the damage the aging process caused to his hair color. "Fuck me." He put his fingers deeper into his hair and held up the strands to look at them in the rearview mirror. "Maybe Ann is right. Maybe I should color my hair."

A rap on the driver's side window jolted him back to reality. Thompson's field representative, Ashley Hampton, was staring at him through the window as he primped his hair. Hampton was used to seeing her boss sit in the parking lot listening to the radio. Thompson had a love for music and a quirky ability to remember lyrics. No day seemed complete without a Thompson reference to some song by Warren Zevon, John Prine or Meat Loaf.

As Thompson rolled down the window, it was obvious Hampton was proud at having surprised Thompson in his car. A cold blast of winter air came in through the open window. "Good morning, boss," she said, smiling. "Are you okay?"

"Yeah," said Thompson, embarrassed one of his staff caught him looking in the mirror and talking to himself. "There's a story coming on the radio about Director Kline returning to work at the CIA today. I just wanted to hear it before I came in."

"Good deal," replied Hampton, tapping her knuckles twice on the truck door. "Don't forget you have a conference call with Griff in about five minutes. We need to start working on your re-elect."

"I'll be in by then," Thompson muttered. "They said on the tickler it was the lead story."

"Got it. And Congressman ..." Hampton leaned closer to the window.

"Yeah."

"I think the gray on your temples makes you look distinguished," she said smartly as she turned and sashayed back towards the office.

"Thanks," Thompson blushed as he rolled up his truck window, "I'll keep that in mind." He turned up the radio as a commercial ended. As promised, the story on Jane Kline was first up.

"Interim Director of the Central Intelligence Agency Jane Kline returned to work today to cheers from coworkers who lined the lobby of CIA headquarters to welcome her back. Kline was seriously injured in the explosion that took the life of CIA Director Ellsworth Steele. Kline's right leg was amputated just below the knee from injuries she sustained in the explosion. She also suffered a severe hearing loss. With the help of a cane, she steadied herself on her new prosthetic leg as she addressed the crowd."

"I want to sincerely thank everyone today for coming out and greeting me," Thompson smiled as he heard Kline's voice on the radio. "The thoughts and prayers you have given me while I've been recovering have been overwhelming. More importantly, thanks for setting up a schedule of dog walks for Hoover while I was in the hospital. He appreciates all of his new friends." Thompson heard laughter in the background. "Finally, a special thanks to President McKinney not only for this antique cane, which was once owned by Secretary of the Treasury John G. Carlisle, but for placing my name into nomination for director. His faith and trust in me helped speed me toward my quick recovery. And, now as the Interim Director … everybody back to work." Again, there was laughter and applause in the background.

The news anchor continued in his no-nonsense voice. "The Senate confirmation hearing for Jane Kline will take place in about a month. However, because of the circumstances under which she was nominated, it is anticipated that her nomination will be approved without serious opposition. In local news, three fire departments responded to a house fire in the seven hundred block…"

Thompson turned off the radio. "You go, Jane," he said as he exited the car. "You go."

As the door slammed shut, Thompson looked at his reflection in the side-view mirror. He tilted his head from side to side. "Meat Loaf was right," he said awkwardly to himself. "Objects in the rearview mirror may appear closer than they are." Thompson just shook his head and walked toward his office.

"Good morning, boss," chirped the red haired receptionist as Thompson entered the lobby of his district field office. "Ashley is back at your desk trying to set up the conference call with Mr. Griffith."

Although separated by distance, from the time Michael Griffith and Richard Thompson roomed together at the Phi Delta Theta house at Eastern Kentucky University, Griffith had been the political yin to Thompson's policy yang. A bald-headed Southerner who annually grew a beard at election time, Griffith looked more like an aging mixed-martial arts cage fighter than a successful DC political consultant. Griffith's recent marriage to a flight attendant he met on the same trip to Romania where Thompson met Kline, seemed to have cooled his legendary angry demeanor a bit. A column in *The Washington Times* recently opined Griffith lost a political step or two along with his sharp tongue and somehow, every so often, he could now suffer fools wisely.

"Thanks, Sheri," replied Thompson. As he made his way down the hallway to his office, he could hear

Hampton talking to Griffith on the phone.

"I don't give a damn if he thinks he doesn't have a race," Griffith's voice resonated through the speaker phone. "This is a funky election year. Voters could turn on him in a heartbeat. We need to be ready."

"I agree," Hampton said. "But right now I think he's more interested in his trip to Dublin with Ann than he is in his re-election bid."

Thompson was not looking forward to this call and hearing Griffith's voice as he walked down the hall wasn't helping his mood. "Talking about me behind my back?" Thompson asked as he entered his spacious personal office. He tossed his briefcase nonchalantly on the black leather couch.

"Not about anything I wouldn't say to your face," came the voice over the speaker phone. "Hey boy, how's Ann?"

"She's great, man," replied Thompson nonchalantly. He moved to his desk and typed his log in into his computer, cocking his head to send his voice in the direction of the speaker phone. "She's still talking about your wedding."

"Yeah?" Griffith asked in a pleased tone.

The home screen came up on the computer. Thompson knew Griffith well enough to speak freely to him as he worked at his desk. "Yeah. And I ain't real happy about being constantly reminded you had a wedding on a beach in Hawaii and we didn't."

"I introduced you two," snorted Griffith. "It wasn't up to me to plan your wedding. I can't help it if you have no imagination or class."

"Bite me."

"I can't. You're a congressman now. I think that's a federal crime," Griffith replied, laughing as he spoke.

Thompson chuckled at Griffith's quick retort. "So what were you two talking about when I came in?" he asked.

Hampton looked over at Thompson and tried to summarize the discussion they were having prior to his arrival. "The filing deadline is coming up," she said. "Griff thinks we aren't ready."

"You're not ready," Griffith huffed over the phone line.

Thompson imagined the wrinkled forehead of Griffith reddening as he spoke. "Come on, Griff," replied Thompson. "There's nothing to be ready for. After the campaign you put together in our last re-elect, there isn't a viable candidate in the District who wants a piece of us. If anybody files—which is questionable at this point—it will be a kook or a fringe candidate."

"And in an election year, you're going on a vacation to Ireland with Ann," Griffith abruptly cut in.

Thompson rolled his eyes. He argued with Griffith over this issue only days earlier. "It's not a vacation. They call it 'holiday' in Europe. Anyway, it's a foreign exchange trip with the Irish Parliament Josh set up for me." Thompson was referring to Josh Barkman, his former chief of staff who had become the Romanian Embassy's Charge d'affaire following their trip to that country. Thompson and Griffith introduced Josh into politics and they followed his career with the pride of parents. When he changed jobs less than a year earlier to become the Congressional liaison for NATO, Thompson wrote his reference letter.

"Save it for the television response, pal," Griffith barked. "It's a freakin' vacation. You know it and I know it. And I can't imagine that you'll get a free pass in your re-elect either."

"I think we just might." Thompson got up from the desk and sat down on the edge of the conference table.

"What about that old Irish lawyer down in Covington?" asked Griffith. "Ashley tells me he's going to file."

Thompson scowled at Hampton for passing along the information about Sullivan's potential candidacy to Griffith. "He's nothing, Griff. He's a classic fringe kook. Hell, all the party bosses on the other side are trying to talk him out of it. They're afraid his candidacy will cause you to put together a campaign that will drive up our turnout in a couple of other races they think they can win."

"But he's gonna file, isn't he?" Griffith persisted.

"Who cares?" shouted Thompson, throwing his hands in the air. He hopped off the table and marched around the room.

"I do," Griffith shouted back. "And you should too, damn it."

"Why? This will be one of those races where you tell me to leave town for the last two weeks so I don't screw it up."

"Do I have to recite the Godfather Rules to you?" asked Griffith, referring to the rules he put together over the years of campaign consulting, each of which had their origins in the trilogy of *Godfather* movies. Griffith believed that, had the Corleone Family not been in the olive oil business, they could have been top-notch political consultants. He regularly used references to the book and movies to explain political strategy to candidates. "Remember Luca Brasi got whacked because he didn't see it coming. He didn't see it coming."

"Well this old guy in Covington ain't no Solatzo," scoffed Thompson.

"He's a potential enemy and that's all you need to care about."

"He wears fuzzy pink slippers to court," Thompson replied, ignoring Griffith's sarcastic tone.

"I don't care if he wears ..." Griffith paused. "What? Really? He wears fuzzy pink slippers?"

"Pink fuzzies," said Thompson. There was a long pause as Griffith took in what he just heard.

"Well, anyway, poll numbers suck out there right now," said Griffith. "People are anti-incumbent and want to throw all you bums out. You could get caught up in that mood and lose ... even to an old coot who wears fuzzy pink slippers to court."

"So, I assume you want to run this like a real campaign?" Thompson sighed as he sat back down at his desk.

"Absolutely," replied Griffith. "Fundraising, opposition research, parades, direct mail—the whole ball of wax."

"Shit." Thompson put his elbows on his desk and laid his head on his hands.

"And I want The Fat Man doing some opposition research on this guy. Where is he today anyway? I thought he was supposed to be on the call."

The Fat Man to whom Griffith was referring was Joe Bradley, Thompson's former law partner who was so named for his large figure. A hard-assed trial lawyer, The Fat Man became interested in campaigns when Thompson first entered the political fray. He caught on quickly and earned the respect of Griffith.

"Joey's working on a presentation he's doing for the Kentucky Equine Law Seminar," replied Thompson.

"Horsey law?" Griffith said, laughing.

"Yeah," replied Thompson. "The Fat Man is one of the state's experts on equine law. And in a state like Kentucky, there actually are quite a few lawyers who give a damn about horses. He teaches a continuing legal education class every year following the spring sale. He's been spending a lot of time getting ready for it. By the way, we may have to quit calling him The Fat Man. He's still losing weight."

"What's the number now?"

"Down 87 pounds."

"I gotta give it to him," said Griffith. "I never thought he'd stick with it."

"The heart thing gave him a helluva scare," interjected Hampton. "He was in here the other day. He's looking good."

"Speaking of sticking with it," Thompson said, "are you still off cigarettes?"

"Yup," said Griffith. "I've gone 67 days without a smoke."

"Not that you're counting," laughed Hampton.

"Baby. If I chew one more stick of nicotine gum, I may kill somebody."

"Sue told Ann you've picked up a little weight," Thompson said, leaning back in his chair as he spoke.

"Well, hell yeah. I chain-smoked since college. You know that. I've never reviewed poll numbers without tobacco in my hand. Now, I'm chewing nicotine gum and eating Ho-Hos by the box. I'm up to 210."

"Did you know The Fat Man is down to 238 pounds?" Thompson smiled to himself.

"Damn," Griffith replied quietly.

"I'll let you know when you pass him," said Thompson gleefully.

"Well, whoever gets labeled fat or skinny, I need Joey to get to work on this Sullivan guy. I want to know everything about him. I want a review of every case he's ever filed. What does he own? Who are his clients?"

"Come on, Griff," pleaded Thompson, as he sat back up at attention. "You can't be serious about all this shit."

"As serious as Michael Corleone was about offing his own brother."

Thompson slumped down in his chair. "I'm the one dying here. You're killing me, Griff."

THREE

Alligator Alley connects the east and west portions of lower Florida with a straight shot of concrete and blacktop jutting out of a briny swamp. Before the Florida Everglades became a national park, side roads off the Alley led to Seminole Indian reservations and an occasional small, ill-developed residential subdivision. When the government bought the land for preservation, they razed the houses. The roads were left in place to deteriorate in the harsh Florida weather. A driver has to look hard to find the remnants of these old side roads, but they are there.

The man who requested the summit drove down Alligator Alley, careful not to exceed the speed limit. The old side roads were perfect places for Florida Highway Patrol and Park Police to hide and set up speed traps. He did not need the complication of law enforcement at this point in time. The sun was nearly setting and it cast an orange glow across the green mix of mangroves and water. He picked out the old road several days in advance of the meeting, and he knew exactly where to turn. Still, he wanted to be there hours early to ensure the location was secure.

Once he was at the site, he drove his rental SUV to a small opening—probably an old driveway—which was hidden behind some brush. As the sun set and complete darkness fell on the Glades, he tried to wrap his brain around the horrifically bad turn of events that brought him to this desolate piece of land.

Zafer Javeed never really liked the darkness. Growing up in Iran during the Islamic Revolution, he associated the night with the sounds of a city torn apart by violence and turmoil. Gunshots that had awakened him from his childhood sleep were now frequently replayed in adult nightmares. The chill of fear and nausea at the moment of awakening was always the same. Except now the reality to which he adjusted every morning was different. Nevertheless, the darkness and the sounds of the swamp on this particular night were giving Zafer a creepy feeling causing the hair to stand up on his forearms.

Slowly, the demons of a childhood past were exorcised by Zafer's concerns for his current circumstance. Over the past several days, he scoped out several of these old drives, and this was the one that worked best for the job that lay ahead. Whatever body parts that were not devoured by alligators would simply sink in waters where living humans never wandered. An automobile could be easily ditched in a canal and never found.

Zafer ruefully shook his head, knowing his own bad judgment was responsible for him being here— sweating miserably in a swamp in southern Florida. He should have never dealt with an amateur. He should have followed his initial instincts. Still, at the time, it all seemed so foolproof. Unfortunately, the time had come to end the relationship.

The situation was being worsened by the fact Zafer's back-up plan was in jeopardy by yet another unanticipated circumstance. He found a secondary source for the supplies his business partners coveted and those parts were small enough to be laundered through existing shipping channels. Now, as they were getting ready to move the parts, a computer hard drive documenting the illegal transactions had gone missing. The lawyer in Kentucky who possessed the hard drive would not normally have given Zafer much pause. Yet, because it could uncover Zafer's entire operation, he feared the information on that hard drive as much as the darkness of the Everglades.

As Zafer sat in his vehicle contemplating the troubles plaguing him, the sounds of the Everglades and the blackness of the night began to play games with Zafer's mind. He thought he saw movement where there was none. The more he sat, the more convinced he was that vicious beasts surrounded his vehicle. Still, he sat for hours—watching and waiting. When the headlights appeared on the road, Zafer looked at his watch. It was a good sign the man was fifteen minutes early. People who were wired by the authorities tended to be right on time.

Before the driver of the approaching vehicle was close enough to hear the door open, Zafer exited his SUV. The newly arrived sedan pulled to the side of the road and the lights shut down. The driver of the other vehicle exited, walked toward the front of the car and leaned back on the hood. He lit a cigarette and nervously puffed away, his head snapping from side to side following the sounds of the night.

The tiny red glow of the cigarette acted as a beacon for Zafer as he walked slowly toward the dim light. As he walked, his finger moved nervously along the edge of the trigger on his FN Five-seveN pistol. Zafer got to within 20 yards of the car before the man heard his approach.

"Jesus, Zafer," he said in a Florida cracker accent. "Is that you? You scared the living shit out of me."

Quickening his pace, Zafer approached and raised his gun. He fired a single shot shattering the man's right knee. The man fell to the ground and screamed out in pain. "That is a greeting from my bosses," Zafer snarled. "They do not like the situation you have placed them in."

The man writhed around on the ground in pain, holding his knee as he rolled from side-to-side. "Motherfucker," the man shouted. "You were supposed to be bringing me money for a lawyer, you God damn motherfucker."

"I have your money," Zafer sneered, as he knelt about four feet from the man. He swatted a mosquito from his neck. "But first, we need to know what you told the prosecutors."

"Nothing," the man said. "I told you before, not a God damn thing." The man was now sobbing between his curse words. "I didn't tell them a fucking thing."

Zafer shook his head and laughed. He quickly raised the gun and shot the man in the foot of the leg not wounded. The shot echoed in the darkness as the man screamed out again. "Sorry, I do not believe you."

"Motherfucker, you cocksucker," the man screamed. "You're fucking nuts."

"I am also excellent at picking out a liar," he said and pointed the gun at the man's crotch. "Now, you can either tell me the truth or I can shoot you in the testicles. I am remarkably accurate with this weapon." When the man only continued to cry and curse, Zafer made an indifferent nod with his head. "Very well," he said as he leveled his gun at the man's crotch.

"No, no … okay, okay," the man yelled, holding his hand up to stop Zafer from firing another round. "I told them a little bit, not much," he panted out between sobs.

Zafer smiled and lowered his gun. "And what do you consider 'not much'?" Zafer asked coolly.

"I didn't tell them any names, I swear. I swear to God I didn't give you up." The man stuttered and continued to sob as he spoke.

"That is what you did not tell them," Zafer replied. Zafer raised the gun and waggled it back and forth in the direction of the man's face. "I need you to tell me what you did say." He slowly moved the aim of the pistol around the man's body as he spoke. "Now, be honest," Zafer said.

"Oh God … I told them … I told them a foreign man approached me … Jesus Christ … to buy the F-14 parts," he spoke haltingly between breaths. "Just like you said, I told them I wasn't even sure of the name. I told them he spoke like he was Indian."

"Really?" Zafer cocked his head.

"I swear," the man cried. "I swear I did."

"Very good," Zafer nodded. He stood up. "I believe you. I am sorry for the tactics, but my people had to know before we could complete our deal."

The man relaxed slightly, his sobs quieting down to low moans. As Zafer started to walk away he paused for a moment and turned. "One more thing," he said as he walked back to the man.

The man started to scream again as Zafer stepped back, raised the gun and shot two quick rounds into his head. The fact the body shook violently on the ground only served to piss Zafer off further. He walked over to the body and fired two more rounds.

"Shut the fuck up," Zafer mumbled. It was going to be a long night.

FOUR

WELCOME BACK DIRECTOR KLINE!!!

The words on the electronic smart-board against the south wall of the conference room startled Jane Kline as she hobbled into a meeting of the top brass at the Central Intelligence Agency. Kline went to the head of the large mahogany conference table and smiled as the twenty or so men and women stood and applauded her successful return. As she balanced herself on her cane, she noticed the eyes of several of the older agency veterans were a bit moist.

Kline herself was fighting back tears, but they were not generated by emotions. The pain in her lower back was excruciating. *Breathe deep*, she thought to herself as she clenched her teeth to hide the pain. *Don't let them know you're hurting.* Kline pulled out the black leather chair and sat down. She closed her eyes briefly. The change in position offered some much needed relief to her back.

As she adjusted herself in her chair, she looked around the windowless but well-lit room. Her new chief deputy, Zach MacKenzie, a round-faced and 50-ish CIA policy veteran, sat to her right. Well-versed in the inner workings of the organization, MacKenzie handled all things administrative at the Company for years. Kline's first order was to put him in charge of the morning briefings.

"Good morning," Kline said. She motioned with her hands for everyone to sit. "Please everyone, sit down."

When everyone was settled, Kline looked around the table. "This agency is not a stranger to the heartache of losing our colleagues. Since our establishment in the '40s, uncounted, nameless patriots have made the ultimate sacrifice for the Company and our mission." Kline looked up at the faces around the table. "However, until this time, all of those who have been dispatched were killed in the field. They were operatives and they took their jobs knowing the dangers. They were killed in a war in which they voluntarily participated."

Kline made eye contact with several people before she clenched her teeth. "Never have we lost our leader. Never." Putting her right fist on the table for emphasis, she said the word a third time, slowly. "Never."

Relaxing the taut muscles in her face, Kline spoke from her heart. "Ellsworth Steele may have been a political appointee, but he was a man of vision and commitment. He never let his political background interfere with our core mission. Instead, he used his knowledge of the political process to bridge our gaps at the Capitol and at the White House. He was our advocate at the highest levels of government. Ellsworth Steele will be missed at this table and cannot be replaced." She cocked her head. "Nevertheless, I will try to earn your respect as I make an attempt to fill his shoes."

"Let's move to today's reports," she said. Her attention was diverted as she looked over again at the greeting on the smart-board. "This may be my first day back at the office, but all of you know Deputy Director MacKenzie has been keeping me up-to-date throughout my recovery.

"Madame Director," said MacKenzie, "the assassination of Director Steele is not on the agenda, but ..."

"Nor should it ever be," Kline snapped. Her attention was quickly drawn back to the meeting. "Don't forget we are not supposed to be involved in domestic law enforcement. Steele was killed on American soil and his murder is out of our jurisdiction. Nothing we discuss regarding this matter should ever be on the agenda or put in writing. Understand?"

"Yes, Director Kline," MacKenzie replied. "Nevertheless, as you know all of the usual foreign suspects have taken responsibility for the hit. However, there is still no corroborating evidence any of them actually did it."

Kline spent her entire career as an operative in covert field operations. She knew the assassin was trying to remain underground. "This was a very professional hit," Kline replied. People around the table took mental notes of her every word, but put nothing on paper. "I can assure you anyone who takes credit for killing Director Steele didn't actually do it."

"Agreed," affirmed MacKenzie. "There was nothing exceptional about the hit indicating the origins of the plotters. The FBI is keeping us up to date."

"The FBI has not found anything to link the bomb to the killers, and it is unlikely they ever will," Kline replied. "There was a ton of forensic evidence that has kept the FBI busy since the attack. They'll spend another couple of months running down leads. The evidence they have uncovered told us how they did it, but did nothing to identify the killers. The assassins were pros who don't brag and who don't leave traces."

"We are conducting a full, albeit quiet, investigation into what Director Steele was working on in the months leading up to the hit," said Kline. "That's the only way we'll figure out who did this. We've made reviewing his files our top priority." Her eyes narrowed. "I want these fuckers."

Everyone stared at Kline. The F-bomb was not unheard of coming from a former field agent, but rarely uttered by the person sitting at the head of the table.

"And I want them before the FBI figures it out," Kline affirmed. "I don't care where we find them, either in-country or the field. There will be no trial of the people who killed Ellsworth Steele. Got it?"

MacKenzie looked around the room and saw all heads nod in silent affirmation. Whoever killed Steele was going to have to face the star chamber sitting around this table.

Kline picked up the agenda in front of her. "Now, people, tell me what's happening around the world this morning. I see here that the arms dealer the FBI arrested in Miami has gone missing."

It was 9:30 in the evening at Jane Kline's townhouse as Leo Argo put the finishing touches on a shrimp and penne dish he prepared for a late dinner. A soulful saxophone version of Steve Goodman's *California Promises* played softly as he rubbed the neck of a bottle of white wine between his palms, forcing the larger portion of the bottle down into the ice bucket. Hoover lay in a corner of the kitchen, patiently waiting for his mistress' return. Argo and Hoover both knew Kline's day had been a long one.

"What do ya think, Hoover, old pal?" Argo spoke to the dog as if he was expecting some witty retort. "Me, too. She needed another week or so in rehab. But you know Jane. She's one tough broad, and she has to make damn sure everyone in the room knows it."

Argo flipped the shrimp around in the skillet, sautéing them in the oil. Hoover stayed in the corner, his head on his paws and his eyes sleepily focused on

Argo. "Oh, you think I'm going to stop her?" Argo laughed. "Not a fucking chance, pal. Once your mom decided she needed to be back at work, no one was going to change her mind … not you … not the doctors … and apparently not me."

Argo poured some wine, swirled it around the glass and took a sip. "Don't look at me like that," he warned Hoover. "Hell, the way she's been reacting to me lately, you may be walking yourself soon. She nearly bit my fucking head off the other night when I suggested she should wait another week before she went back to work. You were there. You saw how she tuned me out."

Argo looked at Hoover as if he said something really outlandish. "Well, of course she's been through a terrible trauma. Her boss was killed. She lost her leg and half of her hearing."

Argo took another sip of wine, looked at the glass and then chugged the remainder of the cool liquid. "I just wish she'd let me in."

As Argo was discussing his love life with the dog, a new black Ford Explorer with tinted windows pulled up in front of the townhouse, and a square-jawed man exited the vehicle from the front passenger side. He made a quick survey of the surroundings before opening the rear door for his new boss, Jane Kline.

Hoover ran to the door and jumped up and down on the tile of the foyer as Argo peered out the front window of the townhouse. He watched nervously as Kline steadied her cane before bringing her good foot to the concrete driveway. The prosthetic leg followed. Once Kline was firmly planted, she paused and spoke to the man before making her way to the brick steps leading to her townhouse.

Kline looked up at the steps as if they were a mountain trail waiting to be conquered. A year-and-a-half earlier, the trendy townhouse in Old Towne Alexandria seemed like a fantastic buy. It was small and needed a lot of work, but Kline picked it up at a great price. Having lived on the road most of her career, Kline squirreled away a lot of housing money, which she recently put to good use. She modernized the kitchen and bought some nice furniture for the living room, dining room and bedroom. It had become a comfortable landing spot. Now, as Kline had been using the services of an occupational therapist to learn how to climb the steps leading to her own home, she was questioning her decision to buy it. Kline flipped up the collar of her coat to keep the cold night air off her neck and climbed the steps.

Hoover's tail wagged as Argo opened the door, but Argo kept a firm hold on the dog's collar to make sure he did not cause a problem for his owner as she navigated the steps. "Hey, Leo," Kline said without emotion as she approached the door. "Thanks for coming over to let Hoover out."

Both waited for Kline to be inside the door before they exchanged a kiss. Kline put her briefcase on the floor, and she took off her winter coat. As Argo took her coat and placed it in the closet, he couldn't help but interject his views on Kline's arrival home. "You shouldn't talk to that guy after you exit the car. You know that don't you? You need to get out of the vehicle and get secure as quickly as possible."

Kline lived through a rough first day back at the job, and she was irritated by Argo lecturing her soon as she entered the house. "Me? I had a good day," she replied sarcastically. "Thanks for asking. How about you?"

"I'm sorry," Argo replied. "I'm not used to worrying about someone like this. I've been comfortably single all my life. I saw you get out of the car and I started looking around for perps. I nearly pulled my service revolver and came out myself."

"I know you're not used to a relationship, but this is my job, Leo. This is my life," Kline replied as she limped from the hallway. Her voice was stern. "I don't need your input."

"Okay, fine" said Argo. He turned his back to Kline before walking down the hallway back into the kitchen without uttering another word. He went to the sink where he washed off a few utensils before putting them in the dishwasher.

Kline closed her eyes and she sighed in regret over her harsh words. She knew she snapped at Argo unnecessarily. Kline slowly followed Argo into the kitchen, put her hand on his back and then she hugged his muscular body from behind. "I'm sorry, Leo. You didn't deserve that."

"Thanks," Argo replied without turning to face her. He focused his attention on the food he had been preparing on the black, glass-top, brushed-chrome stove.

"This is hard for me too, Leo," Kline continued. "No one has worried about me since my dad died twenty years ago. But you've got to remember I've got a lifetime in the field. I know what I'm doing." She paused. "And, yes, I know I'm now a public target and I realize I need to start acting like one."

"All right then," Argo said. He turned around, hugged Kline and kissed her. "Apology accepted." He kissed her deeply a second time before releasing her. "Let's just drop it."

"Thanks."

"So how does the leg feel?" Argo asked. He reached for an empty wine glass on the counter and he filled it before passing it to Kline.

"Thanks again," Kline replied as she took the wine from Argo. Her face winced in pain as she turned and walked the few steps to the great room that housed the dining and family rooms. "My leg feels fine, but my back hurts like hell."

"It's the new leg and the cane. You've changed your gait. The therapist said it's going to feel that way for a while until you get used to it." Argo pulled out a chair at the table for Kline to sit in before returning to the kitchen. She sighed in pleasure as she sank down on the upholstered chair.

"I felt really, really old today," Kline said as Hoover came up to her and put his head on her lap. She ran her finger down his nose and then rubbed him behind his ears. "I had to have a masseuse come into the office around three and give me a rubdown because it hurt so damn bad." Kline removed her suit jacket and hung it on the back of her chair.

"You want a rubdown now?" Argo asked. He turned away from the stove and glanced behind him at Kline sitting at the dining room table.

Kline shook her head. "No. I'm starved. Something sure smells good."

"It better taste as good as it smells," Argo laughed as he walked out of the kitchen with two plates of food. He set one plate in front of Kline and set the other at his place. "I made us some shrimp pasta with olive oil and lemon."

"Sounds yummy." Kline took a small bite. "Damn, Leo, it is yummy."

Argo grabbed Kline's cane, which leaned against the table, and placed it next to a leather chair by the wall. Before he sat down, he stepped into the kitchen, grabbed the bottle of wine and refilled both of their glasses. "So how was it?"

"Weird," replied Kline. "It was really weird."

"How so?"

Kline thought briefly of talking to Argo about the FBI investigation into the hit on Steele, but quickly disregarded the urge. She didn't want him knowing the CIA even had it on their radar screen. She decided to keep the discussion general. "Well, there was the big press conference to start the day."

"But you knew that was coming. You prepared for that, right?"

"That was easy," said Kline. She continued to pick at her food. "I just said what the public affairs guys told me to say."

"So what was weird?" asked Argo as he swirled his wine before drinking.

Kline took another bite of the shrimp pasta and pointed her fork at Argo, smiling softly as she spoke. "You're going to make someone a nice little wifey someday."

"Funny."

"No, what was weird was when I walked into the conference room across from my new office. Someone had programmed 'Welcome back Director Kline' on the smart-board."

"So?"

"Director Kline." Kline put an emphasis on the word director, "Ellsworth is my Director."

"Ellsworth is gone, babe."

Kline shrugged. "I know. It just seemed odd to see my name up there."

"Get used to it," Argo replied. "You're the boss now."

Kline shoved her glass across the table at Argo. "Gee, thanks for reminding me. With that comment, I'll need more wine."

The pair continued with small talk throughout dinner. Argo sensed Kline was a bit distant, but shrugged it off to her being tired after her first day back at the office. He shied away from the thought her mood might relate to some deeper relationship issues. It had been a long day for both of them and he didn't want to go there. Kline stayed seated at the table while Argo cleaned up the dishes.

"Thanks, Leo," Kline said as she watched Argo move around the kitchen. "I really appreciate everything you've done through all of this."

"You said that in a tone indicating I'm going home again tonight," Argo said quietly as he turned and faced Kline while leaning back on the kitchen counter. He struggled to not look disappointed, but the tone of his voice implied his true feelings.

Kline bit back her words. "I'm just not ready yet, Leo."

As the very topic Argo was hoping to avoid was now out in the open, he decided to go ahead and say what was on his mind. "If we're going to move forward with this relationship, Jane, I've got to see you naked someday," he blurted out.

Kline was somewhat shocked at Argo's directness and looked down at where her calf used to be. "I know," she replied.

Argo put it out there, so he decided to keep going. "Jane, I don't give a damn whether you have one leg or three. I just want to be with you." Argo walked to Kline, helped her up and embraced her. He kissed her brow. "But, I'm not sure you still want to be with me."

"Leo, you've been great." Kline placed her head on Argo's shoulder. "I couldn't have asked for anything more from any man and I want to be with you. Really I do."

"But…"

Kline, too, knew it was time for honesty. She looked deep into Argo's eyes. "People at the Company think I'm some tough, cold, iron maiden. That's my reputation and, with my colleagues, I'm fine with that image. But, even though I've been a CIA operative all of my adult life, I'm still a woman. Before the explosion, you helped me understand just how much. Somehow, these days, I feel that I'm, well, less of a woman because of this," Kline fanned her hand down towards her missing leg.

"All right," Argo said, releasing his hug and digging in his pants pocket for his car keys. He pulled them out and pointed them at Kline. "I'll wait. You just need to know I'm ready when you are."

"Just wait for me."

"I will. I promise." Argo leaned forward and kissed her brow again, before heading down the hallway to the front door.

"And Leo."

Argo paused as he heard her speak. "Yeah."

"It's one and a half legs, not one or three."

He turned toward her and smartly saluted. "Get some sleep," he chuckled.

FIVE

A smartly dressed, olive-skinned man smiled politely when the heavily armed IDF officer asked him to step out of line at Jerusalem's Ben Gurion International Airport. The smile was not superficial. The man had become used to the additional scrutiny he had to endure when he traveled in and out of Israel.

Time spent in the Royal Air Force taught Wasfi Al Ghazawi to travel light. He flew with one small carry-on piece of luggage. Anything else he needed was either shipped in advance or provided to him upon his arrival at a particular location. Even with just one piece of luggage, Wasfi knew he would still be pulled from the line. Palestinians flying out of Israel just expect the delay.

A Palestinian, Wasfi's father worked for the International Petroleum Company in Haifa as one of its chief engineers. The political disruption of the region caused the company to move its engineering department to London following World War II, where the elder Al Ghazawi became the chief of IPC's engineering personnel. After Israel was established, the family never saw the need to return to Haifa. London was where their youngest son, Wasfi, was born in 1962.

A British citizen by birth, Wasfi served in the RAF as a pilot. Initially trained in fixed-wing aircraft, he switched to helicopters when a superior officer suggested it as a path to advancement. In the mid-nineties, on a mission over Bosnia, Wasfi flew his craft through heavy enemy fire and was wounded in the leg. Although the Queen gave him a medal for his valor, the incident ended his career in the cockpit. It also left him with a noticeable limp in his left leg.

Upon retirement from the RAF, Wasfi decided to do what his father had chosen not to do ... return to Haifa. There he established Abraham's Olive Tree, a think tank aimed at a peaceful resolution to the Palestinian-Israeli conflict. Initially, people on both sides scoffed at the concept. Still, through passionate determination, Abraham's Olive Tree survived the financial hardships and political turmoil of its early years and was now prospering.

When Wasfi was led into the security office, the officer behind the desk recognized him. "You again?" he chuckled.

"Yes, me again." Wasfi held his arms and hands open in an inviting gesture. "I am in here often enough that I should have my own desk."

The officer put his hand out to greet Wasfi. "You would think at some point we would put you in the system as a safe traveler," he said. "It would save both of us some time."

"I do not mind," Wasfi smiled as he handed his passport and travel papers to the officer.

"I know," the man replied and he scanned Wasfi's passport into the computer. "You may be the most polite person I have ever met in this place. Some of the people who are led in here get so angry."

"I am far too busy to waste time getting angry." The officer handed the papers back to Wasfi, who placed them in his suit coat pocket.

"London this week? It's awfully cold there this time of year."

"London for a week," Wasfi replied, "but then I am going to Dublin for a conference in the spring. I am very much looking forward to that trip."

"Well, enjoy London."

"Thank you. I will be reentering in about two weeks. I am sure I will see you then." Wasfi turned to leave the office.

The officer gave a casual half-salute. "I am sure you will."

SIX

"Hey Cuz," the voice on the other end of the phone was eerily cool.

"What the fuck?"

The caller expected the response to his greeting to be jittery. He took delight in knowing the person on the other end of the phone felt uncomfortable. "That's not a very friendly greeting for family," he replied.

"I thought we were going to set up times to talk. You aren't supposed to call me. I'm supposed to call you. Remember?"

"Not to worry," the caller replied. "It's all cool. I'm on a stolen cell phone. I procured five of them today. You want me to get a few for you? With the money we've got coming in, I can get more."

"No," the second said, his voice gasping. "We shouldn't be talking right now. Things are still really, really hot here." He heard some noise in the background. "Where are you?"

"I'm just out getting a hot cup of Joe. I wouldn't call if it weren't important. We've got a problem."

"Good God … are you kidding me? I didn't want the last problem. And now you're calling me with a new one."

"It couldn't be helped. You told me that yourself."

"I know, I just never expected …"

"What? Expected what? Thanks to me, you're getting your dream. Someday you'll be able to retire to a life of luxury."

"I just never expected people to die … people I knew."

"People die every day, cuz."

"Never because of me, though."

"Don't be so dramatic. You never killed anyone."

"That's easy for you to say. You did this stuff for the military." He paused. "I'm sorry I ever got involved."

"Oh, but you are involved, Cuz." The caller was confident. "Now, I need some information on a lawyer in Kentucky and his daughter."

"Why?"

"They may have something we need."

SEVEN

Sean Sullivan had a little spring in his step as he walked along a cold street in Covington's Main Strasse entertainment district. His laundromat/law office was located in an old three-story brick building on the southernmost corner of the avenue. Everyone waved at the old man as he walked by. Sullivan had been a staple in the unique German village-style neighborhood for the past two decades.

Twenty years ago, Sullivan was a different man. He had been a young attorney with a powerful law firm and was an up-and-comer in the local political scene. Whenever anyone spoke of those with a future in politics, Sullivan was always the name first mentioned. He and his wife, the daughter of a local African-American minister, were a striking couple and A-listers in the local social and political scene. With magic skills he learned as a kid, it was not unusual for Sullivan to pull a coin from the ear of an unsuspecting guest to the delight of others at a cocktail party.

A criminal trial of a local man accused of murder changed Sullivan's life.

While the prosecution was questioning a family member who witnessed an altercation between the defendant and the victim, Sullivan sat at the defense table taking notes. In a flash, another family member of the victim jumped from the gallery and hopped over the railing behind Sullivan. The defendant jumped up just in time to be stabbed by the knife-wielding family member. Pandemonium broke loose in the courtroom, and Sullivan attempted to grab the man with the knife. The man turned and hit Sean Sullivan squarely on the jaw.

Sullivan bellowed in pain and fell backward, falling into a bailiff who was rushing to the confrontation. Sullivan spun and fell forward, hitting his forehead solidly on the corner of the prosecution's desk. His head snapped violently backwards and Sean Sullivan fell unconscious onto the courtroom floor, bleeding from a gaping head wound.

Rushed to the hospital, Sullivan lay in a coma for several days. The blow to the head caused severe swelling of his brain. When he finally surfaced to consciousness, he was confused and disoriented.

In the months that followed, Sean Sullivan's personality changed. The changes were slight at first and were only noticeable to Sullivan's wife. The doctor who handled his case in the hospital explained to her that head trauma sometimes caused minor to severe personality changes. Tests were run and treatments suggested. But, as time passed, the personality changes became more dramatic. Eventually, the changes were too much for Sullivan's wife to withstand and the couple divorced. Even their seven-year-old daughter could not keep them together.

The week the divorce was final, Sullivan's law firm fired him …something about differing directions. He moved his personal and business possessions into an old building with a laundromat on the first floor. Out in front of the laundromat, he hung up his law shingle and began a new career, representing the poor and the indigent of the inner city. He grew his hair long and started to dress in a manner that embraced his Irish heritage.

As time continued to pass, it became clear the Sean Sullivan who once was the future of law and politics in the county had become a parody of himself.

Despite the change in personality, Sean Sullivan's legal skills remained among the best in the courthouse. And he found a new passion within the practice of law. Along with representing needy clients, Sullivan began filing federal lawsuits with the frequency of a crack addict on a binge. The suits were not trivial by any means, but generally revolved around matters of individual rights or government fraud. Civil rights actions under Section 1983 of the United States Code generated out of Sullivan's detergent-smelling law office, were filed on the average of about once or twice a month. And, though he filed more cases than any other lawyer in the district, he still won more than he lost.

Despite his busy schedule, each Monday was reserved for dinner with his daughter, Tiana. This Monday evening, when he entered his favorite restaurant, Sullivan proceeded to their normal table. Within minutes, without placing an order for it, a fresh-poured Guinness was set in front of him.

Sean Sullivan sat at the table in Chez Nora nervously tapping his fingers on the plexiglas covered green, checkered tablecloth. He adjusted his gray Irish wool cap and watched intently as droplets of condensation rolled down the side of his glass of Guinness and made a small puddle of water around its base.

"It's too damned cold," Sullivan shouted at Jimmy Gilliece, the former stand-up comic who owned the trendy restaurant with his wife, Pati. Gilliece strolled over from his normal corner spot at the bar to Sullivan's table, lighting a cigarette as he walked.

Gilliece and Sullivan had been having the same argument over the temperature of Guinness for years. "I can't control the weather, Sully," said Gilliece flippantly.

"Still trying to be a funny man, are ya now?" replied Sullivan, lifting the glass and pointing at the water on the table. "I'm not talking about the weather and you know it. Look at this."

Jimmy nervously puffed on the cigarette as he talked. Sullivan was one of his regular customers, coming into the bar almost every night. He really didn't mind the customary argument. In fact, he liked getting Sullivan riled up. "I know, I know. The beer is too cold for your taste," Jimmy said, knowing such a comment would get Sullivan excited.

"This is not beer. It's a stout. It's mother's milk from the Homeland. And it's not simply my taste. Guinness is meant to be consumed at room temperature." Sullivan swept the water off the table with the sleeve of his heavy green sweater.

"Then wait a while. It'll warm up," Gilliece said, laughing, as he exhaled smoke and flicked some ashes into an ashtray.

"Don't you think I won't, boy-o." Sullivan paused and, leaning back in his chair, let out a sound of displeasure. He looked over at Luke, the young bartender who was drying some of the glasses he just washed. "And, Lukey-boy, go ahead and pour two more so they'll warm up by the time I want them."

Luke was filling up the coffee cup of a man sitting at the bar who was talking on his cell phone and did not immediately look over. "Yes, sir, Mr. Sullivan," replied the young man as he turned and grabbed two glasses off the shelf.

"And how long do you wait between the first and second pour?"

"One hundred nineteen and one-half seconds," Luke replied while starting the first pour.

"Good lad," smiled Sullivan. He personally taught the young man how to pour a Guinness by filling the glass three quarters full and waiting for that pour to settle before topping off the remainder.

"Tiana joining you for dinner tonight?" asked Gilliece, happy to change the topic from the proper temperature of Guinness to the old man's daughter. He put his cigarette out in the ashtray.

"It's Monday night, isn't it?" said Sullivan, referring to the weekly meal tradition the two had maintained since Tiana was in grade school. "And as usual, my daughter is late."

"Aw, give her a break," Gilliece smiled. "She's young."

"Gives me time for my stout to warm up," mumbled Sullivan, frowning.

"Give it a rest, Sully," Gilliece replied, laughing at the old man's surly nature.

Just then Tiana appeared from behind a heavy green curtain put in place around the front door of the restaurant during the winter as a blockade to the cold air from the street. As she walked to the table, heads turned noting her attractive figure. She was wearing tight blue jeans and a white, ribbed, long-sleeve sweater and a leather coat. She kissed Gilliece on the cheek and brushed her hair off her brow. "Hi, Jimmy."

"Hey, babe," Gilliece returned Tiana's welcome with a light kiss on her cheek. He pointed at Sullivan. "Tiana is far too pretty to be your daughter, Sully. Thank God her mom has the looks in the family."

"You're sweet, Jimmy," said Tiana. "Think you can mix me up a Cosmo?"

"Sure." He looked back at Luke who heard the request. "On me," he mouthed to the young bartender before turning back to the table. "How goes the practice of law?" he asked.

"Good," replied Tiana. Before sitting, she reached across the table and gave her father a big kiss and hug and then hung her jacket on the back of her chair. "Interest rates are low so I'm getting lots of title orders these days. I'm keeping busy."

"Practice of law?" interjected Sullivan with mock outrage in his voice. "She's wasting away in the dusty confines of the record room."

"I like real estate law, Daddy. Not every lawyer is meant to be a courtroom attorney."

"But you'd make a great litigator," said Sullivan, his Irish eyes sparkling with pride as he spoke about his daughter. "You're smarter than most attorneys in any courtroom. Those young boys I face every day don't have half your talent."

Like Sullivan's regular debates with Gilliece over the drinkability of his Guinness, Tiana's real estate law practice had been a thorn in Sullivan's side since she graduated from law school. She was hoping it wasn't going to come up tonight. "Please don't start, Daddy." Tiana rolled her eyes and looked at Gilliece for some relief.

Sullivan too looked at Gilliece and pointed at Tiana. "With her brains and my training she could be a female Johnny Cochran."

"If she's an Irish mick, you must acquit," mused Gilliece, doing his best Johnny Cochran impersonation for the pair before he walked away from the table.

"No wonder you opened a restaurant," mused Sullivan loudly. "You're a shitty comedian." He raised his voice louder. "And if you don't start serving a better Guinness, you'll shut down this place—just like your jokes shut down the Ding Ho."

"Daddy, you're funny," laughed Tiana shaking her head.

"Why?"

"Because you've been telling Jimmy the same thing for twenty years, yet you still keep coming here." Luke left the bar to bring Tiana her Cosmo. She took a sip and thanked Luke with a smile and a nod.

"I live under the enduring dream someday he'll get it right."

"I heard you had another good trial last week." Tiana put her glass back on the table. She looked squarely at Sullivan. "Did you get paid for it?"

"It isn't always about money," Sullivan replied. He took a large gulp of his Guinness and frowned at its still-too-cool temperature. He wiped some thick foam from his upper lip. "Sometimes you have to do what is right and worry later about getting paid."

"So, you didn't get paid?"

"No, I did not," Sullivan replied matter-of-factly.

Tiana put her elbows on the table and cradled her head in her hands. "I swear I don't know how you get by."

"Did you know Cicero spent most of his career as a lawyer defending for free those wrongfully banished from the city of Rome?" asked Sullivan, defending himself like he was in front of a judge and jury.

"What firm did he practice with?" responded Tiana jokingly as she looked up.

"Despite your poor attempt at humor, he did."

"Okay then, did Cicero need money for his insulin?"

Sullivan stuck out his tongue and blew a raspberry at his daughter. "I live a simple life and I am quite happy doing so. I have all the money I need."

"And what the hell happened after the trial?" asked Tiana, leaning forward in her chair. "I heard there was an incident outside the courthouse with that kid I watched you do the closing argument on."

"It was nothing." Sullivan emphasized its insignificance with a swish of a backhand in the air.

Tiana was told by one of the young attorneys in the record room that Antwone Mason approached Sullivan outside the courthouse and forced a confrontation. The young man yelled at Sullivan before pushing him to the ground.

"That's not what I heard," replied Tiana looking very seriously at her father. "I heard that kid you got an acquittal for was waiting for you when you came out of the courthouse."

Sullivan lowered his gaze and spoke deliberately. "I said it was nothing."

"Daddy, being pushed around and threatened with violence by an angry former client is not 'nothing.' By anybody's standards it's something. Did you report it to the police?"

"Good Lord, no," replied Sullivan, incredulous at even the thought. "That young boy does not need the police back into his life. He'll get over it."

Tiana heard the whole story from her colleague, but wanted to hear how her father explained it. "What happened?"

"He thought I disrespected him in front of his mother. He's probably already forgotten about it."

"Did he push you down?"

"I slipped."

"And I heard he threatened to kill you," she doggedly continued.

"... a threat I do not take seriously. This conversation is over." Sullivan lowered his head until his chin was resting on his chest. He crossed his arms defiantly. There was an uncomfortable pause as both challenged the other to see who would look away first. Tiana knew once her father declared a conversation finished, there was no going back. She looked away and Sullivan spoke first to declare victory in the visual duel. "So have you thought about my offer?"

Great, thought Tiana. *Now we have another uncomfortable topic to discuss.* "What offer?" Tiana nonchalantly took another sip of her drink.

"Don't be coy with me, my dear," Sullivan replied, uncrossing his arms. "It's a trait your mother taught you. I didn't like it from her and I don't like it from you. You know damn well what I'm talking about." He paused. "Be a part of my campaign for Congress."

Sullivan was relentless in his pursuit of trying to get her to agree to work on his campaign for Congress. "I still don't understand why you want to do this, Daddy," she said. "You can't win. Why do you want to run for Congress against Richard Thompson when you know you can't win?"

"You may have finished in the top five of your class at Chase Law School," Sullivan said as he shook his head, "but there are things you desperately need to learn. Law isn't all about money, and campaigns aren't always about winning, Tiana."

"This wouldn't be like working a jury, Daddy," Tiana quipped. "You can't pull a quarter out of somebody's ear and expect to get their vote."

"But that's exactly what Richard Thompson is doing, honey." Sullivan's laugh carried across the entire bar. "He's using tricks to get people to vote for him."

"What do you mean?"

"When Thompson ran the first time, he was an anti-government populist who believed answers lay in individual rights rather than government action."

This was a new line from her father. He was apparently being straight with her, but she was not getting the reference. "I'm not following you."

"All right, do you remember his first campaign?"

"Kind of," Tiana replied. "What was the old guys's name ..." Her voice trailed as she tried to remember.

"Garrett Jackson," Sullivan completed his daughter's thought. "Thompson's old boss, Garrett Jackson died in office and Thompson won the special election to fill the unexpired term. He ran that year on a platform of limited government. He rallied people who distrusted the federal government and preyed on the fears of those who worried the government was out to get them."

"I'm still not following you."

"Did you see the bill he helped push through the House last month on education?" Sullivan folded his arms.

"No. What was in it?"

"What was in the bill is unimportant. The lad ran on a platform that we should distrust the federal government. Now that he *is* the federal government, he thinks we should all follow him. He should be introducing bills to abolish the Department of Education, not make it better. But no, now he has power, he thinks he can reform the very government he opposes."

"But you don't believe that," insisted Tiana, shaking her head. "You believe there is a role for the federal government in education."

"It doesn't matter what I believe," said Sullivan. He dipped his finger in his beer to test the temperature before taking another swig. "As you have so rightfully pointed out, I have no earthly chance of winning. What's important is that somewhere, deep inside Congressman Richard Thompson's psyche, he believes government is beyond reform. I am going to force him to run for re-election on his true beliefs."

"Thompson will portray you as a whack-job," said Tiana.

"Yes," Sullivan replied. "And how brilliant will it be when a whack-job forces him to come face-to-face with his own values?" His booming laugh filled the room.

"And just how do you plan to do that, Daddy?"

Sullivan reached across the table, put his fingers next to Tiana's ear and magically produced a quarter. "Come to my announcement on Wednesday and I'll show you."

"Let's order," Tiana replied. "Politics spoils my appetite."

EIGHT

It was early in the evening when Tiana Bolton started the walk back from Chez Nora to her old brick townhouse on Second Street, just south of the Ohio River. When Tiana decided to move to the region's urban core following graduation from law school, her mother expressed concerns for her safety. Sullivan, delighted at his daughter's decision, calmed his ex-wife's fears by agreeing to teach Tiana to be "street smart." Following his lessons, Tiana always looked one block ahead and behind and crossed the street regularly to follow the safest routes home. No matter how many times she walked the streets at odd hours, Tiana rarely felt unsafe. Even when she headed out on her early morning jogs, she did so confident in her own safety.

Tiana took in a deep breath of the cold fresh air as she made a right on a busy street that crossed under a railroad trestle. She was in full stride when a buzzing sound emitted from the back pocket of her jeans. She pulled out her phone and looked at the Caller ID screen.

Tiana knew her mother worried about her walking home from her weekly dinners with her dad. She called Tiana every Monday night at about the same time to make sure she was on her way home before it

90

got too late. Tiana slowly looked back and forth, up and down the street as she spoke. "Hi, Mama. What's up?"

"Nothin' much on my end of the phone," Tiana's mother, Shirley Bolton-Sullivan, replied. "Are you on your way home?

"Yes, Mama," Tiana shrugged.

"Good. I don't like you out walking around too late, especially in the cold. How was dinner?"

Tiana looked up the street and crossed. She wanted to be on the same side of the street as the woman who was walking her dog. Tiana switched the phone to her other hand as she jogged across the street. "Great," she replied. "They have such a good walnut salad."

"How you could be raised by your old man and me and end up a vegetarian is beyond belief," said Shirley.

Tiana enjoyed the fact she grew up in the ultimate diverse family. Her mother was the daughter of an inner-city black minister and her father was the consummate son of St. Patrick. "Of course I ended up like this," Tiana laughed delightedly. "We used to have shepherd's pie and greens. I was the only kid at my school who ate Irish soul food."

"It wasn't that bad."

"The hell it wasn't." Tiana knew the woman who was walking the dog. She kneeled down to one knee and let the dog jump up against her leg as she petted it. "I started on a straight veggie diet as soon as I got to college," Tiana said as she stood up and continued her walk.

"How was your daddy?"

Shirley kept up on her ex-husband via Tiana's weekly dinners with him. There was still a connection. "He was good. He's not eating right for a diabetic, and he drinks too much, but he's fine."

"Good."

She knew her mother still cared for her father just as much as he cared for her. "He asked about you like he always does and sends his love."

"Crazy old man."

"He still loves you, Mama."

"And you know I still love him. There just came a point where he made it too hard for me to like him anymore, I guess."

"Whatever…" Tiana looked a block up the street as she crossed at a light by a liquor store.

"So, are you going to do it?" Shirley asked her daughter.

"Do what?" Tiana replied.

"You know what," Shirley countered. "Are you going to work on your father's campaign?"

Tiana was irritated her mother was asking her about the topic. "You know about the campaign offer?"

"Of course I know about that," Shirley said. "Baby, I told him to ask you to do it."

"You're in on this?" Shocked, Tiana stopped momentarily on the sidewalk.

"Me and your grandpa discussed it last week."

"Damn. Gramps is in on this with you, too?" Irritation with her family diverted Tiana's attention from her immediate surroundings. She didn't pick up on the man following her from a block behind. He stopped and was looking at a storefront window.

"Well, Gramps is going to help with his campaign," said Shirley. "The campaign kickoff is going to be at the church. Your grandfather is going to introduce him."

"Gramps is introducing Daddy?" Tiana expressed her confusion as she crossed the street. "Your father, a black inner-city minister, is introducing to the press, his only daughter's ex-husband, who is a white Irish Catholic?" The man crossed at the next intersection and quickened his pace.

"Yeah, baby, you know Sean and Gramps are still friends."

"Holy crap. Look up dysfunctional in the dictionary and there'll probably be the picture from our family Christmas card."

"Look," said Shirley, "your father can't help what happened to him. Whatever happened between us was between us. It doesn't affect you. Sully's still a good man, and he has always been a good father to you. Your Gramps knows that."

"But introducing him?" Tiana huffed out as she continued to walk quickly down the busy street.

"Baby, Sully has probably represented half the congregation down at Gramps's church at one time or another and never sent anyone a bill. He tells them all just to pay what they can."

"I know."

"And Gramps and I thought a campaign with your dad would be good for you," Shirley continued.

Her parents raised Tiana to be an independent woman and the fact they were now trying to push her into her father's campaign was contrary to all their prior tutoring. "This is my life you know," said Tiana. "I'll decide if I want to be in Daddy's campaign. It's my call, not yours or Gramps's."

"I know baby, but Gramps and I think a little social conscience would be good for you."

"What the hell is that supposed to mean—a little social conscience?" asked Tiana. Irritation flooded her voice.

"Well baby, let's face it. You've never wanted for anything. Whatever you wanted, your daddy got it for you. He even gave you my last name so you wouldn't have the stigma of a black girl growing up with an Irish name. You told me about it yourself when you went to that trial of his. Those young folks down in the record room you work with don't even know Sully is your father. He's made life easy for you."

"So?"

"So you owe him," said Shirley.

"I should go play politics with Daddy because you think I owe him?" asked Tiana.

"No, baby," said Shirley. "That's not what I think. This is your chance to see inside his soul. Sully gives a lot to others. He believes he can personally absolve human suffering. You owe him the chance to put that into action. Hell, baby, you owe yourself that opportunity."

Tiana softened. "I'll think about it."

"Think seriously."

"I said I will," said Tiana, rolling her eyes at her mother's relentlessness.

"Be careful walking home. I worry about you down there. It's cold and I wish you would just once take a cab home."

"I'll be fine, Mama," Tiana sighed into the phone.

"I love you, baby."

"I love you too, Mama."

Tiana shoved the phone back into her jeans as she made a left down a tree-lined street. The street lights shining through the naked tree limbs cast evil-looking shadows across the center of the road.

As she walked, she heard a noise from behind her. Tiana suddenly tuned back in to her surroundings. The hair stood up on the back of her neck and a shiver ran down her spine. She stopped and faced the street, reaching in her pocket as if she were looking for her keys. About a block behind her, on the opposite side of the street, a man stopped, turned away and lit a cigarette. Tiana turned back toward her house and started walking.

"Paranoid," Tiana mumbled to herself as she licked her lips. "My mom has made me paranoid."

Still, as she walked, the thought she was being followed planted itself in Tiana's mind. At the corner she stopped and looked back again. The man, who was closer this time, stopped, bent down and tied his right shoe.

"Fuck me," Tiana mumbled to herself. She crossed at the corner and quickened her stride.

Tiana could feel her pulse race as she saw her townhouse in the distance. She looked to both sides of the street as her breathing quickened. "Damn," she mumbled, noticing the streets were empty but for her and the man behind her.

Reaching into her pocket, she grabbed her keys. As Sullivan taught her, she allowed one key to protrude out between her middle and index finger, so she could use it as a weapon if the man tried to grab her. The walk down the last half-block to her townhouse seemed to take forever. It reminded Tiana of a bad dream where each step took her one step farther from where she was trying to get. She was panting as she reached the stone steps leading to her door, her hand trembling as she stuck the key in the thick antique doorknob. Tiana quickly slid inside her townhouse, slammed the door, and flipped the deadbolt. Catching her breath, she went to the front window and peeked around the frame staring into the darkness of the night … one side, then the other and back again. There was nothing. Tiana let out a heavy groan.

"Damn, that woman is making me crazy."

NINE

Ann Thompson twirled her blonde hair as she sat up in bed reading the novel she just picked up at the bookstore. A reading light over her right shoulder outlined an exceptional body for a woman with two kids and twice as many campaigns under her belt. When she heard the garage door open, she looked over at the clock. "11:45," she mumbled to herself before exhaling. Hearing the voices outside in the driveway, Ann surmised someone from the staff had driven her husband home from yet another late-night function.

The consummate political wife, Ann Thompson's days on Capitol Hill as an executive assistant to a Florida Congresswoman seemed a lifetime behind her. With blond hair and blue-green eyes that danced when she laughed, Richard Thompson had been smitten with her when Michael Griffith first introduced them years ago in Washington. Today, her life was a delicate balance between handling the schedule of their kids' school and sporting events, and being the number one supporter and image consultant to her husband. In interludes that seemed to be further and further apart, she was also a wife.

As Thompson entered the hallway, he noticed the light visible under the bedroom door. He steadied his gait in an attempt to keep his wife from noticing the effect a few too many Maker's Mark Manhattans were having on his stride. "Hey, babe," said Thompson as he walked into the couple's bedroom. "You didn't have to wait up."

"I haven't seen you all day," Ann replied. "I've barely seen you this week. It was either stay up tonight or call Lisa tomorrow to request an appointment." Even from across the room, Ann could smell the bourbon on her husband's breath. As a recovering alcoholic, she had a heightened sense of smell for booze.

"I don't know," said Thompson as he took off his tie and started unbuttoning his shirt, swaying a little as he did so. "We're awfully busy at the office. I may be able to fit you in next week."

"Funny. So how was the Chamber dinner?" she asked as she set her book aside.

The dinner circuit for a politician is continuous. There was really no need to describe the meal as they both had eaten the same type of monotonous menu hundreds of times. "They served the same semi-warm mystery meat as last year. In fact, I think my filet was left over from last year's dinner. The dessert was good though," Thompson replied.

"I'm glad I didn't go," said Ann, who had a once-a-month "opt-out" agreement with her husband regarding public appearances. "Thanks for giving me a hall pass tonight. I really didn't feel like going."

"People asked where you were."

"What excuse did you use ... migraine?"

"School function with the kids."

"Good call. I think we used migraine last month with the state party executive committee lunch." Ann reached over and put the book on a bedside table. "Hey, speaking of the kids, don't forget they're singing in the youth choir at church on Sunday."

Thompson winced, put his hands on the top of his head and let out a low growl under his breath.

Ann shook her head in disappointment. "Oh Richard, please don't tell me you planned something on Sunday." She asked the question even though, from observing her husband's body language, she knew the answer.

"Kind of," Thompson said lowering his head slightly. "I told Reverend Lovan I'd stop by the adult Sunday school class he teaches."

"Richard ..."

"I forgot about the kids and the choir thing. Damn." Thompson was truly remorseful for his scheduling indiscretion. Unfortunately, for his family, this kind of slip-up was happening with greater and greater frequency. "We can make this work," he said. "We'll just drive separate cars. I'll listen to the choir, and then hustle out to Florence for Reverend Lovan's Sunday school."

"Rick, it's not about making the schedule work out. You said when we started this political thing Sundays would be a family day. This is the second time this month you've gone to some church other than ours."

"I know," Thompson replied as he slipped his pants off and went to the closet to put them on a hanger. "But this is the biggest church in one of the biggest counties in the state. The Reverend wants me to come out and talk to his adult class. I've got to do it."

Ann paused before she spoke. "Richard, this is not cool." Her displeasure coated every word.

"I know, I know," Thompson replied. "I should have told Ashley check with you first before scheduling it." He walked to the bathroom to brush his teeth. It was one thing to come home reeking of alcohol, but quite another to climb into bed reeking.

"No, that's not the point," Ann raised her voice so she could be heard over the running water. She took a deep breath, trying to deliver her response in a controlled manner. She did not want another late-night fight. "I shouldn't have to call Ashley to get the kids on your schedule. Sunday is family day."

"Look, I know I screwed up on this one," said Thompson as he returned to the bedroom and slid in between the sheets. "I'll make it up to you. In a couple of weeks we'll be in Ireland." He reached over to Ann and slid his hands along her side. "And then, we'll be all alone…"

Ann tried to push her husband's hand away as he reached her breast and pulled at her nipple. "I can see where this is going," she said. "You're going to get me all revved up and you won't be able to complete the transaction because of whiskey dick."

Thompson kept his hand on Ann's breast and playfully pulled at her nipple. He licked his fingers and did it again. "Stop it," Ann protested, but this time she did not push back her husband's hand.

Seeing Ann's protest melt away, Thompson leaned over and sucked her ear lobe into his mouth, eliciting a low moan. He removed his hand from her nipple, grabbed Ann's hand and directed it to his hardening crotch. "Still think I'm having whiskey dick?" he asked.

Ann reached over and turned out the light.

TEN

It is said if God bets the ponies (and most Kentuckians believe he does), then he cashes his holy tickets at a "$50 and Up" teller window at the Keeneland race track in Lexington. The Kentucky Derby may be held the first Saturday in May at Churchill Downs in Louisville, but in the spring, during the weeks preceding the Derby, Kentucky's race fans flock to Keeneland for the finest in racing traditions. Keeneland is racing's Yankee Stadium, Wrigley Field, and Fenway Park all rolled into one.

Located directly across the street from the Bluegrass International Airport, the lush green grounds of Keeneland are bordered by white fences and gates made out of hunter green wrought iron. The stone buildings that form the outside walls of the stately clubhouse and grandstand could well be a stone house in some old European city. When viewing the sport of kings from the stone edifice of Keeneland, men still must wear a coat and tie and women must wear a dress or pant suit. Denim and athletic attire are saved for those lesser life forms who wager via simulcast at the Red Mile, a trotter race track within Lexington's inner-core.

About a half mile down the road from Keeneland, across the street from the white and red barns of the famed Calumet Farm, is a small roadside hotel. A beat-up old two-story structure, the former stop for traveling salesmen stands out in the neighborhood of expensive horse farms like a sore thumb. This is where Padrig Neal, an aging backside horse groom, chose to stay whenever he was in Lexington. A knock at the door of his first-floor room caused Neal to get up slowly from his chair. Just a bit too tall and thick to be a jockey, Neal was known in the States as the trusted groom for County Mayo Stables, a major horse farm just north of Galway in Ireland. In Ireland, Neal was something larger.

When Neal opened the door, a distinguished olive-skinned, Iranian man stood before him. His three-piece steel-blue suit, with French-cuffed shirt and flamboyant silk tie, stood in stark contrast to Neal, who appeared at the door in jeans, riding boots, and a flannel shirt. Red hair stuck out from underneath Neal's yellow County Mayo Stables ball cap.

"Good morning, Paddy. It is good to see you again," the well-dressed man said in precise English, but with an accent and meter clearly indicating his Persian heritage.

"And you, Zafer," Neal greeted in a heavy Irish brogue as he firmly shook Zafer's hand. "Come on in then." Neal walked over to the bathroom where a bottle of whiskey sat on a counter. He raised the bottle backwards toward Zafer, turned and flashed a friendly Irish smile. "Could I interest ya in a bit of the Irish this mornin'? Jameson's?"

"Pat," exclaimed Zafer, his blue eyes widening in disbelief. "Drinking already? It is nine-thirty in the morning."

"Aye, and I've already been over at the track muckin' stalls. I had a big meal at the track kitchen before you even got up this mornin'. On a cold American mornin' like this, you need a little nip to get your joints moving." Neal poured some whiskey into a cheap hotel water glass. He raised the bottle in both a toast and an offer. "Anyway, it's almost quittin' time in ol' Dublin."

"In that case," Zafer replied with a laugh before holding up his hand, "… no."

"Suit yourself then," Neal said as he lifted the glass a second time. "May the hinges of our friendship never grow rusty." He sipped a mouthful, swirled it around his mouth and swallowed. "Sure and I'm ready for it now. Let's talk business."

Zafer was clearly nervous. He walked around as he spoke. "That last horse we got from you, she ran very well … better than we expected." Zafer moved to the window and peeked through a crack in the closed drapes to make sure he had not been followed.

"It's glad I am to hear that. Did she break her maiden then?"

"I said she ran well," Zafer replied. He continued to look back and forth through the drapes as he spoke. "I did not say she ran great. She placed."

"Calm down, will ya?" Neal moved over to the window from which Zafer was surveying the parking lot, and took the drapes out of his hand. He pushed a chair forward for Zafer to sit in. "This place is clean. Look around ya. Why do ya think I stay here?"

Zafer looked around at the room, which had the sleazy feel of a motel used mostly by wayward spouses hoping not to get caught. The dark green shag carpet hadn't been replaced since, well, dark green shag carpeting had been in style. The bedspread and drapes were crushed velvet. The only item that might have been replaced in the last decade or two was the shower curtain, and its substitution was long overdue. The whole room smelled as moldy as the shower curtain looked.

Zafer was still not convinced the room was secure, but sat down in the chair. "What about that green panel van outside in the parking lot?" He nodded toward the window.

"'Tis fine." Neal took another sip of whiskey and laughed. "A bunch of illegals who move from track to track for backside work. They're nuttin' to worry 'bout." He paused. "So then, the filly ran well, did she? Did ya get some of your money back then? How'd she handle the stretch?"

"She had it until there. She faded." Zafer still looked nervous and gently pumped his right leg repetitively up and down.

"Too bad," replied Neal as he rubbed the stubble on his chin. "Hold her out of a race or two. That'll get her there. But don't drop her down a class."

106

"We cannot. We know that. With what we paid your boss for her, we cannot put her in a claiming race."

Neal raised his glass as the two men laughed. Neal took another sip of whiskey. "Sure you don't want a wee bit of Ireland? It'll calm down that damn nervous jig in yer leg."

"You are not going to let up until I drink one, are you?" Zafer asked.

"Aye, and ya can be sure that I'll have another." Neal went to the dressing table where he left the bottle. He grabbed another glass and poured each of them a generous shot. He crossed back across the room and gave one of the glasses to Zafer.

Zafer took the glass and raised it in a silent toast back at Neal. "Bisehtak," he said before taking a sip. Zafer paused, knowing the request he was about to make would not be taken well. He set his jaw. "We need another horse at the spring sale."

"You're mad," Neal said as he sat down on the bed. He spoke without looking at Zafer. "'Tis impossible. It can't be done a-tall. We've done three sales in a row already."

"It is imperative," Zafer insisted. "Our friends are very, very close."

"Too risky," Neal replied, finally looking at Zafer. "We discussed this at the last sale. We need to sit out this season."

"Circumstances have changed. We have a major setback. One season later may be one season too long."

"You're daft, man. You can't be serious?"

"There is a storm brewing and you know that."

"How about the other channels? I thought you were going to move the big stuff through other channels." Neal was now the one who was showing his nerves. He got up from the bed and began to pace. "Sure and I thought that ya had someone in Miami for that."

"That is our setback. The FBI caught him and our distribution chain is gone. I personally ended the relationship myself. You are it, my friend."

Neal had not expected Zafer's request and contemplated his words carefully before he spoke. "Aw, bloody hell," Neal exhaled slowly through clenched teeth. "I'll talk to my boss back in Galway. I'm going home later this week. He'll be wantin' a premium, ya know. The last time we had shipment issues through Turkey."

"I know," Zafer replied. "And so do our friends. They have money and I can assure you they will pay whatever it takes."

Neal gulped down the last of the whiskey in his glass. He looked at Zafer. "I'll be back at the end of next month, just before the sales. Come over to the barns and we'll talk then."

ELEVEN

The Right Reverend James Bolton sat behind the lectern of the First Evangelical Church of Covington, tapping his foot in time as the gospel church choir sang a rousing version of the *Battle Hymn of the Republic*. The elderly minister looked quite distinguished in his purple silk robe. Tufts of cotton white hair popped out on either side of his bald head. A red leather-bound King James Version of the Holy Bible sat in his lap, his hands folded on top of it.

When the choir got to the chorus, Reverend Bolton began singing along with them. He kept time by clapping one hand against the red Bible like some holy metronome. Here, in the exposed brick walls of his inner-city church, he was in his element. The sunlight shone through the beautiful stained-glass windows, casting a warm glow across the wooden floor. The church was so old the aisles separating the pews had subtle grooves worn into them from the endless parade of worshippers who made their way down them over the years. Reverend Bolton did not raise enough money annually to keep the place in perfect repair, but it was a respectable place of worship for his congregation.

Sean Sullivan sat at the side of the man whom he still called his father-in-law. He was wearing the same suit he had worn in court, sans the fuzzy pink slippers.

His former wife, Shirley, was in the choir. Sullivan smiled down at his daughter Tiana, who sat in the first row of the pews in a conservative gray pinstripe business suit and gray silk sweater. She smiled and waved tentatively at her father. The church was filled with congregation members and a couple of the die-hards from party politics.

Camera crews from all but one local television station, a couple of radio reporters and two print journalists stood behind the pews. One cameraman in the crowd was a local videographer hired by Griffith to film the speech for future use by the Thompson campaign. A videographer who shoots an opponent's campaign events—known as a "trailer" in campaign circles—has a consistent paying gig for weeks or months at a time. The newly selected trailer was still in sales mode and eager to please. He texted back and forth to Michael Griffith as the choir sang.

"Otta b here. Quite a show." The cameraman hit send and waited.

"How many?" came Griffith's response on the phone's screen.

"Decent crowd. Good media coverage." The cameraman replied, as he again looked around the church.

"Get some crowd shots. I want to see who is there." Griffith instructed.

"Starting soon. Will call when over."

Just as the choir was blasting the final "Glory, Glory Hallelujah," a television cameraman nudged in next to the trailer. They recognized each other from other local events they covered together. "Did I miss anything?" he whispered.

"Not yet," the trailer replied as he folded up his phone and stuffed it into his pocket. "The choir's just finishing up. They should be starting soon."

"Good. I don't want to miss this."

The trailer was not a political junkie. He wanted the work, but knew very little about campaigns. He was honestly shocked by the number of local media outlets covering the announcement. So he asked the guy the question on his mind. "Sullivan is a fringe candidate, right?"

"Yeah," said the cameraman from a local network affiliate as he continued to set up his tripod. "Why?"

"So, why are all you guys giving him so much coverage?" he asked, truly confused by the all the commotion.

"Sullivan's got no shot," the cameraman whispered as he tightened the camera atop the tripod. "Hell, we all know that. But I've covered the courthouse beat for a decade and you can bet on one thing for sure."

"What's that?"

"Sean Sullivan will put on a show," he chuckled.

When the choir stopped singing, Reverend Bolton took full advantage of the pause, then stood up and strode to the podium. He placed his Bible on the dais and carefully surveyed the room. Sullivan looked at Tiana and winked. Bolton was one of the city's most respected ministers, and the congregation hushed as he looked around.

"It is said that a man's life is measured not by what he takes, but by what he gives back. Those lessons of giving rather than taking go back to the Good Book," Bolton raised the Bible with his right hand as he spoke. "Jesus did not take. He gave."

An older woman sitting behind Tiana mumbled an "Amen." Tiana looked around. It was Antwone Mason's mother, wearing the same blue dress and pillbox hat she had worn at the trial. Tiana looked for the angry young man who attacked her father, but he was not with her. Tiana caught the woman's eye, and she respectfully acknowledged Tiana's presence with a nod of her head. Both looked back at Reverend Bolton. Tiana was silently seething at the thought of confronting the woman about the actions of her son. She calmed herself down and tried to focus on her grandfather.

"Jesus gave Lazarus life. Yet, when his own life was in jeopardy, he gave up his very earthly existence so we could all be free. It was more than a simple gesture. Jesus could have easily asked his Father to spare him, but he chose to fulfill the Scriptures and die for our sins."

"Today, I get to introduce to you a man—a man who, in the Christian tradition of Jesus of Nazareth, is a giver. Sean Sullivan is not a member of my flock. He attends church somewhere else. Yet, he is as important to this church and its mission as I am through my services as its pastor.

"Sean Sullivan serves this congregation, and he serves many others in this inner-city community, by giving to those in need. If I had to count the number of times Sean Sullivan came to the aid of someone in need, I would have to use a calculator to tally them all up.

"When children have gone barefoot, Sean Sullivan gave them shoes. When their parents needed food to put on the table, Sean Sullivan made sure they did not go hungry. And when the oppressive arm of government comes down upon those who are least able to defend themselves, Sean Sullivan stands by their side in the courtroom. He soothes their fears and defends their liberty."

The congregation nodded their heads to the rhythm of Bolton's voice. Even some of the members of the media were starting to succumb to the cadence of the presentation and began nodding ever so slightly along with others in the room.

"My dear friends, Sean Sullivan is a giver. But today his role will change. Today, I will introduce him to you as a man who has given. But he will leave this podium as a candidate for the United States Congress."

Applause rippled through the church, but Reverend Bolton raised his hands to quiet the crowd.

"Now before you applaud, I need you to ask yourself a question. Are you ready to give? Because now is our time to give back to Sean Sullivan. We need to help him in his journey."

"Yes, sir," shouted the woman sitting behind Tiana. Others joined in.

"Are you ready to give?" Reverend Bolton asked as the applause began again. "Are you ready to give this community new leadership?" As the applause got louder, people began to shout and stand in the pews. "Are you ready to give this great country new hope and direction?" Bolton himself was shouting, but in a manufactured way. "Then ladies and gentlemen, I give ... I give ... I give you the next Congressman from Kentucky's Fourth Congressional District ... Brother Sean Sullivan."

"I told you," the camera man whispered to Griffith's trailer, "it would be a show."

The choir stood up and began to sing a gospel hymn, clapping in rhythm as Sean Sullivan rose and hugged Reverend Bolton. He then walked back to the choir and enveloped Shirley in a loving embrace. As he turned to the podium, he looked at Tiana and blew her a kiss. The choir continued to sing as Sullivan slowly, dramatically, made his way to the dais. He pulled out a small pair of wire-rimmed glasses and put them on. Unfolding a piece of paper he took from his coat pocket, Sullivan looked over at the choir director, who lowered his hands. The voices in the choir faded in response and the choir members sat down.

"Brother Bolton," Sullivan began, "thank you for that kind and far-too-generous introduction. I appreciate your good wishes, but there's an old Irish proverb that says you should praise the creek only after you've crossed it."

Reverend Bolton chuckled while thrusting his Bible in the air. "And cross it we shall, Brother Sullivan. Cross it we shall."

"Amen," Sullivan quietly affirmed. "Now everyone has told me when you announce as a candidate for public office, you're supposed to give a political speech." Sullivan held up the papers he pulled from his jacket. "This is what they've written for me."

Tiana put her fist to her mouth and silently chuckled to herself, knowing no one had written a speech for her father. She knew he was holding up racing results he printed out from the computer earlier in the day while checking the bets he made with his bookie.

"They tell me I am supposed to stand before you and read these words with great vim and vigor, as if somehow these words will convince you I am the man you should send to Washington to represent you in Congress."

Sullivan paused and held up the multiple pages of paper, looked at them momentarily and then, with great dramatic flair, tore them in half. The crowd erupted in wild applause as Sullivan declared, "But then again, they don't know me very well, do they?"

Sullivan waited for the crowd to quiet down and then resumed.

"I don't want to give a political speech to you fine folks. Political speeches are where a candidate comes before you and tells you what you want to hear, so you'll vote for him. I cannot, nay I will not, do that to you.

"I have been to your homes for dinner.

"I have watched your kids growing up on the street outside my office.

"I hate to say this, but for many of you," Sullivan pointed his finger at no one in particular, "...for...many...of ...you, I have even helped fold your laundry."

The crowd laughed and applauded.

"No. I know all you all far too well to give you the political speech they wrote for me."

"Many years ago, Richard Thompson gave you a political speech. Richard Thompson told you he was a new voice. He told you he would be by your side. Well, my friends, it seems in the years since he was elected, he has forgotten those things. But I can assure you I have not forgotten ..."

TWELVE

"I'm really proud of you, Joey," Thompson said to The Fat Man as he entered his office. "You've really stuck with this diet thing."

The Fat Man stood up, shook hands with Thompson, and then stepped back holding his arms wide and palms open to show off his new body. Known for years as "The Fat Man" because of his rotund figure, Joe Bradley attended a come-to-Jesus meeting with his own lifestyle. When told by a team of doctors he could choose between food and life, he adopted a new "fishes, but no loaves" menu. Eliminating half a dozen Mountain Dews and three "biggie" cheeseburger meals from his daily intake of calories had elicited a remarkable effect on his physique.

"Look at you," Thompson exclaimed, then laughed out loud watching The Fat Man do an awkward pirouette. "A new suit and everything."

"Old suit," replied The Fat Man as he sat back down behind his desk. "Luckily, I held onto all my old suits and shirts. They're all starting to fit again. It's like I have a whole new wardrobe."

"And wide ties are back in style. What a bonus," Thompson said with a smile.

The Fat Man chuckled. "Yeah, I'm a real trendsetter."

Trendsetter was hardly the proper word to describe The Fat Man. His scruffy beard and former pear shape often lulled visiting lawyers into a false sense of superiority. But lawyers in the community knew him as one of the smartest attorneys in the local bar, with true obsessive-compulsive tendencies. Judges rarely checked his research—they knew they didn't have to.

When Thompson left Washington as a staffer to return home and start a family with Ann, he joined the law firm where The Fat Man was already a partner. They immediately became close. Thompson took on causes in which The Fat Man also believed. When Thompson jumped into politics, The Fat Man followed along, bringing his anal retentive personality to the aid of Thompson's campaign endeavors. As a result, Thompson's campaigns were always fully informed about the issues that really mattered, as well as a great many background facts and remote contingencies most human beings would not find significant.

Thompson considered The Fat Man his closest friend, next to Griffith. He was truly proud of him for losing weight. "Seriously, you're looking really good. Have you lost 100 pounds yet?"

"Not yet, but I'm closing in on it," The Fat Man replied proudly.

"Well, keep at it."

"I have to," The Fat Man replied, pointing to the lunch in front of him—thin sliced turkey, without bread, a small bowl of edamame and a bottle of vitamin water. "Doctor Larry told me it was either this or I was gonna check out before I hit sixty. Want some?"

"No … uh, no thanks." Thompson sat down in the chair across from The Fat Man's desk. He looked around the room. His friend had been working in this office for years, yet his framed law license still rested on the floor, leaning against the wall. Redweld accordion folders of files were piled up around the desk. "How goes the research for the equine law class?"

The Fat Man pointed to twenty or so three-ring binders on the floor next to his desk. "It's all right there. Those binders contain all of the data on Keeneland sales for the last decade."

"Damn. That's a lot of horsies," Thompson replied, truly impressed by the sheer volume of sales.

"Damn is right. I've had our new intern spend a couple of weeks plugging all that information into Excel spreadsheets. I've come up with some interesting data, but I'm not really sure what it all means yet. All I know is there are a lot of people who are still paying a lot of money for horse flesh these days."

"So, what're you looking for?"

"Trends mainly," The Fat Man replied as he grabbed some turkey and stuffed it into his mouth.

He washed it down with vitamin water as he spoke. "I want to see how the swings in the economy have affected the price of horses."

"Like, do the rich and famous hold back in a recession?"

"Precisely," said The Fat Man. He used his computer mouse to click on one of the numerous windows he minimized at the bottom of his computer screen, and a graph suddenly replaced a still photo from the movie, *The Princess Bride,* he used as wallpaper. "This is pretty interesting," he said moving the mouse pointer around the graph for emphasis. "I'm comparing the increases and decreases in money spent at the horse sales against investment in high-price commercial real estate during the same time periods."

"Bottom feeders come out during a real estate recession," said Thompson. "They end up buying real estate out of foreclosure for pennies on the dollar."

"That's right," The Fat Man replied. "Except investment in real estate is a long-term proposition. Horses, by their very nature, tend to have a very limited useful investment life. The recession hasn't affected it as badly."

"Makes some sense, I guess. The horse has to win a few races before he goes to stud ... and then eventually dies."

"Right. We should be so lucky." The Fat Man minimized the graph on the screen. "So I'm going to compare the two and see if I can come up with any interesting correlations."

"Or contrasts?"

"I expect I'll find some of them, too."

Thompson reached over to The Fat Man's desk and grabbed the most recent copy of *The Blood-Horse*, a periodical devoted entirely to horses. A beautiful one-year-old thoroughbred wandering through a vividly green field at some Lexington, Kentucky horse farm was on the cover. "And every year there are the anomalies," Thompson said as he thumbed through the magazine.

"Yup," replied The Fat Man, chewing on more turkey. "I can never understand why some of these horses end up going for seven or eight figures."

"Expensive hobby." Thompson looked at the book shelves behind The Fat Man's desk as he spoke. A framed autographed photo of former Cincinnati Reds great, Tony Perez sat on one shelf right next to a picture of The Fat Man's wife and daughters snapped during one of their vacations in England. He mused to himself idly, wondering which photo The Fat Man valued more. "Well, I hate to do this to you," Thompson said, "but I've got to put one more thing on your plate."

"Name it." The Fat Man sat back in his chair.

"I got an official opponent today."

The Fat Man's obsessive tendencies compelled him to follow local politics closely ever since

Thompson first run for office. He knew the game and the players as well as the head of either local party. "Don't tell me Sean Sullivan has actually filed? I thought you'd get a free pass this year."

"There's apparently no such thing as a free pass," replied Thompson. "The old man is making his announcement right now at Reverend Bolton's church down in Covington."

The Fat Man rolled his chair back up and put his arms on the desk. "I'm really sorry to hear that. Word around the courthouse was that he was thinking about it, but no one thought he was serious. Then again, you always say you're only as good as your last two years in office."

"Thanks for reminding me. Sullivan is in."

"I wouldn't worry about him too much," said The Fat Man.

"I'm not worried," said Thompson, tossing the magazine back onto The Fat Man's desk. "But, Griff sure as hell is. He wants me to treat Sullivan like a real opponent. And, of course, he wants you to head up the research about the opposition."

The Fat Man grabbed his bar association directory and opened it up to Sullivan's information page. "Sullivan has represented a ton of criminal defendants at the trial level. He's down there every day looking for poor folk who can't afford lawyers. If someone approaches the bench without a lawyer, he just steps up and jumps right in."

"Yeah, so I hear."

"And," continued The Fat Man, "he's got a reputation for filing a shitload of pro bono cases in federal court."

"Exactly. Griff wants you to look at each one of them and find out what they're all about."

"Hang on," said The Fat Man as he swung around in his chair back to his computer. "Let me pull up the federal docket online." The Fat Man clicked a couple of links on his computer. "All-righty then ... lawyer name ... S-U-L-L-I-V-A-N ... enter." He clicked his mouse. "Holy crap." The Fat Man stared in stunned amazement at the computer screen.

"What?" Thompson asked as he leaned forward to get a glimpse.

"Look at all of these," said The Fat Man as he clicked down the list of cases. "I haven't worked on this many cases in my entire career, and this is just one court. I bet he's filed some in other districts, too. It'll take weeks to go though all of these cases."

"Sorry, man. I had no idea."

"Don't worry." The Fat Man began clicking to print the pages that appeared on his screen as he read them. "It's the price I pay for being your loyal sidekick." He glanced at Thompson. "Can you get me an intern or something to help me out? I've already used up my free-spin cards here at the firm by tapping into the kid who's been helping me with the research for the equine law seminar."

"That shouldn't be a problem. We've got a lot of college kids who want to volunteer."

The Fat Man again turned his attention back to his computer screen. "I'd heard he filed a lot of cases, but damn ..." He continued to scroll down the list. "1983."

"Civil rights violations," replied Thompson. "I expected a bunch of those."

"Qui tam," The Fat Man continued.

"That's a whistleblower cause of action, right?"

"Yeah," replied The Fat Man. He stared at the screen and continued to scroll down. "He's filed dozens of those."

"Well, here's an interesting case." The Fat Man paused and looked up at Thompson. "Have you been visited by a federal process server today?"

"No," replied Thompson, puzzled. "Why?"

The Fat Man rotated one of his two computer screens around for Thompson to view. "Here's his latest case ... it's styled, In re: Congressman Richard Thompson."

"What the fuck?" Thompson stood up and walked around the back of The Fat Man's desk to get a closer look, carefully stepping over and around case files spread out on the floor.

"You've been sued in federal court this morning. Sullivan's filed a lawsuit against you." The Fat Man looked at the information screen for the case. "He's asking the court for a writ of mandamus against you."

THIRTEEN

Press events for a political candidate have a lot in common with a traveling medicine show. A snake oil salesman, cure-all product in hand, sells his wares to a crowd of consumers who know up-front they are about to be had. Media representatives are often a similarly skeptical audience, so the campaigns do what they can to put their sometimes dubious messages in the most exciting and positive light they can muster.

President John Kennedy's handlers in the early 60s referred to press events as a three-ring circus, and they used all the tricks of the trade to their fullest advantage. If the campaign was expecting a crowd of 200 people, they would stage the event in a room that comfortably held 75. The overflow in the room would make it look more impressive to the press.

Sean Sullivan might have been a trial lawyer at heart, but he knew the tricks of staging press events almost as well as he knew the magic tricks he performed in front of juries. Both involved creating an illusion.

Before the effects of head trauma syndrome brought forth the eccentric changes in Sullivan's personality, he had been very active in politics. He was so astute he even led a so-called "advance team" on a couple of national campaigns, traveling ahead of the candidates to insure everything at each event was set up and running properly. He remembered those old lessons as he carefully planned the formal announcement of his candidacy for the United States Congress.

As he made his way ever so slowly through the supporters who came to the church to kick off his campaign, Sullivan shook hands with each of them. He tried to position himself at a perfect angle to the cameras covering him as he moved.

When he determined the press finally had enough "B-roll" for their story, Sullivan quit glad-handing and turned his attention to the press. "Thanks for coming by today. It must be a slow news day." A few of the reporters chuckled. "Seriously, I really appreciate it. Now, I'm sure you have a few questions?"

The reporters closed in tightly around Sullivan, thrusting their microphones and camera lenses into his face. "Why are you running?" asked an attractive brunette in a royal blue business suit.

"I am running for United States Congress because this country is headed in the wrong direction," said Sullivan, sound-biting his reply for future editing like a pro. "Richard Thompson is AWOL in the war against the forces that are holding back poor and middle-class Americans. Sean Sullivan is the voice of change. The working people of Kentucky know I stand with them in the battle for justice and equality."

"Thompson has strong name identification and

he won his last election by a large margin," said a young man who seemed to be hiding behind his own television camera.

"That's right," said Sullivan. "He does. So what?"

"Well, do you expect to win?" the man asked.

"Of course I do," snapped Sullivan. "I wouldn't file for this office if I didn't expect to win. The people understand what's at stake in this election, and they will vote accordingly."

"Mr. Sullivan," interjected a young blogger in a tattered button down shirt, who scribbled on a pad as he spoke. "Campaigns need money to get their message out. Congressman Thompson has amassed a good sized campaign war chest. Can you raise the same kind of money?"

"No," said Sullivan sternly, waggling his finger at the cameras for emphasis as he spoke. "In fact, I intend to go in the opposite direction. The people are tired of elected offices being bought and sold with the wallets of those who have. I represent the voices of those who have not. I will not accept any campaign contribution over $100 and I will send back any PAC check I receive."

Sullivan paused two beats for effect, and then continued. "Richard Thompson has become a slave with unclean hands, hoarding the funds he extorts from his buddies up on Wall Street like a miser. I will take my campaign directly to the people."

"Then how do you expect to win?" the young man

behind the camera followed up.

"I was wondering how long it would take someone to ask that question," Sullivan said, a sly smile on his face as he spoke. "Ladies and gentlemen, please meet my press secretary, Ms. Tiana Bolton." Tiana entered the fray and began to hand out a fifteen page document to the reporters. The look of confusion among them was universal.

"What is this?" asked the brunette in the business suit.

"Ms. Bolton has just given you a copy of a federal lawsuit I filed today against Congressman Richard Thompson," Sullivan announced proudly.

"You've sued Richard Thompson?" a radio reporter replied, sticking her microphone closer to Sullivan. "For what?"

"While the complaint is a bit lengthy, the principle behind the lawsuit itself is quite simple," said Sullivan, now controlling the press corps just as he controlled so many juries over his lifetime. "I filed an equity action asking the sitting Federal Judge to issue a writ of mandamus against Congressman Richard Thompson."

"What's a writ of mandamus?" Sullivan was not sure even who asked the question, but he knew they were all thinking the same thing. He shifted slightly from one foot to the other before answering.

"A writ of mandamus is a seldom used legal action. It is so rare those of you who cover the courthouse beat have probably never seen it used. In Latin, it simply means 'We command.' Such a writ is issued when the Court orders a government entity to take a specific action."

"And what are you asking the court to command?" the print guy asked as he thumbed through the lawsuit.

"I am asking the Federal Court issue a writ of mandamus ordering Congressman Richard Thompson to vote in opposition to the Energy and Water Appropriation Bill."

"You're what?" asked an amazed reporter.

"Congressman Richard Thompson ran on a campaign he was against action by the federal government. As I point out in the lawsuit, his exact classification of his own political views is ...," Sullivan opened the lawsuit to a dog-eared page and read, "... 'a Goldwater conservative with a mean streak of populism.' Yet, when he had the opportunity to vote accordingly, he has not done so."

"You're going to have to give us more than that Mr. Sullivan. I know I'm not following you. And I bet no one else is either."

"It's quite simple. Congressman Richard Thompson has fraudulently induced the people of the Fourth Congressional District into voting for him. In order to get out votes, he promised us one thing. Then he got to Washington and has done another. I want the court to hold Richard Thompson accountable for his words and mandamus him to vote in opposition to legislation he has promised to oppose."

Tiana got caught up in the excitement of the moment and blurted out, "And, we're asking for an emergency hearing."

All heads suddenly turned her way. She froze until she heard Sullivan's voice. "Yes, Ms. Bolton, why don't you explain that to these folks?"

"Well," Tiana stuttered. She was suddenly rendered speechless from several microphones being thrust in her face. Then she looked up and saw her father beaming with pride. She straightened her shoulders and addressed the media. "The Energy and Water Appropriation Bill is scheduled to be up for a vote on the floor of the United States House of Representatives when Congress returns from its next recess. The response and discovery time for a normal lawsuit would take us outside that window. Therefore, we are asking the court for an emergency hearing. We are asking that a hearing be held during the recess in order to allow timely consideration of our request for a writ of mandamus before the vote."

"I'm sorry. I didn't catch your name."

"Tiana. Tiana Bolton."

Tiana looked up again, and noticed her father was tearfully focused on her. Her mother moved in next to him. She carefully considered her next words.

"Strike that." Tiana notched her chin up ever so slightly. "My name is Tiana Bolton-Sullivan."

FOURTEEN

As the big black Ford Explorer made its way down King Street in Old Town Alexandria, Jane Kline sat, eyes closed, in the back seat. A stack of neatly folded international newspapers sat unopened at her side. Kline was tired. She felt she did not have the strength to pick up even one of the newspapers, let alone read and comprehend it.

The padded headrest on the black leather back seat cushioned Kline's head as the car approached The Potomac River. She slowly rolled her shoulders backwards and did some deep breathing to try to relax, but Kline's back was killing her. So she restlessly opened her eyes and looked out the window at the college kids and tourists making their way in and out of the bars, shops and restaurants. She spied a pair of Raggedy Ann and Andy dolls in a shop window. Kline was not sure if she looked like a crumpled rag doll, but she sure as hell felt like one.

Ease back into it. That was the advice Kline's doctor gave her about returning to work. But anyone who knew Jane Kline knew she did not "ease into" anything. Instead, she was the kind of person who tended to dive in without first dipping her toe in to test the temperature of the water. People with Type A personalities were envious of her drive. When she was a teenager in high school, her father used to tease her about her gung-ho nature. "Full tilt Bozo" was what Mick Kline called his youngest daughter.

But the explosion, and all the injuries Jane Kline sustained from it, had taken a physical and emotional toll on her. When she felt the time was right, she jumped head first back into work, whether she was truly ready or not. It turned out that maybe she was not, but that was her nature. Kline knew it was a crucial time for the Agency. The CIA lost its leader and the Agency deserved a full-time director—whether she was personally up to the challenge or not. She would force herself to perform.

The pressure was tremendous. Something had to give and Kline decided that "something" was her personal life. She told Leo Argo it was time to step back from their relationship for a while. Magazine articles advising women on their love lives would call it "personal space." Kline thought of it as a couple of hours in the day she needed to take back in order to regain control of her life. Argo argued with her, but Kline was firm in her resolve. She was America's top spook now and, despite her desire to the contrary, she just did not have time for a boyfriend.

God, how childish that phrase sounded to her when she said it to Argo ... "boyfriend." When she first let the word slip from her mouth, she felt like some teeney-bopper experiencing a school-girl crush. Now, as she headed home to a townhouse devoid of any human companionship, she felt an emptiness she never suffered before in her life. She spent most of her days in the field, and before Argo, had never been committed to any real or deep relationship. Now that she had experienced it, she found it hard to let go. Some would consider her decision to choose her country over herself a noble decision, but at this moment in her life the decision left her empty and alone. Noble and proud would come later, she silently supposed.

Kline determined that standing as the resolute, albeit lonely, leader was her lot in life. Perhaps it was God's punishment for the unspeakable things she did as a CIA operative. Justifiable as her actions were from the standpoint of America's security, she long ago came to a personal realization that Judgment Day for her would be painful. She believed God would judge her more harshly than the old men at the CIA who gave her the orders. With this as the morbid foundation of Kline's belief in her personal salvation, imagining she was entitled to something more personally fulfilling seemed like another of life's rewards out of her reach. It was so complicated, and yet, so simple at the same time... she just missed Leo.

"Director," the voice of her driver and bodyguard, Jim Day, shook her from her reverie. "Director Kline. You're home now."

"Thanks, Agent Day," Kline replied, quickly focusing. She grabbed her cane and pulled at the car door handle at the same time.

"Whoa, Director." Day reached into the back seat and put his hand on Kline's cane. "You shouldn't be exiting the car until I get to your door first."

Kline chuckled sarcastically at the agent's overly protective gesture. "Agent Day, you do realize I was fighting the fucking Cold War before you were even born, don't you?" She snatched her cane away from Day's grasp.

"Yes, Director." Day begrudgingly let go of the cane. "I've read about that Cold War thing in history books." He looked directly at her. Despite his sarcastic tone, his eyes were deadly serious. "But I've got my orders, Madame Director, and those orders are to protect you. Please let me do my job."

Kline smiled to herself at the young man's insistence. *He's got a big set of balls*, she thought to herself. Day was cut and fit, but even missing one leg, Kline thought that, considering her experience, she could take him in an alley fight. Still, she knew Day was making a point she should heed. "Fine, Agent Day. I'll wait. Let me know when you're ready." Kline pulled the cane to her side and waited.

Day exited the car and surveyed a block in either direction to make sure it was secure. As Kline watched the agent casing the block, she noticed, and not for the first time, how attractive the man actually was. She may have decided to get men out of her life for the time being, but she wasn't dead either. Day was an attractive man. His tall frame, square jaw and stone physique could have made him a model for a fitness magazine. In fact, MacKenzie once called him the Agency's "blond boy toy." It was a phrase Kline had forbidden to be repeated, but she thought about it now as Day opened her door.

Kline exited the car and hobbled towards her steps, with Day following closely behind. "That's all for today, Agent," she told Day as she started up the steps. "Thank you."

"Not quite, Director," replied Day. He continued to hover directly behind Kline. "I've been instructed to follow you to the door and then walk Hoover before heading home."

Kline acquiesced in the earlier protective coddling, but the thought that Day wanted to walk her dog pissed her off. "No way," she shot back. "Walking my dog isn't part of your job description."

"Sorry Director, but it is now."

"Says who?"

"Says Deputy Director MacKenzie."

Kline drew her lips tight as she spoke. "Zachary doesn't have that kind of authority over me."

"He said you'd say that," Day replied. "And apparently he does. He told me to tell you that you signed an executive order putting him in charge of security, and he's quite worried about you walking Hoover up and down the streets of Alexandria without cover. I'm under direct orders from

MacKenzie to walk Hoover. I can't check out tonight until Hoover has … ahem … done his business."

"Sonofabitch," Kline gritted her teeth before she said anything further. Chain of command was important at the Agency and, although she was in charge, she was not about to object to MacKenzie's orders in front of a subordinate. "So, your orders are to keep me alive by picking up Hoover's poop? Fine," she replied. "You can walk Hoover tonight. I'll take this up with Deputy Director MacKenzie tomorrow."

"Thank you, Director," said a relieved Day as they reached the top of the townhouse stairs. They could hear Hoover barking inside.

Kline remembered back to her days as a young operative, when she, too, had followed orders she felt were silly or inconsequential. A grin broke out across her face as she suddenly felt some empathy with Day. The kid literally had a shit assignment. "You're right Agent Day. I'm sorry for being curt with you. Come on in and I'll introduce you to Hoover."

FIFTEEN

Papers were strewn all across the right side of The Fat Man's desk. A black binder labeled "Sullivan v Thompson, Writ of Mandamus, Pleadings" sat on top of the pile like a paperweight. On the left side of The Fat Man's desk stood seven three-ring binders containing the research for his upcoming equine seminar. The Fat Man, sitting unnaturally low in his chair, was looking like a bearded, round-faced warrior peeking out from between the two turrets of his paper castle. He sat behind the files and binders and peered at the two young people sitting in uncomfortable chairs on the other side of his paper fortress, Brit Rodgers and Tito Mendes.

The office paralegal, Brit Rodgers, was a fit, attractive, shorthaired blond who spent her free time as a weekend warrior for the local Army Reserve unit. The Fat Man was not shy in mentioning to others at the law firm how he was smitten by the combination of her good looks, keen intellect, and vivacious personality. Rodgers had been assisting The Fat Man in the compilation of economic data regarding the horse sales held throughout the year at Keeneland race track in Lexington, Kentucky. She sat in her chair, clutching her cup of coffee with both hands as The Fat Man began to fumble around with the mouse, maximizing and minimizing some of the numerous windows he had active on his dual-monitor computer screens.

Tito Mendes, a third year law student, leaned his left elbow on the arm of his chair in order to look around the binders on The Fat Man's desk. From Brazil, Mendes was visiting the local law school via a foreign exchange program. Mendes had been so impressed with a lecture Congressman Thompson had given at the law school that he volunteered for the campaign on evenings and weekends. The brown-eyed Brazilian soccer player had a bright smile that stood out under his curly black mustache and matching hair. At Thompson's request, Mendes got the campaign assignment of assisting The Fat Man with the research on Sullivan's writ of mandamus lawsuit. It was clear from his rigid posture Mendes was uncomfortable at being the "new guy" in the room.

"All right," said The Fat Man in a matter-of-fact tone. He turned away from his computer screens, leaned forward and placed his elbows on his desk. "It's the bottom of the ninth and I've got to decide who I have left on my bench."

"Excuse me, sir?" Mendes spoke up with a confused look on his face. He had a legal pad on his lap, but he did not write down any notes. It was clear Mendes did not understand The Fat Man's baseball reference.

"He speaks a lot in baseball analogies," murmured Rodgers, hoping to help the newcomer through The Fat Man's latest ball game laden advice. She took a sip of her coffee.

Mendes leaned in toward The Fat Man with a concerned look on his face. He had only met with The Fat Man a couple of times previously, and Mendes was afraid his lack of baseball knowledge was about to give offense. "I am sorry, sir," he said. "I am afraid I am quite unfamiliar with the game of American baseball."

Rodgers laughed so hard she nearly spit out her coffee. The Fat Man was obsessed with baseball. The thought that someone innocently walked into such a gaffe with her boss caused Rodgers' outburst. "Oh, that's priceless," she said, trying to regain her composure while looking at The Fat Man's shocked face.

"What?" replied Mendes. His expression quickly went from one of concern to one of sheer panic as he glanced back and forth between Rodgers and The Fat Man. "Did I say something wrong?"

"No," said Rodgers as she pointed at The Fat Man. "Joe, here, just loves baseball. The fact that everyone does not share his passion is probably going to be crushing to him." She looked over at The Fat Man with a smile, hoping he saw the humor in the situation as well. Instead, she encountered a completely blank and slightly confused expression.

"Sorry, sir," Mendes replied. "I just don't know the sport."

"Alrightie then," The Fat Man said—his rising angst quite apparent in his voice. "That's going to be a problem," he said as he stroked his scraggly beard. He paused and then found a solution. "Okay, Tito, let's try this. There's a soccer match, or a football match whatever you call it, and it's all tied up. I have to decide what strategy to employ in determining the order of my penalty kicks. So, I've got to know where everyone stands at the end of the game ... how they feel and if they can perform. Got it?"

"Yes, sir," replied Mendes. "I think so."

The Fat Man leaned back in his chair and smiled. "You've got to quit calling me sir," he said.

"Yes, sir."

Rodgers looked at The Fat Man and shrugged her shoulders. "Okay," The Fat Man continued, "we got the brief filed on Sullivan's motion. The hearing is up next. Any idea on how it was received?"

Mendes reached down into his brown leather brief case next to him on the floor. He sifted through several files, pulling out the one which contained his typewritten notes. As he was looking at the file, Rodgers made eye contact with The Fat Man, raising her eye brows in silent and somewhat mocking recognition of Mendes's organizational efforts.

Mendes found his spot and continued. "I spoke with Cassie in the clerk's office, sir. She said Judge

Gunning is going to recuse himself from the case, but is going to wait until the last minute to sign the order."

"So, he's going to punt it?" said The Fat Man.

"Again, sir, I am not catching the reference."

"American football this time," said Rodgers. "Don't try to keep up. He'll be using movie references by the end of the meeting." The Fat Man shot Rodgers a disgruntled look. "I'm just sayin," she said smiling as she spoke. "I'm just sayin.'"

"Does Cassie have any idea who we'll get?" asked The Fat Man.

"They are not sure yet. Apparently, all of the judges who are in this court district like both Mr. Sullivan and Congressman Thompson too much to become involved."

"That's a basis for recusal in our system, Tito," The Fat Man responded.

"Yes, sir. I understand and I find it very interesting."

"How so?"

"Well, sir, in most Latin American countries, friendship is exactly what you seek in a judge, even if the friendship has to be bought."

"They'll probably get some retired circuit judge to come in and handle the case."

"Yes, sir."

"Keep an eye on it and let Brit know as soon as we get a name. She can help you get the scouting report on the new judge."

Without waiting for the question from Mendes, Rodgers looked over and mouthed, "I'll explain it to you later."

"And we're running out of time," The Fat Man added. He pulled the binder with the pleadings off the pile of papers and flipped to the last page. He looked closely at a Scheduling Order as he spoke. "The hearing is almost on us. I'd damn sure like to know who I'm arguing in front of before I walk into the courtroom. All we need is some former appellate judge to walk into this thing and feel compelled to make new law."

"Understood, sir, but what do we do if we get one—an appellate judge who wants to make new law?"

"Who knows … zig instead of zag." Catching himself making yet another reference Mendes might not understand, The Fat Man quickly corrected himself. "I mean I may have to lead off with our best striker instead of saving him for last."

"Got it, sir."

The Fat Man turned his attention to Rodgers. "Okay Brit, how about you? Right after the argument, I've got to scoot down to Lexington for the horse sales."

"Yup."

"Why don't you call me 'sir' like Tito does?"

"Because I've known you too long."

"Fair enough."

"So what's happening at Keeneland? Any good horses listed for sale at the auction?" The Fat Man shuffled through the various binders on his desk looking for something he obviously could not locate.

Rodgers handed The Fat Man a thin, three ring binder. "If you're looking for your sale binder, I came in and got it this morning. I had printouts on three new horses, some late entries to the sale, I wanted to add."

"Good." The Fat Man grabbed the binder from Rodgers and began to leaf through it.

"Check out the one on the back page."

The Fat Man immediately turned to the final entry in the binder. "Finn's Lassie," he said as he scanned the vitals on the filly. "She doesn't look like anything special."

"She's not," replied Rodgers, "except she's being put up by that Irish breeder who had the big sale at the last auction."

"County Mayo Stables," replied The Fat Man. He opened up a drawer on his desk and pulled out a yellow highlighter, popped off the cap and highlighted the name of the breeder on the page.

"Yeah, that's the one," Rodgers confirmed. "Finn's Lassie is another late entry into the auction. They just put her up yesterday."

"That's perfect," said an enthusiastic Fat Man. "I'd like to meet the geniuses at that barn. They've been getting top dollar every time they go to auction. I'd love to know what advance marketing they're doing to get that kind of cash for the nags they're putting up." He scanned the sheet. "They have Clarke Sales doing their marketing for them again. Call around and see if you can find out if anyone will be in Lexington from Ireland for the seller."

"Got it," Rodgers replied.

The Fat Man stood up, indicating to his young colleagues their meeting was over. "Okay, we've all got our orders, and remember no sonofabitch ever won a war by dying for his country."

"I take it that is the movie reference you warned me about?" asked Mendes.

"Yup," laughed Rodgers.

SIXTEEN

Richard Thompson adjusted the speaker buds on his iPod deeper into his ears as he settled back into the first-class leather chair of the big jet carrying him and Ann to Dublin, Ireland. They were just far enough into the flight that the attendant announced that using electronic devices was now permitted. Thompson looked out the window and saw the buildings of Manhattan disappearing on the horizon. The sun was casting a beautiful orange glow as it set to the west of the city. On his right, Ann was quietly engrossed in a new novel she purchased at LaGuardia's New York Times Book Store.

As the plane continued to gain altitude, Thompson hoped the tension he experienced lately would remain on the runway behind him. It had been a long, stressful couple of weeks leading up to the trip. He was glad to be leaving everything—and everybody for that matter—behind him. He breathed a sigh of relief knowing that, if only for ten days or so, he and Ann would be alone.

Each second of airborne travel seemed to put one more mile between Thompson and his reelection campaign, which he correctly identified as the ultimate source of his uneasiness. For a short time, at least, he would not be making calls for campaign cash, giving speeches to some Rotary Club or dodging reporters who were asking questions about Sean Sullivan's damn lawsuit.

When New York's skyline disappeared entirely, and there was nothing to see outside the window but darkness, Thompson asked the flight attendant for a Maker's Mark bourbon on the rocks. Once it was delivered, Thompson swirled the ice around in the glass before taking a sizable gulp. He closed his eyes and could almost feel his blood pressure drop a point or ten as he savored the taste. A second sip quickly followed the first.

After the bourbon settled nicely, Thompson decided to tackle what he hoped would be his toughest decision of this trip: what music he would listen to as he drifted off to sleep on the long night flight across the Atlantic Ocean.

Music was a big part of Thompson's life, and he almost always could identify the perfect tune to fit his circumstance. He frequently changed the lyrics of songs to adapt them to the moment. He always seemed to be humming or whistling some obscure tune—and the more obscure the better. Thompson had a near photographic memory for lyrics that allowed him to pull songs out of his mental juke box at will. Ann often told friends her biggest cross to bear was living with a walking soundtrack.

Thompson fiddled with the dial on his iPod. His first stop on the music menu was his regular play list of John Prine, Warren Zevon, and Meat Loaf tunes. But the list caused him to groan out loud. He begrudgingly realized he was starting to associate this group of songs by his favorite artists—songs he repeatedly played to relax after a long day on the Hill— with the tension in his neck and shoulders that he was trying to escape.

This trip was different. He was going someplace new. He wanted a chance to relax, not just unwind. But he would also have a chance to do something important for himself and his family. Thompson wanted—no, he needed—music on this flight to capture his sense of anticipation and take his mood to the next level.

Thompson looked out the window and thought about the distance he was traveling, and how long it would take by boat. He was on his way to Ireland, the home of his father's ancestors. He had dreamed of visiting there ever since he first read some old family letters—words written a century and a half ago by his great-great grandfather.

The young Irishman and his bride made the journey to America around 1850 from County Galway. Thompson and his wife were retracing those steps in a single night. This was a trip his father had always wanted to take, but never actually made. The awareness of that fact made this more than just an educational exchange or relaxing vacation. Thompson's Ireland adventure was going to be the fulfillment of a family obligation. He decided he should try to listen to some music appropriate to the level of this personal challenge.

Thompson smiled as a sudden thought jolted through him like a stiff shot of Irish whiskey. "Ah, the Pogues," he mumbled while he set the iPod dial and clicked. "Perfect, just perfect."

"What?" replied Ann. Thompson's mumbling disturbed Ann's reading and she looked up from her book and leaned towards her husband.

Thompson removed one of the ear buds and turned in his seat toward Ann. He gently put his hand on her leg. "I said I'm going to listen to some old Pogues music on the flight over the Pond. I want to get in an Irish state of mind. If Shane MacGowan doesn't do it for me, nothing will," he chuckled softly.

"Wow," said Ann, grinning crookedly as she spoke. "That sure brings back some old memories." She paused and cocked her head. In the early years of their relationship, Ann had faced up to a serious drinking problem. Reminded of their dates before her first Alcoholics Anonymous meeting, Ann continued, "Along with a couple of nights I'm more than glad to forget."

In their younger days, Thompson and Ann were regulars at the Dubliner, an Irish Pub in Washington, DC, located a few blocks from the Senate side of the Capitol. The musicians who played there on weekends occasionally covered some Pogues tunes. Like most who frequented the Dubliner, the pair loved to sing along with the musicians. Also, like the regulars, the more Guinness the two had consumed, the louder they sang.

The young couple eventually got to know the musicians so well that occasionally they would let Thompson play mandolin as they sang "Dirty Old Town." It was one of the things that kept them going to the Dubliner even after Ann quit drinking. Thompson rarely picked up his mandolin since being elected to Congress, but he still moved his fingers as if fretting along every time he heard the song.

"Yeah," said Thompson smiling. "Those were some fun times, huh?"

"Or not," Ann replied, holding up her palms as if to stop the bad memories of her past drinking issues from overwhelming her. "Sometimes those wild nights seem like a lifetime ago."

Thompson grabbed her open palm and encircled it with his hands. He remembered the day Ann checked into rehab and the pain her drinking caused them both. Memories like those were usually stored deep within their collective psyche. When they did occasionally surface, they were painful. Ann fell off the wagon when Thompson was first elected to Congress. He was instantly distraught at the thought of those memories arising now, at the start of what was supposed to be a fun trip. He turned and looked deep into her eyes. "I'm sorry, babe. I didn't mean to bring that up."

"That's okay," Ann replied. She smiled in an effort to try to make her husband feel better. "I just hadn't thought about those days in a long while. Not all of those memories are bad, Richard."

"But it's always there," replied Thompson. "It's always just on the outskirts waiting to come in, isn't it?"

"Well, if I were Richard Thompson, I'd probably sing about what a long, strange trip it's been." Ann chuckled, half singing and half speaking the lyrics.

"Oh well, we've turned out okay. We're having a pretty good life."

Ann brought up their hands to her lips and gently … lovingly … kissed Thompson's. "Yes, we are," she replied. She saw the look in Thompson's eyes and knew he was anxious about having brought up old, bad memories. Ann knew the trip meant a great deal to her husband and tried to allay his concerns. "It's okay," she insisted. "I'm fine. Look, what happened back then is a part of us. We never forget, but we forgive and move on with life. You know that as well as I do. And we're both stronger for it. That's what recovery is all about."

Ann grabbed Thompson's dangling iPod ear bud and placed it in his empty hand. "Now, get your tunes on and have another drink." After sobering up, Ann never minded that Thompson continued to imbibe. She understood she had the addictive personality, not him. More importantly, she knew that a snoot-full on occasion did help him unwind his high-strung, type-A personality. Besides, Ann thought Thompson was a fun drunk who could keep her laughing through more than a couple of rounds of drinks.

"You need to get Griffith, Sullivan, and everyone back at home out of your head for a couple of days. It's time for us to build some new memories this week." Ann squeezed the inside of Thompson's thigh and whispered seductively, "Happy memories."

Thompson put the ear bud back, leaned over and kissed Ann on the cheek. He knew what she was feeling, and he appreciated the fact she let him up off the mat. "Agreed." Using the awkward silence between him and Ann as a reason to take a long sip of bourbon, Thompson closed his eyes in order to better savor the taste while his mind attempted to let go of the pressures of his life.

Ann is right, Thompson thought to himself. *I've got to get that son-of-a-bitch Sullivan off my mind. I can't believe I'm even this upset about him. The old fart is a nut, and Griffith is going to bury him. Still, I just can't get that damn lawsuit out of my head.*

And for God's sake, it's just a lawsuit. People file them every day. Hell, The Fat Man and I filed a million of them over the years. The only thing special about this one is that it's against me. No one cares about it, and neither should I. The voters will see it as a stunt.

He swallowed and swirled the bourbon around in the glass before taking another drink. *I've got to get over this. I can't let it spoil Ireland for Ann and me. The Fat Man has it all under control. He's the smartest lawyer in town. Hell, he may be the smartest lawyer in the whole state. I can't get anyone better on the case. If anyone can get the judge to the right answer, it's him.*

And Griffith has the campaign under control, too. My poll numbers are right where they need to be. This lawsuit won't move a single vote. I don't have a thing to worry about.

Thompson flicked his finger at the ice in the near-empty glass. He reached for the iPod and turned up the volume. As he listened to the songs, however, no increase in the degree of sound could drown out the thoughts in his head. *Fuck me. Why is this case bothering me so damn much?*

On the day after Sean Sullivan announced his campaign against Thompson, a process agent dropped by Thompson's local Congressional office and formally served him with a copy of <u>Sullivan v. Thompson</u>. Initially, Thompson was only slightly irritated by the lawsuit and considered it nothing more than a campaign stunt … a very clever one, but a stunt nonetheless. Thompson's level of concern was raised a bit when, following some basic research, The Fat Man informed Thompson the suit actually had some merit.

The legislation at the heart of Sullivan's lawsuit, the Energy and Water Appropriation Bill, originated in the House Committee on Appropriations—or as Members of Congress call it, the College of Cardinals. Contained in the legislation was the funding for all the federal agencies that deal with energy policy and water development. Along with giving lump sums of money to various federal agencies, the legislation also contained line item appropriations for specific projects across the country. People who live in the Congressional districts that get the money often refer to these line-item appropriations as "earmarks." People who live in districts that don't get them generally call them "pork."

Thompson and his staff worked very hard to get a rural water development project into the appropriation bill. One of the counties in Thompson's Congressional district desperately needed water lines, and Thompson thought getting funding for the project into the spending bill was a good return on the tax dollars his constituents sent to Washington. Of course, once the project was in the final bill, the College of Cardinals expected a favorable vote from Thompson when the bill came to the House floor for passage. That vote was scheduled to be taken the week following the current recess.

And the lead up to that vote was where Sean Sullivan caught Richard Thompson "in the act" of breaking a promise Thompson had made in previous campaigns. In each of his runs for Congress, Thompson vowed opposition to any appropriation bill that increased federal spending over the previous fiscal year in an amount greater than the cost of living.

In his early years in Congress, Thompson used that rule as a strict litmus test for voting on spending bills. Of course, in those days, Thompson didn't have the political pull to get any of his district's projects into those bills. Earmarks, quite frankly, had not been a concern. However, that quickly changed for Thompson by the time he reached his second term in Congress. With assistance from another Congressman, Thompson was able to place some specific funding for a local university into the bill that appropriated overall federal spending on education.

Those efforts had been praised by the local Chamber of Commerce. The local media heralded his accomplishment. Before long, Thompson convinced himself the inclusion of good local projects in appropriation bills was sufficient justification for violating his own rules of voting. He still talked about his strict rule on the campaign trail, but no one ever brought up his actual voting record.

The Energy and Water Appropriation Bill posed a larger problem for Thompson. It did contain a Thompson earmarked project. But, it also increased spending on all other related federal programs by nearly 8%. He had to balance his voting values against the needs of some local constituents who really needed water lines. Despite his uneasiness at the size of the overall increase, Thompson publicly stated his support for the legislation.

In his lawsuit, Sullivan alleged Thompson made an enforceable promise to voters. Sullivan contended Thompson's pledge had, in fact, been relied upon by voters in making their decisions to cast ballots for him. As the legislation included an increase in overall spending nearly three times the size of the increase in the cost of living, Sullivan was asking the Court to hold Thompson to his vow and order him to vote "no" on the bill.

Thompson concluded he was not irritated so much by the lawsuit itself. It received only a day's worth of play in the local newspaper, and the article included pictures of people from the rural community who were hoping to get the federally funded water lines. What annoyed Thompson the most, he decided, was the fact Sullivan apparently did not realize how badly the water lines were needed. Thompson felt he was doing something noble for the community, and was being unjustly criticized for his actions.

Now, to add to Thompson's stress, The Fat Man was telling him that, at least technically, the case had some merit. While the concept of Congressional immunity would probably lead to the case ultimately being dismissed, The Fat Man nevertheless felt Sullivan skillfully crafted a valid cause of action against Thompson … or at least one that would survive a motion for summary judgment. In short, Sullivan v. Thompson was going to be around for a while. The lawsuit was going to be a royal thorn in Thompson's side.

Whenever Thompson felt his nerves being frayed by the tension of political worries, Michael Griffith was usually there to talk him off the political window ledge. But never having faced a campaign tactic like this one, the filing of the lawsuit had done a number on Griffith's head as well. Lawsuits are certainly nothing new in politics, but they were generally filed after the campaign to contest the vote count, not to compel votes on the floor of the House of Representatives after an election was decided. And an actual lawsuit about an incumbent's voting record was unheard of. The complaint filed against Thompson by Sullivan had Griffith walking on boggy political ground, and he was having trouble finding a firm foothold.

Initially, Griffith's knee-jerk reaction was to try to get Thompson to cancel his Ireland trip. But then, when the emergency hearing requested by Sullivan ended up being scheduled during the week when Thompson had already planned to be overseas, Griffith changed his mind. In fact, he encouraged Thompson and his wife to take the trip as scheduled. Griffith ultimately decided he was more comfortable with having Thompson unavailable to the press until the hearing played out. In other words, Griffith would rather deal with the bad press from a junket than the possibility of awkward "no comments" from

Thompson himself during the contemporaneous media coverage at the hearing itself.

So here Thompson sat—on a plane to Dublin, Ireland, with the Pogues blasting "Dirty Old Town" in his ears and another freshly poured Maker's Mark in his hand.

Look at her, Thompson thought as he glanced over at Ann. *She's beautiful. Back in the day when we were staffers, she could have had any guy on the Hill. Hell, she still turns heads. But she chose to spend her life with me, some geeky-looking, girl-shy policy wonk from a small town in Kentucky. Forget filing lawsuits, winning campaigns, and passing legislation … forget all of that. Having that woman love and support me is the greatest accomplishment in my life.*

Thompson leaned over and kissed Ann on the cheek two times in quick succession.

Ann looked up from her book with a puzzled smile on her face. "What was that for?" she queried.

Thompson sung his response while playing an air-mandolin.

Kissed my girl by the factory wall,
Dirty old town,
Dirty old town.

SEVENTEEN

"Oh my God, Josh," squealed Ann as she approached Josh Barkman. Josh was waiting for his old boss Congressman Thompson and the Congressman's wife by the baggage claim in Terminal One at Dublin Airport. Ann rushed up and engulfed Josh in a big hug. Neither Thompson nor Ann had seen Josh since he had left Thompson's staff to become Charge d'affaire at the US Embassy in Romania. They had spoken by phone and exchanged emails on a weekly basis.

Pulling back, Ann looked at him. Ann put her hand on Josh's chin and turned his head from side to side. "Look at you. You've grown a beard." Josh smiled sheepishly as Ann released her grip. Despite the fact the facial hair covered most of his face, Ann could see the redness rise in his cheeks. Josh was embarrassed.

Thompson was standing behind his wife, watching the reunion. He was proud Josh developed a solid reputation in the community of America's players in international affairs. Like his wife, Thompson was glad to see Josh and teased him about the new look. "Beard?" Thompson exclaimed. "It's damn peach fuzz. Put some milk on his face and a cat could lick it off."

"Hey, boss," said Josh. He stepped around Ann and put out his hand to greet Thompson.

Thompson bypassed the handshake and hugged the young man with as much enthusiasm as Ann. "Sorry, kid. A handshake just isn't going to cut it." Ann stood back as Thompson gripped Josh in a hug she was sure would break one of Josh's ribs. Thompson gripped Josh as if somehow the hug would release the ache both were feeling about the reunion.

Josh Barkman had been a young, naive kid from the Midwest when he had become the political director for Richard Thompson's first run for Unites States Congress. Michael Griffith took the young man under his wing and taught him the ways of politics. When Thompson won his first race, the curly haired blond followed him to Washington to become the new Congressman's chief of staff. A few years later, while assisting Griffith on a trip to work on a foreign campaign in Romania, Josh was kidnapped by Communist rebels living in the Carpathian Mountains. Eventually freed, the experience left Josh Barkman a confused and shattered young man.

After the dust from the kidnapping settled, Josh returned to Romania, but the demons spawned by the memories proved to be too much for him. The traumatic events in Romania ultimately produced a very natural desire to leave Bucharest, but he found he was not ready to return to the United States either. He was withdrawn and still trying to work through what happened. When a job with NATO had opened up, Josh jumped at the opportunity, packed his personal and emotional bags, and moved to London.

Josh was asked by NATO leaders to attend the conference in Dublin to meet with one of its speakers, Wasfi Al Ghazawi, the Executive Director of Abraham's Olive Tree, a moderate Palestinian organization which advocated resolution of Middle East conflict through peaceful negotiations rather than violence. Once Josh secured his own plans to attend, he was able to get Thompson invited to the conference as a guest of NATO. Josh had not been face-to-face with the Thompsons since he had left for the job in Romania, and he was hopeful the reunion would further his emotional recovery.

Thompson pulled away from Josh and looked at him. Remarkably, after spending weeks considering all of the things he wanted to say to Josh when he saw him in person, the impact of the meeting had rendered Thompson speechless. "You look great," was all Thompson could manage.

Josh laughed and shook his head at Thompson's obvious lack of words. "Go on," he said, pointing to a luggage carousel. "Go wait for your luggage and I'll stay here with Ann. When you find your bags, I'll get us a cab."

"Cab?" asked Thompson, frowning. He expected Josh would have a rental car to use while they were in Ireland.

"Yeah. I know you want to spend a couple of days out in the countryside sightseeing, but I didn't get you a car for the conference. The streets of Dublin are confusing as hell. When you want to head out on your own, we'll get you a rental car from somewhere out on the edge of town. It'll be easier. Trust me." Josh paused and again looked over at the baggage claim. "Do you want me to get your bags?"

"I'll get my own bags, thank you very much," Thompson said firmly. "I'm not that old, Junior."

"You sure couldn't tell from the hair," Josh said jokingly, gesturing at Thompson's gray hair. "As we used to say back home, it looks like there's a little frost on the ol' pumpkin."

"I see you're still trying to be the funny boy."

"I do what I can," said Josh, bowing mockingly at the waist.

When Thompson was out of earshot, Ann stepped next to Josh and grabbed his arm. She had tried to counsel him following the events in Romania. However, having not seen him face-to-face for such a long time, she could not be confident of his successful emotional recovery. Her concern was evident in her voice. "It's great to see you."

"Thanks," Josh replied while staring straight ahead. He knew what Ann was thinking about. He so badly wanted this time with Ann, but he could not make direct eye contact with her. "I've missed you guys."

"Really, Josh, how are you doing?" There was a soft plea in Ann's voice. When Josh did not respond, Ann squeezed his arm and went further. "Come on, Josh. It's me, Ann. How are you really doing?"

"All right, I guess." The smile had disappeared from Josh's face.

Ann noted the unmistakable sadness in Josh's face, especially in his eyes. The events of Romania lurked behind those beautiful blue eyes and expressed an anguish Ann hoped was behind him. "No, you're not. Don't lie to me."

Josh looked down at the floor and planted his hands firmly into his pants pockets. "Still trying to be my mom, aren't you?"

Ann hugged Josh from the side, gently shaking him as she spoke. "You're still a big part of our lives Josh. I'm not your mom, but we do think of you as a son."

"I know that," Josh said quietly. "That means everything to me."

"And because we love you like a son, it troubles me to see you still in such pain." Ann saw Josh looking over at Thompson, who was waiting for the bags to appear on the carousel. She continued. "You know you have Richard's love and respect. You know that, don't you?"

"I need his approval in my life," Josh replied. "I've always wanted to do things that would make him proud of me."

162

"Approval?" asked Ann. "Well, honey, you have that in spades." Ann knew what she said had not sunk in. She repositioned herself so Josh was forced to look at her. "Josh, nothing that happened in Romania will change the fact that he ... no, we are so very proud of you."

Josh was suddenly overcome by Ann's simple acknowledgement. He started to tear up. He had not talked with many people about his Romanian experience, and Ann was one of the few people with whom he could speak frankly. He had needed to talk to someone about Romania for a long time, but he never expected a meeting at an airport baggage claim would be the occasion. "The last couple of years have been hard," he stammered. He needed to be more precise. "They've sucked."

"I can't imagine," Ann replied.

"Ever since Romania, I've been living with a ghost I've loved and hated all at the same time." Josh was referring to Noua Alexandro, a beautiful Romanian woman who had been part of the kidnap plot. Noua had kidnapped, seduced and mind-fucked Josh, then was killed during his rescue. The memories of those events had haunted him. Josh had been unable to come to terms with whether Noua's passion was seduction or rape ... a beautiful act of giving or a brutal effort at mind control.

Josh hesitated as he shared his deepest feelings with Ann. "I've tried to date, but it never seems to work out. Every relationship I've been in over the last couple of years has been a disaster," he said.

"Maybe you just haven't met the right girl yet."

Josh grimaced at Ann's comment. "The girls have been right, but I've been wrong. Things don't work out because of me, not them. Pardon the reference Ann, but I'm still pretty fucked up. I'm hoping that spending some time with you … and him … will help me close the door on Romania and Noua."

Ann put her hand over her mouth as her eyes filled with tears. "I hope so, too."

"That's why I left the embassy in Romania. Everyplace I looked I saw Noua's eyes. Young and old alike … they all had Noua's eyes. They were the eyes I saw when she kidnapped me. They were the eyes I saw when she made love to me. They were the eyes I saw when she was shot dead on the ground."

Ann wiped a tear away from Josh's cheek. "Oh, baby. I'm so sorry … so very, very sorry."

"And when I didn't see her eyes, I saw the eyes of those sadistic bastards up in the mountains who helped her." Josh ran his fingers through his beard. "I could still feel the cold of their floor." He took a deep breath. "So I did my job in Romania, but I stayed pretty much to myself. Then, when the NATO job opened up, I decided London was a town big enough for me to disappear into."

Ann knew she was running out of private time with Josh. The bags were starting to come up from their flight. She wiped her own eyes and nodded over at Thompson. "He's changed too, you know."

Josh looked up, surprised the man he admired so much had any serious problems. "What do you mean?"

"Well, first off, he's never forgiven himself for what happened." Ann wasn't sure if she should be telling these things to Josh, but the moment seemed appropriate. "He sent you on that trip and he still blames himself for what happened to you."

"But it wasn't his fault," Josh protested, looking over at Thompson. "He had nothing to do with me getting kidnapped." Josh looked back at Ann. "You know that, don't you? He has to know."

"You and I know the truth, but he can't get past it." Ann paused. She had gone this far with the confession—she might as well go all the way. She leaned in and whispered. "And …" The words caught in her throat.

"And what?" Josh asked.

"Well … something happened over there, in Romania. Something happened to him the day he went looking for you. I'm sure of it. Every time I've brought it up over the last couple of years, he changes the subject. We talk about everything, Josh. But Richard won't talk about Romania. I finally quit trying to talk to him about it. There are nights when he wakes up screaming and dripping in sweat."

"Damn. I didn't know." Josh looked over again at Thompson, who was retrieving their final bag and placing it on a cart. "I wonder what happened?"

"I have no earthly idea," Ann said. "Whatever it was, one thing's for sure."

"What's that?"

"He's just as fucked up as you are about Romania."

Thompson walked up, pushing a small cart loaded with their bags. He looked at the solemn faces of Ann and Josh. "Who died?"

Ann was a politician's wife and very good at deflection when necessary. "No one, babe. I was just catching up with our boy here. I'm trying to coax him into moving back home. We miss him."

"Good point. Junior, when are you headed back to the States?"

"Knock it off, both of you. Let's get a cab." Josh walked to the cab stand with a lot more to think about than his return to the States.

EIGHTEEN

Wade Clarke took a carrot from the pocket of his green canvas jacket embroidered with the yellow Clarke Brokerage & Sales logo and held it out to a skittish two-year-old chestnut filly. "Here ya go, girl," he said with an English accent Americanized from decades of living in the States.

As the horse hung its head over the stable door to grab the carrot, Clarke spoke in a soft and calm tone to the new arrival. "Welcome to the States, Lass." Clarke patted the horse's head as she munched down on the carrot with great gusto. Several carrots and more soft talk followed before Clarke pulled a peppermint hard candy out of his front pants' pocket. He held the mint out in the flat of his palm and the filly quickly lapped it up with her tongue.

"Atta baby," Clarke said just above a whisper as he continued to rub the horse's neck. "Everybody likes a mint after dinner." He patted the filly a couple more times before he took the leather bridle he was carrying and looped it over a hook by the stable door. The brass name plate affixed to the bridle announced to all that Finn's Lassie had arrived at Keeneland for the annual spring sale.

Clarke was a smallish, older man with a hairline pushed back on his head by 60 years of horse trading.

His forehead was ridged by deep lines and, even when he was happy, his mouth seemed to be permanently drooped down. Based upon his attire of jeans and work boots, a casual observer might not be able to distinguish Clarke from the backside barn staff. Upon closer look, however, Clarke's Rolex watch and Kentucky cluster diamond ring stood out as badges of his success in the horse brokerage business. He had made it a long way from being a young cooldown walker for a farm just outside Warrington, England.

The barns of Keeneland were abuzz with activity, as the agents for sellers of the horses being auctioned at the sale set up their barn areas to impress potential buyers. Wade Clarke was known in horse circles as a specialty agent who focused on representing owners of horses primarily from Ireland and the United Kingdom. The two barns he occupied at each sale were usually stocked with some of Europe's top horses.

The air was ripe with the fresh smell of spring and newly mucked horse stalls as Clarke sat down in a director's chair to quietly observe the activity. He followed his staff's every move, making mental notes of what details remained undone before the start of the sale. Logoed signs were being attached to the barns marking Clarke's sales stalls. Veterinarians were conducting physicals on the horses, and sale sheets advertising each horse's particulars were being set up on display tables offering free coffee, Irish whiskey, and crumpets.

Andrea Norris, a tall, curly haired brunette dressed in dirty jeans and a work vest, worked as Clarke's top aide at the brokerage house. She was walking a jet black horse in Clarke's direction when she made eye contact with her boss. The steely look in her eye matched her purposeful stride. When the connection had been sufficiently established, Norris nodded her head ever so slightly in the direction of the main pavilion. Clarke returned the nod and looked just beyond the sales ring to see Paddy Neal and Zafer Javeed approaching.

Norris walked her horse close enough so Clarke could hear her near whisper. "What do you think they want?" she asked.

"I don't know," Clarke replied. He was trying to keep his actions as nonchalant as possible. He didn't want to convey he was talking to Norris about them. The farm for which Neal worked had been a client of Clarke's for years, but he never fully trusted Neal. "I'm not sure what these boys are up to, but I bloody well don't like it."

"What do you mean?" Norris asked. The black horse bucked slightly and Norris yanked at the lead of the horse as she spoke. "We've made some damn good money off County Mayo over the last couple of years."

"Yeah we have," Clarke replied, kicking around some dirt as he spoke. "But something doesn't feel right about those sales."

"Why?" Norris walked the horse in a quick circle.

"Farms with Arab connections have been buying too many horses from County Mayo," Clarke replied.

"Isn't that whole thing over?" Norris heard of the feud between the Arabs and the Irish over horse sales. Several years ago, a couple of Irish breeders kept raising the price of horses that Arab buyers were bidding on. It didn't take the Arab buyers long to discover the bids were being placed for the sole purpose of driving up prices. In several of the subsequent sales, the Arabs refused to bid on any Irish-bred horses.

"For a few, it's over," Clarke said, continuing to follow the pair closely. "But for most on both sides, it will take a generation of breeders before the feud really ends. The wounds of that auction season run pretty deep."

"Sad," said Norris.

"Arabs haven't been buying from the Irish for years," Clarke continued. "Now, suddenly, the boys at County Mayo Stables are getting top dollar from Arab buyers. Something doesn't feel right."

Clarke repeated his previous dire assessment to Norris after he lost sight of the two entering the pavillon. "No sir, I sure as hell don't like it at all."

"So, what the hell happened down in Florida?" Neal asked Zafer as he placed two cups of self-serve coffee on the table. The pair were seated at a table away from the others in the restaurant at the Keeneland sales pavilion. Located directly opposite the room that houses the sales stage, the sales pavilion restaurant is a place where the regular breakfast patrons are accustomed to people speaking in low whispers. Normally, however, the conversations are about the sale of horses.

"What is it to you?" Zafer responded to Neal's question with a question. "I have things covered."

Zafer's smug tone caused an instant and intense reaction in Neal. "I'll tell you what it fuckin' is to me, boy-o," replied Neal. His anger rose so quickly his Irish brogue impaired Zafer's ability to discern what was actually being said. "This fuckin' sale was not supposed to happen. I'm not supposed to be here, don't ya know. This batch of supplies was supposed to move through your other channel in Miami. But something got fucked up down on da' coast and I want to know what. I still have time to head me plane back to Ireland with nuttin' but a horse on it."

"Calm down. Calm down," Zafer reached across the table and patted Neal on the arm. "I can barely understand you."

"Well, you better understand this." Neal looked squarely at Zafer and pointed his finger. "I'm dead fuckin' serious, mate. Either you tell me what happened in Miami, or me and da' Lass are goin' home tonight."

"Fine," Zafer replied stiffly. He had done deals with Neal before, but had never seen him quite so agitated. Personally, he thought it best that Neal did not know Zafer's other source for F-14 Tomcat airplane replacement parts was now alligator bait in the Florida swamp. But Zafer feared Neal's threat to go home early was not an idle one. County Mayo had been reluctant about offering up Finn's Lassie at the sale. Telling Neal selective facts from the story might be Zafer's best chance to keep the deal alive.

"Okay," Zafer leaned forward over the table and spoke in a hushed tone. What he was about to tell Neal implicated him in a criminal conspiracy. He sure as hell did not want anyone else to hear his story. "About two years ago I set up a shell import/export company in India. It had all the airs of legitimacy. I even conducted a few proper import deals so we would have a record and a history when we came to the States looking for a partner. My finance partners in Dubai decided we were going to take a direct approach and have my Indian shell buy the parts from a military scrap dealer here in the States."

"Direct?" Neal didn't quite get the reference.

Zafer chuckled. "Direct is a relative term, my friend. We were going to be as direct as we could be in conducting an illegal purchase. Do not forget. We are all doing this because it is illegal to export military replacement parts to Iran."

"Go on." Neal had been instructed by the owner of his stable to get the entire story before finally releasing the new horse for sale. He didn't want to interrupt Zafer with too many questions, but he did want him to cut to the chase. "So, where was the problem then?"

"It turned out that our problem was in America, not India." Zafer looked around the room again and leaned back in. "At this point, we are down to needing smaller specialty parts … parts that are particular to an F-14. Metal wraps for a fuselage or a wing can be manufactured to fit. We are able to buy these parts from Russia. But in every airplane there are certain parts unique to that singular design. The manufacturers do it to make sure they have a monopoly on replacement parts. Usually they are engine parts or electronics. They will use a special 33 point coupler instead of a standard 31 point or design an odd length and circumference on a drive rod. Those are the kinds of items we need now. We get those to Iran and we can have a few F-14s operational within weeks."

"Got it," Neal confirmed his understanding with a nod.

"The most likely place to get specialty Tomcat replacement parts these days is at a graveyard on a military landing strip in Arizona. When the American military grounded the F-14 a couple of years ago, it was not profitable for companies to manufacture parts anymore. So we contracted with a man in Florida, Jared Seebree, who buys salvage from military auctions. We hired Seebree to go out and get us what we need. We did not want to do anything to raise attention, so we paid him top dollar, but not a premium."

"And they catch this Jared Seebree guy at the auction then?" Neal anticipated the next line in Zafer's story.

"No." Zafer's voice indicated he was caught up in the story now. "Seebree got through the auction fine. He got us just what we needed."

"Then what the fuck happened? How'd he get caught?"

"The stupid son of a bitch let his export license expire. I spent two years of my life setting up the Indian shell company and crafting the deal. Seebree gets us what we need and we pay him for it. The shipment is scheduled and all is going as planned. Then an inspector at the loading dock in Miami runs Jared Seebree's name through the computer and discovers he has an expired military export license. So the inspector starts looking at what is being shipped. When he figured out they were airplane parts, he flagged the shipment for further inspection and discovered they were F-14 parts."

"So this fella got pinched for shipping illegal parts on an expired license." Neal looked blankly out the window at a horse being walked by a groom. "How did your hooligans bag out? Why weren't you and the other lads arrested?"

Zafer pondered the question over a long drink of his coffee before continuing. He did not want to tell Neal the fate of Seebree. "I told you. The Indian company was a true shell, which is why it took so long to establish. There is no one behind it. There are no records of the owners having ever actually existed."

"These parts we're talking about now aren't from Arizona, are they?" Neal's curiosity was peaked. His eyes grew wide. "If you're going back to Arizona, you've got to believe the government is tracking the parts."

"No," Zafer reassured Neal. "I said Arizona was the most likely place. I have found a secondary source for the parts. I have someone on the inside of the original manufacturer. There is still a limited supply of parts they have as unused inventory. The United States government isn't ordering any new parts these days. So, it has been pretty easy to steal a part here and there."

"So when I go back to Ireland, I suppose my airplane will have these specialty parts on board hidden in the straw?"

"Precisely."

Neal still had concerns about the deal and pushed Zafer for more information. "And who is this insider?

Is it some other dense bloke who could make me a prison waster for the rest of me life?"

"Do you really want to know, Paddy?" Zafer had told Neal about Seebree, but he felt uncomfortable about revealing the source of the parts. "Perhaps the less you know about the source, the better."

Neal did not understand Zafer's reluctance. "I want to know, yes. In fact, I need to know. The new source has to be secure. You may want to go tits-up for your cause, but I sure as hell don't."

"Very well," Zafer realized he had to put a good many of his cards on the table to get the deal done. "The parts you will be taking back to Ireland were bought as extra inventory by the engine manufacturer. We have a person in the company's management who is removing parts from inventory and can cover our tracks. This is not some idiot we are trying to scam. The parts are in control of a true partner and are being delivered by him to the sale this week before you head home."

Neal thought for a minute about the structure. "I'm thinking your fingerprints were well hidden on the Florida deal. Fuck this up and we may both end up out in the open on this one."

"And for that, as in the past, you are being well compensated." Zafer now pushed back a bit.

"Aye, but I'm not waiting for a Miami situation here."

"Our partner has as much to lose here as we do, my friend."

Neal took a final sip of coffee and stood up. He nodded in agreement and reached out to shake Zafer's hand. "It's all fine then, but this is absolutely the last one, to be sure," he said firmly as they shook.

"Not to worry, my friend," Zafer replied as they walked to a trash bin to throw away their coffee cups. "After this transaction, Allah be praised, we will not need another."

Neal exhaled. "Let's go down to the barns, then. I'll introduce you to Finn's Lassie."

"I will be down in a minute," Zafer replied while pulling out his cell phone. "I have to make a call first." Zafer waited until Neal was out of ear shot, then sat down on a bench away from the show ring and dialed. "It is Zafer," he said when the man picked up. "Do you have what we need?"

"Yeah," he replied. "The parts are secure. I'm ready to deliver at your command."

Zafer looked around to make sure no one was listening. He was nervous about the deal going smoothly. Neal's interrogation had not helped his concern about this one exposing him to the authorities. "What about that damn lawyer? Did you find the hard drive with the phony destruction orders you prepared for the parts?"

"Don't worry," the man replied. "One way or the other, the old bastard will never file that lawsuit."

NINETEEN

The Thompsons stood on opposite sides of the bed as they unpacked their belongings into the dresser drawers of their multi-room suite. The cab through Dublin had weaved its way through streets every bit as confusing as Josh promised. The roads seemed to have been built with no particular destination in mind. Even the most seasoned traveler could easily get lost in the streets of Dublin.

When the airport cabbie driving the trio into town discovered Thompson was an American Congressman, he talked without pause about politics in the States. Thompson swore the cabbie had driven around the city for an extra ten minutes or so just to chat. Thompson thought he recognized a couple of pubs as they passed them a second time and he noticed the cabbie discounted the cab fare once they arrived at the hotel.

As confusing as the city seemed, Thompson could feel the tension and his worries slowly disappear as they drove. The morning sky had been uncharacteristically clear, and the sunlight painted a fresh look on an old city. While the cabbie chatted on and on about American politics, Thompson simply looked out the window in awe, realizing he was finally visiting the country of his father's family.

When they reached the hotel, Thompson's mood was as fresh as the spring morning greeting him outside. Thompson felt like the man he had been in his youth, alive and invigorated. Ann noticed the change in Thompson as she unpacked.

"You're certainly feeling chipper," she observed as she hung up a dress.

"Yeah. I feel like a kid. I can't wait to get out and kiddy-hawk around." Kiddy-hawking was what his grandfather called the exploring they had done together when Thompson was a child.

Ann hadn't heard him use that reference in years. "Kiddy-hawk?" she laughingly replied.

"Oh yeah," he said. "Kiddy-hawk. I really want to explore this place. In fact, I don't even want to sleep while I'm here. I'd be wasting precious time."

"Let's take it one day at a time," warned Ann. "It's going to take us at least a day to get over the jet lag."

His wife's comments were lost amid Thompson's excitement as he grabbed his toothbrush and razor from the suitcase and walked into the bathroom. "And Josh, it's so great to be here with him. Can you believe he's grown a beard?" He looked at the razor before coming back into the room. "Maybe I should grow a beard."

"Griff would never allow you to grow facial hair," laughed Ann. "Beards on politicians went out with Rutherford B. Hayes." Like Thompson, Ann was digging through her suitcase, but placing clothes into drawers with a bit more care than her husband.

"Josh is such a good kid," Ann started. She decided to let Thompson know what was going on in his life. "It's really hard to see him hurting so much."

"What do you mean?" Thompson paused in his unpacking. "Hurting?"

"Hurting, Richard," Ann insisted as she continued placing her clothes in drawers. "Romania almost ruined him. He's still torn up about what happened." Ann wanted to add "like you," but thought better of it. Thompson was in a great mood. She didn't want to open that particular door. "That's why he left Romania for the job with NATO in London. It was too much emotionally for him to stay there."

"What does that mean?" Thompson queried. "I thought he went to London just for the job. How do you know Romania was too much for him emotionally?"

"He told me so."

"He never said anything to me."

Ann stopped and looked at Thompson. "Of course, he's not going to tell you, honey," she replied. "He worships the ground you walk on. He doesn't want you to know he's anything less than perfect. He wants you to think he's just like you ... perfect."

The ringing of the telephone startled both Thompson and Ann. Thompson walked into the sitting area of the room and answered the phone on the desk. "Hello?" Ann heard him answer. "Hey, Josh.

What's up? Yeah, I'd like that. Okay, I'll see ya down there in a half hour or so."

When Thompson walked back into the bedroom, Ann asked, "That was Josh?"

"Yeah, he wants to have a Guinness downstairs in the lobby bar in a bit."

"You're not going down until we initiate the room, are you?" Ann asked invitingly.

"I thought you were tired," Thompson replied with a hopeful smile on his face.

"Not too tired for hotel sex. It's our tradition, Richard. We have to initiate the room."

Thompson grinned evilly and reached into his suitcase. Ann watched as he pulled out one of their favorite sex toys and held it up. "Oh my God. I can't believe you put that in your bag," a shocked Ann laughed. "What if they pulled that out at Customs? You would have caused an international political incident." Ann collapsed on the bed in a fit of giggles.

Thompson turned on the device and it made a high-pitched buzzing sound. Thompson wiggled his eyebrows at Ann as she laughed even harder. He jumped on the bed with a laugh and said, "Welcome to Dublin."

TWENTY

"Two Guinness, please." Josh placed the order when he saw Thompson saunter off the elevator into the lobby of the conference hotel. Thompson stood looking around, trying to find his young friend in the mingling crowd of name tag wearing conference goers. Josh waved his hand in the air. Thompson saw the signal, spied Josh and headed for the bar.

"You said the lobby," said Thompson. "I didn't expect to find you here in the bar. I don't remember you being much of a drinker."

"It's a habit I've picked up from Griff, I'm afraid," replied Josh with a forced laugh. In fact, Josh had been spending a lot of evenings in bars since he moved to London. Heavy drinking at the city's pubs had the self-medicating effect of washing away bad memories of Romania. "I ordered us up a couple pints."

"I haven't been a Guinnie drinker for years. I'm more of a whiskey man now," Thompson replied, nodding at the bartender who placed two foamy pints in front of them. "But, I guess a snoot full of Guinness is what's required when you're in Dublin."

Josh reached over and grabbed both glasses, handing one of the pints to Thompson. "Here's to looking up your old address," Josh toasted. Both raised their glasses before taking sizable gulps.

"They're right," said Thompson with a pleased smile on his relaxed face.

"Who?" Josh used his shirt sleeve to wipe the foam from his upper lip.

"Everyone who's been to Dublin," replied Thompson.

"About what?"

"Guinness." Thompson said as he took another drink. "Everyone said it tastes better when it's shipped straight from the St. James Gates. And, I'll be damned. This tastes awfully good."

"You need to go to the brewery while you're here," Josh insisted. "They give a tour that ends up in a bar on top of the building that has a 360-degree view of Dublin. The Guinness is really fresh there. I think the conference has a bus going over there after tomorrow's meetings. You should go."

"Well, we're here for ten days. If we don't go with the group, I'll definitely head over on my own. That's one tourist stop I'll be glad to make."

"Good. I have to head back to London the day after the conference, but I can give you some tourist tips. I've been over here a couple of times since moving to London."

Josh took a drink of his pint and changed the subject. "Griff emailed me about this nut running against you. What's his name? Sullivan? He sounds like a real piece of work."

"I'm not too worried," Thompson lied. He didn't want Josh to know how concerned he was about the lawsuit. "Griff will deal with him."

Josh continued with small talk as he worked on his beer. "How's Griff doing without cigarettes? I didn't think he could run a campaign without smokes." Both of them laughed out loud. "So, how's Mr. Bradley? Griff says he's handling the nut job's lawsuit against you."

"Joe's doing great," Thompson replied. "He's lost a bunch of weight. We won't be able to call him The Fat Man too much longer. And yeah, he's my lawyer. Griff let me get out of town, probably so I wouldn't be around for the hearing."

"Griff's the man," Josh chuckled. He paused and took a deep breath. "Anyway, thanks for meeting me down here. I wanted to talk to you about Wasfi Al Ghazawi before you meet him."

"That's not a problem. It's a good time to meet." Thompson remembered Ann's comments about Josh being troubled by Romania and he looked for any crack in his otherwise light-hearted façade. "Ann didn't sleep much on the plane, so she's taking a little nap before we go out tonight. I read the file you emailed to the office last week. This Wasfi fellow sounds like a pretty impressive guy."

"He's a real impressive guy." Josh nodded and looked around the bar making sure Al Ghazawi wasn't in the vicinity to hear his praise. "I met him in London.

He's a British citizen of Palestinian descent who lives in Haifa these days."

"And I read he's former RAF. Did he fly?"

"Yeah," replied Josh. He looked down into his near empty glass. "He was a Royal Air Force helicopter pilot in the 90s. He apparently got an audience with the Queen for some rescue mission he ran in Bosnia in 1995 where he took a lot of fire. He flew his Hewey right through it … landed, picked up some men and got the hell out of there. He took some shrapnel in the leg in the process."

"Tough dude," said Thompson nodding his head. He knew Josh was impressed with Al Ghazawi, so he continued the conversation. "I'm curious. Why here? Dublin, I mean? Ireland isn't a part of NATO."

"There's a pretty interesting history behind Ireland and its relationship with Israel and Palestine," Josh replied. He leaned in toward Thompson. "The whole conflict has always been high priority on the collective Irish consciousness. Initially, the Irish supported the Zionists. They found parallels between Jewish suffering and their own under English rule. But as time passed, the Irish came to view Israel in a different light."

"What happened?" asked Thompson, taking another drink.

"Northern Ireland," Josh replied. "Ireland began to view Israel in the same light as the British crown."

"Oppressors."

"Precisely," Josh continued. "The Irish began to view the policies of Israel through the bifocals of their own divided island."

"So Israel became to Palestine, what the Queen was to Northern Ireland."

Josh nodded his head in agreement. "Still is today. A year or so ago, the leader of Sinn Fein called Israel the most despicable regime on the planet. There's a mural in Belfast entitled *IRA-PLO One Struggle*.

"Damn." Thompson had a puzzled look on his face. "So, tell me about the foundation this guy runs. What's it called? Abraham's something-or-another?"

"Abraham's Olive Tree is the name of it." Josh broke eye contact, leaned forward and placed his elbows on the bar. "It's a foundation he set up to bridge the political gap between the Israelis and the Palestinians. He believes there can be a peaceful solution in Gaza. The basis of his solution is that Palestinians and Jews are all children of Abraham and should be able to live together in peace. He works with moderates on both sides to try and bring them together in the spirit of compromise."

"Yeah, so how's that compromise thing working out for him?" Thompson smirked sarcastically.

"Don't laugh," Josh said. "He's actually had some success. The Israelis respect him because of his military background."

"And his own people?"

"That's another story," said Josh. "Some think of him as a hero and others a traitor."

"How about you, Josh? What do you think of him?"

"Personally, I like him," Josh replied.

Thompson noticed the hesitation in Josh's voice. "But …" Thompson prompted.

"Well, he's a bit idealistic," Josh said with a little pity in his voice.

Hearing Josh label someone as idealistic in that tone caused Thompson's gut to clinch. He closed his eyes and remembered Josh as the idealistic kid he and Griffith laughed about. Back then, Josh might have actually believed Israel and the Palestinian Authority could implement a democratic resolution to Gaza. "I see he's speaking to the attendees at our closing session?" Thompson continued.

"Yeah. They want him to talk about his model and how it could work for other conflicts across the world." Josh sucked down the last bit of his Guinness and pounded his glass down on the bar. "I'm out," he declared. "How about another?"

"You hit that pretty quickly," observed Thompson.

"Come on, boss. You're in Dublin. It's time to drink like an Irishman."

TWENTY-ONE

Michael Griffith fumbled nervously as he paced around behind the wood railing which separated the lawyers from the gallery in the richly appointed federal courtroom. Jingling his keys in his pocket as he paced, Griffith seemed to be a bouncing collection of nervous twitches. He badly needed a cigarette, but promised his new wife he wouldn't light up. Wearing a pair of black jeans, snakeskin boots, a white button-down shirt and a black sport coat, Griffith was about as dressed up as he ever got during the week.

Precinct polling places were Griffith's courtrooms. This real courtroom was a political venue that made him even more antsy than normal. He looked around the wood paneled room and surveyed the situation. The Fat Man, dressed in an ill-fitting grey suit, which was obviously purchased before his recent weight loss, sat at one of the tables. Dressed in a smart brown suit, Tito Mendes, the Brazilian law student who volunteered for the campaign, sat at The Fat Man's side.

Wearing the same suit he wore at his campaign kick off, Sean Sullivan sat at the other lawyer's table. Sullivan was not wearing his trademark pink slippers, but when Sullivan opened his briefcase, Griffith noticed he brought them—along with his other legal supplies.

Seated next to her father was Tiana Bolton-Sullivan. A smile broke across Griffith's face as he looked at Tiana and Tito sitting ever so properly between The Fat Man and Sullivan. He scratched the back of his neck and shook his bald head as he thought of the old saying about roses between thorns.

Other than the combatants, there was no one else was in the courtroom except one print journalist sent by the local newspaper to cover the hearing. He sat in a corner looking pissed that he had to attend. Griffith was happy the media appeal of Sullivan's lawsuit had already worn off.

Despite the lack of immediate media attention, Griffith still believed he made the right political decision by telling Thompson to head on off to Ireland. As a candidate, Thompson was now unavailable to make a comment on the hearing and the press did not much seem to care. He had three different press releases in his coat pocket, ready to use according to whatever happened in the next couple of hours. He felt he had covered all of the political contingencies.

Still, Griffith was nervous. He leaned over the rail and tapped The Fat Man on his shoulder. "I thought you said we had to be here promptly at 2:00," he whispered.

"Calm down, will ya," The Fat Man instructed, shaking his hands, palms down as he spoke. "You're starting to make *me* nervous. Take it down a notch."

"But it's almost 2:30." Griffith pointed at his watch, tapping the crystal repeatedly. "This joker is a half an hour late. You told me we had to be prompt."

The Fat Man looked forward, speaking out of the side of his mouth. "I said we had to be on time. I didn't say anything about the judge. He can get here whenever the hell he wants." He cupped his mouth and looked at Griffith. "And for God's sake don't call him a joker. The microphones on the tables may be open. He might be listening to us back in his chambers."

Griffith grimaced and chewed at the fingernail on his right index finger. "Looks like I picked the wrong campaign to stop smoking cigarettes."

"Sniffing glue," interjected The Fat Man, turning sideways in his chair as he spoke.

"What?"

"It looks like I picked the wrong day to quit sniffing glue," repeated The Fat man. "It's a line from the movie *Airplane*. Lloyd Bridges said it."

"A joke," said Griffith rolling his eyes. He looked at Mendes while shaking his head. "Can you believe this guy? I'm dying a thousand deaths over here and you're telling me one-liners from some damn movie."

"Apparently that's what he does, sir," replied a stiffly formal Mendes.

The Fat Man chose not to question Griffith's inaudible reply. Normally not inclined to get into a pissing contest with Griffith, The Fat Man was getting irritated with his attitude this particular day. "Griff, what is your problem?" he asked.

"I'm a control freak," said Griffith, his arms crossed in defiance. "That's what I do in politics. I control things. This …" Griffith unlocked his arms and waved them around for emphasis. "This is out of my control."

"I've got this under control," The Fat Man urged.

"You got it under control?"

"Yeah."

"Yeah?" Griffith repeated. "Then what's the judge here for? You want to explain that one to me? It seems to me the guy in the black robe is the only one with things under control. And he's not even here yet." Griffith threw his arms up in frustration.

The Fat Man shrugged his shoulders. He had no reply and turned back around just as Judge Chris Meuhling entered the courtroom. Sullivan and Tiana stood up at their table, as did the uninterested reporter. Griffith turned and put his hands at his side in a very formal position. The Fat Man and Mendez also stood. Meuhling was a tall, balding, older man whose mother probably spent a lifetime defending him as "big boned." What little hair the judge had left atop his wrinkled head was dyed black, with small white roots separating the dyed portion from his scalp.

Meuhling, an appointee of President Jimmy Carter, was sitting as a special judge on the case of

<u>Sullivan v. Thompson</u>. The case had been assigned to him when the regular judge recused himself because he knew both of the litigants too well. The Fat Man was aware of Meuhling's reputation as a surly, no-nonsense adjudicator. Thus, he was not surprised when Meuhling told everyone to sit down and went straight to questioning the attorneys.

"Sit down, people," Meuhling instructed as he shuffled through papers in the file, peering over his gold wire-rimmed glasses as he spoke. Everyone in the courtroom sat. Meuhling looked at all four attorneys before speaking. "We're here today on the motions filed by Plaintiff requesting an expedited hearing and decision on his requested remedy of a writ of mandamus. Mr. Sullivan, you filed this lawsuit *pro se*, but I noticed there is someone else at the table with you today."

Sullivan stood up and placed his hands firmly on the table. This was federal court and he was not about to pull any pranks before this judge. There would be no magic tricks in Judge Meuhling's courtroom. "Yes sir, your Honor. If I may introduce to the Court, this is Tiana Bolton-Sullivan, my daughter and co-counsel." Tiana stood upon the introduction. "We entered an appearance for her this morning."

Meuhling scrunched up his nose and squinted at the pair. He was obviously confused by the large white Irishman introducing a petite African-American as his daughter. "Your daughter, huh?" He looked back down at the file. "Very well—it's nice to meet you."

When Tiana and Sullivan sat back down, Meuhling turned his attention to The Fat Man. The Fat Man was up and speaking before the sour, old man could say a word. "Your Honor, may I introduce to the court Mr. Tito Mendes. He's a law student from Brazil who is attending some classes at the law school. He is here today observing our system, but he will not be appearing formally."

"Welcome," said Meuhling with no real indication he meant it as a sincere greeting. He peered at The Fat Man. "Mr. Bradley, you seem to be short a client. Where is Congressman Thompson today?"

The Fat Man anticipated the question and quickly shot back. "Congressman Thompson is out of the country on official business."

"Excuse me?" Meuhling raised his eyebrows at The Fat Man's response.

"This is an attorney argument on plaintiff's motion. It is not an evidentiary hearing. Congressman Thompson was not subpoenaed nor was he otherwise ordered to attend."

"Humph," mumbled Meuhling, seemingly unimpressed by whatever business was causing Thompson to be absent from the hearing. He placed his folded hands on the bench. "I've read the briefs in this case and really don't need you to repeat your arguments orally. Mr. Sullivan, you have asked for extraordinary action by this court."

"Yes sir," replied Tiana, standing as she spoke.

"Mrs. Sullivan," said the Judge.

"Ms. Bolton-Sullivan," Tiana replied.

"Right," said Meuhling frowning. "You've asked for this court to grant emergency relief for your motion, but I don't understand why this case could not be heard in the normal course of litigation."

Tiana stood tall as she spoke. "Your Honor, because the pending legislation which is the underlying subject of this litigation will come up for a vote in the United States House of Representatives when Congress returns from its recess next month. And …"

"So, why should this court care about that?" Meuhling interrupted. "That's a matter for the legislative branch, is it not?"

"No, it isn't, your Honor," insisted Tiana, tapping her pencil on a legal pad as she spoke. "This is a matter for the voters of the Fourth Congressional District who are under your jurisdiction." Sullivan smiled as Meuhling leaned back in his chair, contemplating Tiana's legal argument. "Those voters will suffer irreparable harm if Congressman Thompson votes in a manner contrary to what he has otherwise promised."

"But isn't it the place of the people to decide the consequences of Thompson's vote?" Meuhling wrote some notes as he spoke.

"That is precisely the point, your Honor," Tiana said confidently. "They have already decided. Based on a promise they relied upon, the voters sent Congressman Thompson to Congress. His breaking of that promise upon which they relied, is in fact the irreparable harm they will suffer if you do not intercede and grant the requested relief."

Griffith noticed Judge Meuhling nodded his head as Tiana spoke. He was convinced the judge was buying her argument.

Meuhling then turned his attention to The Fat Man. "Mr. Bradley, is she right? Is that irreparable harm?"

"No, your Honor," replied The Fat Man, who stood as soon as Tiana finished. "We live in a republic, a representative democracy. Voters sent Congressman Thompson to Washington to execute his best judgment on their behalf. Circumstances change. There are no enforceable promises."

"But isn't that precisely the problem, Mr. Bradley?" Meuhling pressed. "Aren't public officials promising one thing and doing another?"

"Quite possibly," replied The Fat Man. "In the Federalist Papers, Madison identified the possibility of citizen legislators doing things which may not be in the best interests of the collective whole. But the remedy is the ballot box, not judicial intervention. In fact, any such action by this court mandating a vote would be unprecedented in American jurisprudence and clearly in violation of the line of cases delineating separation of powers amongst the three branches of the federal government."

Griffith sat nervously and watched the ebb and flow of the arguments being made before Judge Meuhling, unable to tell from the questions being asked exactly where the old man was heading. He was relieved when the judge said he had heard enough, announced he would have a decision prior to the time Congress would reconvene, stood and left the courtroom.

"Well, that sure was fun," Griffith declared to The Fat Man.

Following the hearing, The Fat Man, Griffith, and Tito Mendes were standing in the hallway outside the courtroom, talking about the case, when Sean Sullivan and his daughter approached. Tiana still had her game face on, but Sullivan was wearing his customary big Irish smile. His eyes danced as he approached, holding his hand out to The Fat Man in greeting.

"Damn good argument in there, Joe," Sullivan declared loudly. "Thompson may have run out on me, but I'm glad he sent in the First Cavalry. I love being up against the best."

"Good to see you, Sean," The Fat Man replied as he shook Sullivan's hand. He looked down at Sullivan's feet. He had changed into his pink slippers. "How do the feet feel? I see you've changed out of your good shoes already. Those leather ones can't be comfortable for you."

"They hurt like hell," Sullivan winced. "I appreciate you asking." Sullivan put his arm around The Fat Man and acted like he was whispering in his ear, but his voice was just as loud as before, maybe more so. "You still doing that horse law stuff?"

"Yeah," replied The Fat Man. "I'm going down to the sales in a couple of days. You'd love it Sean. There's an Irish farm getting top dollar for their horses these days."

"Never bet against an Irish horse on the turf," replied Sullivan.

"So I'm told," The Fat Man responded. "It's a good thing I don't bet."

"Hey," Sullivan changed the subject, "can you believe we drew that old dinosaur Meuhling today? I didn't know he was even still alive."

"You're not griping are you?" asked The Fat Man, trying his best to duck out from underneath the larger man's grasp. "He's old enough to have been appointed by Carter. You're suing a Congressman using a populist theory. I'd figured you were dancing an Irish jig as soon as you heard we got Meuhling."

"Good liberal judge, for sure, but I'm afraid he won't remember the arguments by the time he gets home." Tiana shifted her weight from side to side, obviously uncomfortable at talking with the opposition. "Oh Joe, where are my Irish manners? This is my daughter, Tiana."

Tiana reached out and shook The Fat Man's hand. "Pleased to meet you," The Fat Man said. Returning the courtesy, The Fat Man introduced his colleagues. "This is Tito Mendes, a law school student who is helping out on the campaign." Mendes nodded at both Sullivan and Tiana. "And this is Michael Griffith."

"Ah, the great Michael Griffith," Sullivan smiled sharply. "The bane of my very existence. I wish I could say it was a pleasure to meet you, but it really isn't."

"Likewise, I'm sure," replied Griffith. He begrudgingly reached out and shook Sullivan's hand.

The Fat Man felt the tension growing between Sullivan and Griffith. He decided to quickly change the topic. "Hey Tiana, nice argument in there."

"Thanks, Mr. Bradley."

"Call me Joe, please," responded The Fat Man. He pointed at Sullivan. "You're learning litigation at the feet of the master. As painful as the feet may be, they still belong to your dad and he is the master of litigation in these parts."

"You're full of shit, Joe," Sullivan laughed heartily as he turned to walk away. He stopped and looked back at The Fat Man. "Are you sure you're not Irish?"

Tiana looked at her father as they walked away. "You were awfully friendly with them."

"Bradley is a good man," Sullivan said. "He's probably the smartest lawyer in this community. It's a lawsuit honey, not life and death. An opponent in there doesn't have to be an enemy out here." Sullivan put his arm around Tiana as they walked. "Never let your emotions overtake your better judgment, Tiana. You'll never know. There might come a day when you want to be on the same side with someone like him."

As Sullivan and Tiana headed for the elevator, Griffith expressed similar concerns about The Fat Man's familiar tone with Sullivan and his daughter. The Fat Man smiled. "I'm surprised at you, Griff. I'm just following your Godfather Rules."

"And just which one is that?"

"Remember Godfather III? Don't hate your enemy. It affects your judgment."

"Yeah." Griffith mumbled. "That's why they should have stopped with the second movie."

TWENTY-TWO

Laughter erupted from the cab when its doors swung open in front of Kelly's Pub. Wasfi Al Ghazawi charmed his guests at dinner, and the Thompsons were more than glad to have him accompany them and Josh out on the town for an evening of authentic Irish folk music. As they exited the cab, it was apparent Ann and Wasfi were the non-drinkers in the bunch. Josh and Thompson had each been hitting the Guinness over dinner just hard enough to need help steadying their gaits.

With an international flair apparent in his voice and manners, Wasfi had proven to be a delightful dinner guest. Wearing a custom- made silk suit and shirt that fit his frame like a glove, the distinguished looking, olive-skin Arab captivated Ann with his charm. While listening to Wasfi modestly weave his stories of wartime heroics, Thompson came to understand why Josh's superiors at NATO respected him so much. Wasfi Al Ghazawi had charm that could bring enemies together, and the bravado that could make them stay that way.

While Josh paid the cabbie, Ann noticed the thirty plus people gathered on the sidewalk outside the pub smoking cigarettes and drinking beer and cider. "I can't believe the Irish have passed an indoor smoking ban," she said.

"Yes," replied Wasfi, pointing to a group of middle-aged men laughing and smoking wrinkled, self-rolled smokes as the four entered the pub. "It's pretty amazing in a society that still values the skills of a man who can roll his own cigarette."

The air was damp outside the pub where the men gathered for a smoke. The street was lined with shops long since closed. Except for those heading out for a pint, the streets were vacant. This was not the tourist section of Dublin.

The cabbie who drove them to Kelly's claimed two things. First, he guaranteed Kelly's had the best music in Dublin. He said it was where he went when he had a night off. Secondly, he warned the bar might be crowded. He was correct on both accounts.

As promised, the inside of the long and narrow pub was jammed. People stood four and five deep against a long mahogany bar that lined three quarters of the entire room.

Immediately upon entering the bar, a ruddy-faced local with grey hair recognized the four as visitors and politely gave up his seat at the corner of the bar to Ann, tipping his cap as he did so. Ann accepted the man's gesture with a pleasant smile. "Is every Irishman as polite as you?" she asked.

"Sure and they better be," the man replied. "If anyone isn't helpful to a pretty lass like you, they'd not be Irish."

Ann thanked him again and sat down.

Leaning in over Ann, Josh ordered two Guinness, two fizzy waters for Ann and Wasfi, and whatever the kindly local who gave up his seat wanted to drink. When the libations were delivered, Thompson placed a British fifty pound note on the bar. Kevin Kelly, the 50ish proprietor of the pub, looked at the English currency resting on the bar and snarled at Thompson. "I don't take foreign currency." Thompson stood, nonplussed, not quite knowing how to react.

Josh laughed, took a hearty drink of his Guinness, and pulled two twenty euros from his pocket. He handed them across the bar to Kelly, nodding his head in Thompson's direction. "Sorry, he's a Yank." Unamused, Kelly snatched the euros from Josh's hand and went to the cash register to ring up the sale.

"I didn't realize that would be an issue," said Thompson.

Josh got his change from Kelly in Irish pounds, threw a couple of coins on the bar and placed the rest in his pocket. He was amused at how little his old boss actually knew about the harsh feelings between Ireland and England. "You wanted authentic, boss. This is as authentic as it gets. And part of being here is these folks don't care much for the Brits."

"Can I tell them I'm a Congressman from the States?" he asked.

Josh laughed. "You can tell them you're anything you want as long as you don't say that you're the Queen of England."

At the front of the bar the musicians began to gather from their smoke break on the street. The two guitar players were older men, but the man playing the five-string banjo was a beaming young redhead with bad teeth and a penny whistle sticking out of his shirt pocket. Thompson began to follow the musicians' every move. A big-breasted woman with flowing brown hair set aside her bodhran and squeezebox before sitting down. She ordered up a cider for herself and round of Guinness for the others.

An old man, dressed in a coat and tie, sat proper and rigid on a small stool to the side of the couches where the musicians were lounging. He offered to pay for the drinks of the musicians and ordered a cider for himself.

As the musicians got ready to play, Josh excused himself and headed back to the toilet. Before heading to the rear of the bar, he looked at Thompson. "Don't get arrested before I get back."

One of the musicians shouted for someone named Bryan. From the loo to which Josh was headed came a pepper-bearded man in jeans and a red flannel shirt. He had a mandolin strapped over his shoulder which he tuned while he walked to the front of the pub to join the others. The man sat down on the couch closest to the proper old man, who patted Bryan on the knee as he sat.

With all of the musicians present, the young redheaded man began slapping a beat on his knee and, in a beautiful baritone voice, began to sing. Conversations ceased.

In eighteen hundred and forty-one,
Me corduroy breeches I put on,
Me corduroy breeches I put on,
To work upon the railway, the railway.

When they got to the chorus, the ruddy-faced old man who gave his seat to Ann pounded his glass on the bar and sang along. The big breasted woman picked up her squeezebox and began to play.

I was wearing corduroy britches,
Digging ditches, pulling switches, dodging hitches,
I was workin' on the railway.

As they started into the second verse, all the musicians began playing in earnest. Thompson was instantly enthralled in the folk symphony taking place before him. A lover of folk music all of his life, he was listening to it at its most basic level. The musicians played with a spirited passion that spoke to his soul. "Poor Paddy" was a song Thompson's father used to sing, and Thompson suddenly found himself singing along.

The next song started with Bryan working a lick on his mandolin. Thompson looked over at Ann in a silent plea for permission to leave her side and move closer to the players. She smiled and nodded her head yes. Like a kid, Thompson gleefully moved forward and sat on a short stool between the proper old man and the mandolin player.

Wasfi watched the silent exchange between Thompson and Ann. "So is that what it is it like being the spouse of an American Congressman?" Wasfi asked Ann as Thompson tapped the beat with his foot.

Ann took her eyes off the musicians. "What do you mean?" she replied.

"Knowing instinctively what he wants and needs at any given time," Wasfi said. "He wanted to leave your side and get closer to the music. All he had to do was look at you and you knew what he wanted. I suspect mind-reading is a very important quality for a politician's wife."

Ann set her fizzy water on the bar and leaned toward Wasfi. "It's an important quality all wives share, I suppose. Still, it seems like mind reading is my full-time job anymore."

"How so?" Wasfi queried, as he leaned in closer to hear her words.

Ann smiled and pointed at Thompson. "Half my time is spent keeping him in the game, and the other half is spent keeping our family out of it."

"You sound like my wife," Wasfi chuckled. "She is always worried my passion for my work will put me into harm's way. Luckily for us, though, our children are grown."

"She didn't come with you to Ireland?" Ann asked as she picked up her drink again.

"No, she hates to travel," Wasfi frowned. "I do not like being away for long periods of time, but conferences like this are crucial to our mission of Middle Eastern peace."

"That's a pretty large mission for one man," Ann said frankly, and then thought twice about having been so forthright with her views. She started to try to clarify her statement when Wasfi stopped her.

"That's why you are a good political wife. You say what you think and that keeps your husband grounded, I'm sure. My wife says the same things to me. I am not so naive as to think I will totally change the peace process with my efforts. But if I can change a few minds among those who control the process, then I will be happy."

Josh had just returned from the loo and was listening in on the conversation. "Quite a difference from your military days, I suspect," he interjected.

"Very different," Wasfi said. "When I flew for the RAF, I knew everything I needed to know about the instruments of battle. There was not a single plane I could not identify on sight. Now I spend my time focusing on … intangibles—personalities and the like."

Josh caught the attention of Kelly and ordered another round of drinks for everyone. The trio sat listening to the music and watching Thompson enjoy himself as he swayed in rhythm with the music. When the drinks were delivered, Josh paid for them and distributed them accordingly. He also took a fresh cider to the red-haired man who sung earlier. He handed him the bottle along with a note he scribbled out on the bar.

"What was that?" Ann asked when Josh returned.

"A song request," Josh replied.

A new song was beginning and it was one Wasfi recognized. "Listen," he instructed. "Do you know this song, Ann? It is called *The Dutchman*."

"I think I've heard it before," Ann replied. "I'm sure Richard probably has it on a folk collection somewhere."

Wasfi leaned in as the man began to sing the lyrics. "Listen to the words. It's about a wife taking care of her husband who was shell-shocked from the war. She loves him so much that she sacrifices every day for him. Even though he lives his life in another world, she takes care of his every need." Wasfi joined the others in the bar who were softly singing the chorus.

Let us all sing a song for the Dutchman
As the walls rise above the zider zee
Long ago I used to be a young man
And dear Margaret remembers that for me.

As Ann listened to the words, she looked over at Thompson who was singing along with the crowd.

Ann wasn't surprised he knew all the words, and she focused on the lyrics as he sang. In a moment of absolute clarity, the lyrics to *The Dutchman* touched her. She was, in fact, the old woman from the song ... taking care of a man who was in a world understood only by him. She didn't feel the tear as it ran down her cheek.

He's mad as he can be, but Margaret only sees that sometimes,

sometimes she sees her unborn children in his eyes.

Wasfi saw what was happening and silently handed Ann a bar napkin to dry her eyes.

"Thank you," she said, slightly embarrassed at such an emotional reaction to the song.

"It's alright," Wasfi whispered. "The song has powerful lyrics."

Ann nodded her response. She never quite understood her husband's love of folk music until that very moment.

When the song ended, the man to whom Josh handed the note stood up. "Ladies and gents, thanks for being with us tonight. We're the No Time Players ... so named because, as the regulars here know, we have no time to practice." The crowd laughed as the man looked at the note. "I've been informed we have a celebrity in our pub tonight," he shouted. The crowd hooted and hollered in response. Several pounded their glasses on the bar. The man looked again at the note. "His name is Thompson and he's a Congressman from over the pond in the States."

Thompson blushed a bit, but stood and toasted his glass to the crowd. He watched Josh pass the note to the man, so Thompson shook his fist at Josh in a mock threatening manner. Josh let loose the heartiest laugh he had in months. The musician continued, and he shocked Thompson with his next announcement. "Apparently, the Congressman plays a little mandolin and his favorite song is Dirty Old Town."

"I think we know that song," said Bryan, as he handed his mandolin over to Thompson.

Thompson shook his head and tried to sit back down, but the crowd started shouting their encouragement. Ann laughed and started to shout with them. "Come on, Richard," she hollered. "Just like the old days."

Thompson laughed at his wife and put the instrument's strap over his shoulder. He quickly picked away at a couple of strings to get comfortable with the neck. Bryan slapped a beat on his knee which Thompson counted out loud. He shook his head to the half-beat as the group began to play.

"God, I hope no one posts this on YouTube," Ann laughed as the song began. Then she cupped her hands around her mouth and shouted out, "Go get 'em, Richard. Play that thing, boy."

Hours later, the four were walking back to their hotel when Josh's phone rang. There was a light rain falling and Josh had to wipe the water off the screen to see the caller ID. "It's Griffith," Josh announced, before hitting the talk button. "Hey, you old married fart, what's up?"

Josh stopped in his tracks and his jovial demeanor vanished. The call sobered Josh up in an instant.

TWENTY-THREE

The Main Street Laundromat in Covington, Kentucky was home to 32 washing machines, 23 dryers, 2 mega-washers, a coin changer, a gum ball machine and the law offices of Sean Sullivan, Esq. On any given day, the residents of the close neighborhood entered the building to clean their clothes or to get legal advice from a man who was truly committed to the people he represented in court. The business had regular business hours and purported to open at 8:00 a.m. and close at 10:00 p.m. However, even though Sullivan turned out the lights at closing time, it was not unusual for the doors of the laundromat to remain unlocked throughout the night.

Sullivan lived in a second floor loft above the business, but spent most of his time in a small office in the back of the laundromat. From this perch he could work on his cases and help deal with the occasional washing machine malfunction.

The back room law office was as unkempt as Sullivan was himself. Stacks of files were piled around the room in no particular order. Coffee cans filled with quarters retrieved from the washers and dryers sat on top of the files stacks as paper weights. Sullivan didn't mind working around the intense detergent smell. It smelled like Irish Spring soap to him.

In recent weeks, the storefront of Sullivan's Laundromat had taken on a new third function. It had also become the official headquarters of the Sullivan for Congress campaign. Red, white, and blue bunting hung beneath and above the big plate glass storefront. On a table behind the window which was normally reserved for folding clean clothes, there were stacks of green and white bumper stickers declaring Sullivan's candidacy. Campaign yard signs on metal frames were leaning against the wall next to the table. A big sign was taped in the window and blocked some of the light from the streetlamps.

During the day, Sullivan's laundromat was abuzz with activity. Women in the neighborhood cleaned clothes, and men dropped by to exchange stories. During the evening hours, the store was quiet most nights.

Sullivan was sitting in the dimly lit back room, writing notes to be inserted into one of the many law files stacked around the office. He had done some of his own wash earlier in the evening and was now waiting for the dryers to finish before he retired upstairs to his second floor living quarters for the evening.

The leather suspenders, which earlier in the day held up Sullivan's pants, were now hanging down by his side. Sullivan's dress shirt had long since been discarded and was resting over the back of his desk chair. He still had on his white undershirt, but he had taken off his shoes and socks. Stroking his white beard, he looked like Santa Claus sitting in his workshop making notes on legal pads about who had been naughty and nice.

The bell attached to the front door of the laundromat jingled, a declaration that someone entered the building. Even over the loud hum of the dryers, Sullivan heard the bell. He looked at his watch and noticed it was well past midnight. "We're closed," shouted Sullivan without looking up. "Come back tomorrow."

The lights were out in the front room of the laundromat, but the glow from the street light leaking in around the edges of the campaign signs in the windows was just bright enough for the figure approaching the back office to cast a dim shadow. Sullivan looked up and squinted his eyes as the indefinite shape resolved into a recognizable person. Antwone Mason, the young man whom Sullivan represented recently on a third-strike drug possession, entered the room.

"Hey, Mr. Sullivan," Mason mumbled as he approached. His greeting was barely audible.

"Mr. Mason, it's awfully late. My law office and the laundromat are both closed for the day. If you have business to discuss or dirty clothes to wash, you can come back tomorrow." Sullivan may have represented the indigent people of the street, but he insisted they discuss their business (and wash their clothes) during regular business hours.

"I ain't got no business." Mason stuffed his hands in his pockets. "I just got something to say to you."

Sullivan looked up from his notes. Mason was wearing similar clothes to those he wore in court, but tonight something looked different about him. Sullivan decided his face looked softer than it had after their scuffle outside the courthouse. His eyes were not as menacing. He decided to humor the young man. "Very well," Sullivan replied. "What is it, then?"

Mason looked down, avoiding eye contact as he spoke. "Yeah, well about that thing at the courthouse. Well, my mama found out I yelled at you and pushed you down. She told me I had to come over and apologize to you. So that's what I'm here to do."

"Your mama is a good woman," Sullivan replied. He put the file down on the desk and his pen on top of it.

"Yeah," Mason mumbled, shifting his weight uncomfortably from one side to the other.

"And she wants you to apologize to me?" Sullivan looked directly at Mason, who refused his eye contact.

"Yeah." Again, Mason's voice was barely audible.

"What about you, Antwone … do you want to apologize?" Sullivan stood up and approached him. "Your mama wants you to say something, but what do you want to say?"

214

"Well, I probably shouldn't have pushed you down on the ground. You're an old man and you been nice to me and my mama. I'm sorry I did that." It wasn't a detailed dissertation of remorse. However, it was probably as good an apology as Antwone Mason had ever given to anyone—whether it was at his mama's insistence or not.

Sullivan placed his large left hand on Mason's shoulder. "Very well, Mr. Mason. I accept your apology." Sullivan extended his right hand in a shake which the young man accepted. Mason finally looked into Sullivan's eyes. "You're a good man, son. Don't ever let anyone try to convince you otherwise." Mason nodded. "And tell your mother I said hello."

As Mason turned and exited, Sullivan waited to hear the sound of the bell. When it rang he went back to his chair and picked up the file he was reviewing. He paused briefly and smiled. Sullivan knew it took a lot of courage for Antwone to come into the store and apologize, even if it was at an odd hour. Sullivan chuckled. Hell, it was probably business hours for Antwone Mason. Sullivan decided he would call Mrs. Mason in the morning and see if there was something he could do to assist in finding her son an honest job.

The bell on the front door rang again, acknowledging another entrance. "Don't worry, Antwone," Sullivan shouted, "I shall call your mama first thing tomorrow morning and let her know you properly apologized."

When Sullivan did not hear the bell making an exit refrain, he repeated his announcement. Nothing. "Antwone, please answer me." For the third time no one responded. "Ah, hell's bells," he mumbled, before yelling, "Antwone?"

Sullivan had occasionally found a homeless person trying to use the laundromat for shelter. He stood up, pulled his suspenders over his shoulders, put his slippers back on and headed out of his office to the front. The old wood floor squeaked as he walked. He stopped at the entry to the laundromat. There were no shadows this time.

"Who's out there?" Sullivan looked around the dark room. "The homeless shelter up the street really has much better accommodations than this place."

Silence.

When the hunting knife plunged into Sullivan's massive chest with a violent punch, the old Irishman let out a loud, guttural scream that sounded like the roar of a wounded lion.

Sullivan grabbed the hand holding the knife and pulled it away from him. Blood gushed from the deep wound, immediately increasing in flow with the sudden rise in Sullivan's heart rate. "Get out," Sullivan bellowed at the shadow in the darkness.

The lights from the street made evil silhouettes on the floor as Sullivan stumbled backwards, away from his anonymous intruder. There was not enough light for him to see who stabbed him. The room spun as pain and shock combined. Sullivan's survival instinct kicked in.

When the intruder lunged a second time, Sullivan saw him coming. He tried to parry the attack, but the knife cut the big Irishman's left arm. Sullivan swung his right arm wildly, landing his big, meaty paw squarely on the trespasser's jaw. The man fell hard to the floor.

"You hooligan," Sullivan said as he tried to lift the man up by the neck of his shirt. The man planted his shoulder into Sullivan's stomach and pushed him backwards toward one of the washing machines. The two of them hit the washing machine with such force they knocked the washer off its concrete base. Sullivan slid down the side of the machine, red blood from the wound on his arm smearing a path down the machine's white enamel.

When Sullivan hit the floor, he stared at the knife the silent intruder had again planted firmly in his chest with an indifferent gaze. Blood was now gushing both from his arm and from the two chest wounds. Sullivan's breathing was labored and rattling sounds emanated from his bloody mouth. His hand searched his neck and clutched at the St. Christopher medal on his necklace. He slowly looked up toward the ceiling as he felt his life draining away.

The attacker leaned against the wall and tried to gather himself. Sullivan had hit him hard on the jaw and the drive into the washing machine had broken a rib. He stumbled over to Sullivan, who was struggling to stay alive and muttering the Lord's Prayer. When he pulled the knife from the Irishman's chest, Sullivan let out a loud moan.

The intruder wiped the blood off on Sullivan's pant leg and placed the knife in a sheath on his own belt. The man took another deep breath in order to regain his composure. Closing his eyes, he ran his bloody fingers across his sweaty head and contemplated his next move. Slowly, staying close to the wall and as low as possible, he walked to the front of the store and looked through the gloom of the laundromat out at the street. He saw no movement— the struggle had not attracted any attention. He could get what he came for. Slowly, as the dryers continued to hum, he started back down the aisle towards Sullivan's office.

"I said get the hell out of my store," grunted Sullivan. The old Irishman used all of his remaining strength to get up to his feet and ram the intruder.

Surprised at a counter-attack from someone he thought was dead, the man was knocked off-balance. Sullivan spun his assailant and pushed him face first toward the front of the store. The momentum of the two caused them to smash through the front plate glass window of the laundromat—their bodies sailing out onto the sidewalk in a spray of bodies, glass, and blood.

The man dislodged Sullivan, rolled to his feet and took the knife out of its sheath. He plunged it two more times into Sullivan's chest. He did not get what he came for, but there was now too much commotion. He ran as fast as he could into the darkness of the night. When it was all over, Sean Sullivan lay dead on the sidewalk, still clutching the St. Christopher medal in his right hand.

TWENTY-FOUR

When the phone first rang at Tiana's townhouse, she thought it was a prank call of some sort. Someone awakened her with a rambling message about her father and the laundromat. She hung up the phone and was getting ready to push the buttons to review the caller ID, when the phone rang a second time. She was still half asleep and the ring made her jump.

This time the call was from Tiana's mother, Shirley, who was hysterical. She was speaking rapidly, trying to spit out words in between uncontrolled sobs. Tiana could not make out what her mother was trying to say, but something was definitely going on at the laundromat.

"Mom," Tiana said, her hands starting to shake in response to her mother's hysteria. She closed her eyes and spoke in a slow, even meter, hoping to get her mother to calm down enough for Tiana to understand what she was saying. "Please calm down. What is it? What's wrong?"

"It's Sean," Shirley spewed the words out. When she tried to elaborate, nothing came out.

Tiana's heart seemed to freeze in mid-beat. "Has something happened to Daddy?"

"Yes, God yes, baby," cried Shirley. "Gramps and I are here at the laundromat. It's bad baby. It's really, really bad."

Tiana closed her eyes and opened them again to make sure she was awake. She slowly sank to her knees. Shirley was saying something about a robbery and having the police come to pick Tiana up at her townhouse, but Tiana wasn't listening. Before her mom even finished her sentence, Tiana jumped up. She flipped her phone shut, mindlessly threw on some sweats and shoes and ran out her door without putting on a jacket. The early morning coolness cut into her tears as she took the front steps to her townhouse in one long stride.

Each city block seemed a mile long. Tiana streaked down sidewalks and cut across streets without looking at oncoming traffic. Tiana was a runner, but the panicked nature of her strides quickly had her lungs burning for air. Still Tiana refused to let her legs quit. The pounding of her legs on the pavement was matched by the pounding of her heart. Parked cars whizzed past her peripheral vision in a blur. About a block away from Sullivan's laundromat, a side stitch began to rip at her abdomen. Despite the pain, Tiana did not stop running until she rounded the corner at Main Street.

When Tiana saw the flashing lights of the ambulance and the police cars, she froze. As fast as she had run to be there, she just stood on the sidewalk, her lungs greedily taking in oxygen, unable to move. Then, panting and holding her side, she forced herself towards the flashing lights. Words and sounds around her were muffled and inaudible as she stumbled forward in slow motion. The sidewalk felt like quicksand sucking at her legs to stop her from completing that short walk into the nightmare in front of her.

When Tiana saw her mother and her grandfather talking to a police officer, her stride quickened. Her mouth was so dry she was barely able to get the words out. "Mom? Gramps? What's happened?"

Shirley screamed as she ran to Tiana and grabbed her in an intense hug. "It's your daddy, baby. Oh, Lord, it's Sean," she sobbed uncontrollably, unable to continue to speak. She put her head on Tiana's shoulder and began to rock her back and forth.

"What about Daddy?" Tiana pulled back and shook her mother by the shoulders. Without knowing the answer to the question, Tiana started to cry. She looked to her grandfather who walked over to hug them both. "Gramps. Tell me what happened? Where's Daddy?"

Reverend Bolton put his arms around the two women and touched his forehead to Tiana's cheek. Then he looked up and focused on her eyes. "Tiana, sometimes the Lord challenges us by placing evil in our path."

Tiana looked at him blankly, unable to comprehend what he was saying. Then a noise from behind drew Tiana's attention. She swung around and looked in the direction of the laundromat. A stretcher with a blanket covered body was being raised up off the sidewalk by two paramedics. Underneath the stretcher, blood spread out in a pool across the sidewalk.

"No," Tiana screamed. Her grandfather and mother tried to hold onto her, but Tiana ripped herself from their embrace. "Oh God no, please no," Tiana cried as she ducked under a line of yellow crime tape and started to run to the stretcher. Reverend Bolton and Shirley followed in quick pursuit.

A police officer grabbed Tiana around the waist and swung her around. "I'm sorry lady, but you can't be in here. This is a crime scene."

Reverend Bolton and Shirley caught up with Tiana and also tried to restrain her. "That's my daddy on that stretcher. That's my daddy." The police officer kept his grip on Tiana as she went limp.

The officer knew Reverend Bolton from working the city beat and the sounds of Tiana's cries tore at the seasoned officer. "I'm sorry Brother Bolton, but I can't let anyone near the store until we're through getting all our evidence."

Tiana's head jerked up. "Evidence?" she cried. "Evidence of what?"

Shirley grabbed Tiana's shoulders. "Sean's dead, baby. Someone killed him. Your daddy's gone."

Pleadingly, Tiana looked at her grandfather as if somehow he could change the awful verdict. "I'm sorry, honey. The Lord has called Sean home."

Hearing those horrible words, Tiana collapsed into the arms of her family.

The investigation dragged on through the early morning twilight until the sun came up. Tiana watched the slow progress from atop the front quarter panel of a police car, while the morbid circus expanded to include media and men in blue jackets with FBI emblazoned on the back. A neighbor brought out a blanket, which Tiana now wrapped around her shoulders. Looking at the stretcher sit without moving in front of the laundromat for the past hour left her numb and emotionless. Finally, the coroner began to move the stretcher to his hearse. Tiana got up and met him at the rear of his black vehicle.

The coroner looked up as Tiana approached him. "So, I understand you're his daughter," the man said.

Her hands stuffed in her pockets, Tiana simply replied, "Yes."

The coroner put a comforting hand on Tiana's shoulder. "He was a good man," he said. "Did you know he would buy suits for the homeless people I'd process?"

"No," said Tiana. "He never told me that."

The coroner realized his words seemed shallow compared to the young woman's obvious grief. He hung his head embarrassed at his awkwardness. "Well, he did."

Seeing the coroner's embarrassment, Tiana replied, "It's okay. I understand what you want to say. He was a good man." Tiana nodded at Sullivan's covered corpse. "Can I have a minute?"

The coroner hesitated, then he nodded. "Please just don't touch him. We still have to perform an autopsy and get whatever evidence we can to help us find who did this." He patted Tiana on the shoulder before walking a few steps away. "I'm sorry."

Tiana removed the blanket draped over Sullivan's pale, lifeless face. "Oh, Daddy." She smiled, fighting back tears. She so wanted to brush back his white hair. She fisted her hands to stop them from reaching out and touching him. She tried to speak, but could think of nothing to say. It all seemed so surreal. She covered her mouth and tears flowed down her cheeks. The couple of minutes she stood there seemed frozen in time. Finally, Tiana pulled the blanket back over Sullivan's face. "I love you, Daddy."

Reverend Bolton and Shirley had been watching Tiana from a distance. Tiana turned and walked slowly to them, where she was met and enfolded in her mother's open arms. They were just about to walk away when another police car pulled up to the scene. Antwone Mason, with his arms handcuffed behind his back, sat in the back seat. A witness told the police he had seen Mason in the neighborhood around the time of the initial 911 call. The police picked him up in the projects moments earlier. He sat still, trying to look tough, but his eyes looked scared. An officer threw the car into park and jumped out of the driver's side of the car.

"We got him," the officer shouted to one of the other officers near the door of the laundromat.

"Got who?" Reverend Bolton asked as the officer passed in front of them.

"That kid over there. The one in the car," the officer pointed at the young African American man in his patrol car. "He's been in trouble before, you know."

Reverend Bolton looked over at the car and recognized the young man as someone from his church, the son of one of his loyal members. "Antwone Mason?" he asked.

"Yeah," said the officer. "A neighbor saw him coming out of the laundromat late last night."

Tiana's eyes drew sharp with rage, remembering it was Mason who attacked her father at the county courthouse. Her breathing shortened and she drew her fists. "You motherfucker," she mumbled as she stared at Mason sitting in the police car.

Tiana started for the car, but her grandfather got between her and the vehicle. He knew the look in her eye and he wanted to avoid a confrontation. "Not now, baby. This isn't the place."

"The fuck it isn't," Tiana shouted as her fury shook every inch of her small frame. "That sonofabitch killed my daddy." Despite his efforts to stop her,

Reverend Bolton was unable to keep Tiana away from the police car. She ripped herself away and ran to the side of the car.

Mason saw her coming, but refused to make eye contact. He simply looked down at the floorboard as Tiana pounded her open palm on the window. Incensed that he refused to look up, she screamed at him. "Look at me."

Undaunted by Mason's refusal to look at her, Tiana continued to scream. "Afraid to look at me? You'd better be afraid. You'd better pray they give you the chair, because if you ever get out, I'll kill you. You got that? I'll fuckin' kill you myself."

Reverend Bolton succeeded at getting his arms around Tiana's waist and was moving her back from the car when Mason looked up at Tiana from behind the glass. His eyes looked sad and sincere. His only words, mouthed through the barrier of the police cruiser window, left her frozen in disbelief.

"I didn't do it."

TWENTY-FIVE

Leo Argo stood with his back against the wall of the office hallway. He had his service revolver in one hand and his FBI badge in the other. A dark-haired woman sat at her secretary station, glaring at Argo. He raised his eyebrows at her and brought the gun to his lips. "Shh," he whispered.

"Freeze, you sonofabitch." Leo Argo shouted the words into The Fat Man's office with an enthusiasm he normally saved for a Washington, DC back alley bust. He jumped into the messy law office like he was busting into a crack house, his badge and gun lowered at The Fat Man's eye level. Argo struck a pose that would have made the director of a television police drama proud.

The Fat Man sat at his desk, with his neck crooked forward toward his computer, reading some words he just added to a court document. Argo's sudden and abrupt entry caused him to leap out of his chair and scream in a high pitch worthy of an opera singer. As soon as he did, he reached down and grabbed the back of his right leg.

Lowering his badge and gun, Argo began to laugh hysterically. The Fat Man didn't see the humor. "Jesus, Leo," he said. "You scared the living shit out of me."

"That's the reaction I was going for," Argo replied. He holstered his gun, flipped his credentials closed and shoved them into his back pants' pocket. "I did tone it down a notch. When I do it just right, I can make grown men piss their pants … and apparently make middle-aged attorneys scream like little girls."

"Very funny," The Fat Man said as he continued to rub behind his knee. "I think I pulled a hamstring."

"Dude, you have got to start getting some exercise." Stepping over the piles of folders and binders on the floor, Argo walked behind The Fat Man's desk and extended his hand.

The Fat Man removed his hand from his hamstring and returned the shake. "Getting the crap scared out of you by an FBI agent could be a start," he replied. "You realize a simple knock on my door would have sufficed."

Argo laughed and stepped back to size up his old friend. He cocked his head from side to side and looked at The Fat Man as if he was viewing a suspect in a line-up. "You told me you'd lost weight, but damn Joey. You've lost a lot." Argo gave his friend a thumb's up. With an exaggerated Cuban accent, he added, "You're looking good."

"Thanks." The Fat Man sat down and gestured for Argo to do the same. "I really didn't have much of a choice. When the doctor told me I could either lose weight or die, I chose the former."

"Good call," Argo replied. "I could drop some tonnage too, but since Jane and I split, I've been eating a whole lot of junk food."

The Fat Man scooted his chair up under his desk. Argo e-mailed The Fat Man about his split-up with Kline, but he explained it only in the vaguest of terms. Argo hadn't offered any of the details, and The Fat Man had not asked for them. The Fat Man sensed Argo wanted to talk about it, but was unsure where to start. Often socially awkward, The Fat Man was hesitant at the thought of discussing his friend's love life.

While the two traded emails on a regular basis, The Fat Man had seen Argo only once since they returned from Romania. The Fat Man did not have many close friends, but he developed a close relationship with the big Cuban on that trip. The Fat Man visited Argo once in DC to see a baseball series between the Nationals and the Reds.

Argo's abrupt office entry might have startled The Fat Man enough to make him pull a hamstring, but he was not totally surprised to see him in his office. He knew Argo dealt directly with Members of Congress on behalf of the Agency and thought he might be sent to investigate the murder of Sean Sullivan. "I wondered if you'd be showing up anytime soon."

Argo knew exactly what The Fat Man was referring to and quickly shifted his friendly demeanor to business mode. "Yeah, you had a pretty brutal murder down in Covington. It's a federal crime to kill a candidate for US Congress, you know. We used some local agents for the crime scene investigation, but my division in DC is in charge."

"Was it as bad as I've been told?" The Fat Man winced as he asked the question. While Sean Sullivan had been his opponent in the Thompson case, Sullivan was just as quirky as The Fat Man. He respected Sullivan and was stunned to learn Sullivan had been brutally killed at his laundromat law office. The Fat Man truly liked the old guy and, although he had asked the question, he was not really sure he wanted to know all the grisly details.

"I saw the pictures this morning," Argo replied, shaking his head as he spoke. "Man, it looked like a Freddie Krueger movie scene. Sullivan may have had some years on him, but he put up a good fight. There was blood all over the laundromat. I suspect some of it will end up belonging to our killer."

"It wiped me out when I heard the news," said The Fat Man.

"So, I assume you knew Sullivan?" Argo asked as he pulled out his notebook. "Do you mind if I take some notes?"

"As long as I'm not a person of interest, you can take anything you want," The Fat Man replied. He was only half-joking. When Argo didn't respond, The Fat Man contemplated calling in one of his colleagues from the office to sit in. He quickly remembered he trusted Argo and continued. "Everybody in town knew Sean Sullivan. Well, at least every lawyer in town knew him. He was a big old friendly mick and one helluva lawyer." He paused. "I was just with him in court. It all seems so unbelievable."

"Really?" replied Argo as he jotted something down on his notebook. "Did he give you any indication someone was out to get him?"

"Not at all," The Fat Man said. He looked up at the ceiling as he searched his memory banks. "Naw, nothing."

"What about this kid they have in custody? Do you know anything about him?"

"Just what I read in the papers," The Fat Man replied. He thought he'd explain a little about Sullivan. "You've got to understand, Leo, Sullivan wasn't your typical lawyer. He did a lot of probono work for people in the inner-city. He led a simple life. It wasn't important if you had any money. Sullivan stood up for the down-trodden in society. This Mason kid was apparently one of those cases. According to the folks at the courthouse, Sullivan and this kid had some sort of confrontation a while back."

"I met with Antwone Mason early this morning," Argo said. He folded up his notebook and put it back in his pants pocket before leaning back in his chair. "The kid said he didn't do it."

"Don't they all say they didn't do it?" The Fat Man replied. He was a bit surprised at Argo's statement.

"Pretty much so, except ..."

"What?"

"The kid didn't look like he'd been in a fight. Sullivan and his attacker bounced around inside the laundromat like a pinball machine. Hell, they knocked one of those big washers off its base before they crashed through the front plate glass window. All that and you'd expect to see the other guy busted up a little bit—you know, cuts and bruises and such. Antwone has some marks on him, but I suspect those are from the arrest."

The Fat Man followed Argo's argument, but decided to play the devil's advocate. "The newspaper reported the kid was seen in the vicinity at the time of the murder and the courthouse scuttlebutt is that you guys have his prints on the front doorknob."

"Yeah, once the DNA comes back, we'll know for sure." Argo nodded his head in affirmation. "Do you know Sullivan's ex-father-in-law?" Argo pulled his notebook back out and looked at a name for confirmation before speaking it out loud. "Reverend Bolton?"

"I know of him," The Fat Man said. "He's a minister down in Covington. Why?"

Argo shook his head as he spoke, indicating what he was about to say didn't make sense. "Bolton was coming into the jail as I was leaving. He was going to see the Mason kid. Reverend Bolton thinks the kid is telling the truth. He thinks someone else killed Sullivan."

"He's a minister," The Fat Man said. "The family goes to his church. Of course, he wants to believe someone else did it."

"Maybe, but I just don't think this will wrap up so easily. They're doing the crime scene detail right now and I suspect this case is not as straightforward as the local police think." Argo paused. "But the Sullivan murder isn't the real reason I came to your office. It was just an excuse. I was just hoping we could grab some dinner while I'm in town."

"Crap," The Fat Man pounded his desk. "I'd love to, but I have to head down to Lexington after work today. I'm doing some research on the Keeneland horse sales and a filly I want to see has one of the first auction slots in the morning."

"Too bad," replied Argo, shaking his head. "I'd love to catch up over dinner."

The Fat Man tapped a pen on his legal pad. "Hey, what time do you get done today?" he asked.

"I don't know," Argo shrugged his shoulders as he contemplated what he planned. "I've got one or two more interviews I need to get done." He looked at his watch. "I could be free in a couple of hours."

"Great," The Fat Man replied. His eyes danced at the plan he was plotting. "Why don't you head out and get your interviews. Then come back here and you can head to Lexington with me. In the morning we'll grab some breakfast, watch the sale and be back here in time for your morning report."

Argo rubbed his hands together. "That sounds perfect. I could use some fun these days. What time are you taking off?"

"What ever time you get here."

"Great. Let me get to these interviews and I'll call you as soon as I'm done."

The legislative exchange conference which Thompson was attending was being held a short walk from his hotel at Leinster House, home of the Oireachtas, the national parliament of Ireland. While it has been extended on several occasions, Leinster House is said to be the original model for the White House. The Parliament was out of session and the conference itself was taking place on the floor of the Dail Chamber.

Josh, Ann, and Thompson came to Leinster House early. They sat at a speaker phone in a private office just off the Dail Chamber floor. All three of them were studying a press release while Michael Griffith spoke to them from America on a secure line.

"Paragraph two, line three..." Josh thought out loud as he jumped up and paced around the room. "... let's add Ann and the kids' names to the condolences quote. It makes it sound more personal."

"Agreed," Griffith replied over the phone. "Hey Josh, what do you think about cutting the final sentence? It sounds kind of trite to me."

Josh took a moment and reread the quote. "Yeah. I don't have a problem with that. I can't imagine anyone using that as a quote in their story anyway."

Ann looked pale. News about the death of Sean Sullivan made sleep for her restless at best. Despite Thompson's reassurance that it was some random street crime, Ann felt uncomfortable. She put down her cup of coffee, stood up and walked over to peer out a window. "This all seems so sick."

"What?" Thompson replied, looking up from the papers in front of him.

Ann turned from the window. "I can't believe we're wordsmithing a press release over a man's murder."

"Godfather Rules, Annie." Griffith's voice over the speaker phone cut to the chase. "In the words of Hyman Roth, let it go and remember this is the business we have chosen."

Hoover was sniffing around a telephone pole when Jane Kline's phone rang. She switched her cane to the same hand holding the dog's leash. Looking around before answering, Kline hit the green button on her phone. "Kline here."

"Director, it's Zach." MacKenzie's voice sounded frenzied. "Where the hell are you?"

"I'm out walking Hoover. Why?" Kline knew her top deputy would not be happy by the revelation she was out alone.

"Because I'm over here at your townhouse and you're not here," MacKenzie replied. Kline was correct. He wasn't happy. "You're not supposed to be going outside without protection."

"My dog has to relieve himself occasionally, Zach." Hoover started walking and Kline followed.

"Yeah, but you shouldn't be doing it—at least not alone. We've discussed this."

"No Zach, you've discussed it. I've just listened." Kline paused thinking about what had just been said. "And why are you at my townhouse?"

"I've got to talk to you immediately, boss. It's about Director Steele ... and you."

"I'll be right there."

Paddy Neal sat alone in his room staring at the bottle of Irish whiskey he'd been working on for several hours. The questions he asked Zafer had been a test. He knew what happened in Miami, but wanted to see if Zafer would tell him the truth. Neal's boss may be a believer in Zafer's cause, but Neal was not. Neal did not want his picture on an Interpol wire over some fucking freedom fighters. He was taking all necessary precautions.

Neal took a shot of whiskey and picked up his cell phone.

Zafer was at a local restaurant having dinner. He picked up his cell on the first ring. "Hello."

"One more question about Miami," Neal said while lying down on the bed.

"Paddy?" Zafer replied. "We should not be talking about this on the phone."

"I know, I know." Neal paused for a second. "I'll see you in the morning, then." When Zafer hung up the phone, Neal spoke out loud to an empty room. "But if you sold out the man in Miami, what keeps you from selling me out?"

Tiana walked up to the laundromat and surveyed the scene of her father's murder. Sean Sullivan's law office was a source of many fond childhood memories for Tiana. Now, it was the source of her greatest agony.

The company Shirley hired to clean up the laundromat had just arrived and was unloading equipment from their van. The plywood slab which would temporarily be the front window of her father's store stood in stark contrast to the window draped in bunting on the other side of the door. The broken glass had been swept off the sidewalk, but despite having been hosed down, blood stains remained.

Neighbors and friends started a small shrine to Sullivan on the front steps of the laundromat. Candles burned amongst handwritten notes, flowers, and Irish mementos. Several St. Christopher medals hung on necklaces around the doorknob. Tiana spied a Guinness sitting on the top step in a glass with the

Chez Nora logo on it. She teared up as she read the note attached to the glass: "Room temperature, Love Jimmy & Pati."

Tiana put the note back and stepped over the items and entered the laundromat. She nodded to the cleaning crew as she made her way back to her father's office. Tiana opened the door to Sullivan's back office and flipped on the light. The stacks of files, papers, and coin jars were overwhelming. Tiana sat down in her father's desk chair, laid her head down on her arms and began to cry.

Once Tiana's tears subsided, she again looked around the room. The files were more than she could handle at this moment in her life. She felt empty, lost and useless. Then her father's words came back to her. She searched around his desk and found Sullivan's writ of mandamus file, flipped it open and found what she was looking for … a phone number. Tiana grabbed the phone and dialed the number.

Tiana paused as the person on the other line answered, "Joe Bradley, how can I help you?"

The man stood naked in front of a full-length mirror and pulled away the bloody gauze taped just below his right breast. The first aid he performed on the cut was not working and stitches would be required. He took a shot of vodka, put a towel in his mouth and poured rubbing alcohol over the wound.

The pain dropped him to his knees as he screamed into the towel, nearly passing out. Once he could stand again, he picked up the loop needle off the dresser and pushed his skin together. He screamed again into the towel as he hooked the needle through his skin, but he had no other options. No urgent-care facility in America could close the problems caused by this wound.

TWENTY-SIX

Richard Thompson lay motionless on his bed, staring aimlessly at the ceiling of his well-appointed Dublin hotel room. The day was still young, but Thompson felt like he had been awake for a lifetime. Despite the fact Josh and Thompson had both been drinking heavily at the pub, the news of Sullivan's demise sobered them up quickly. After receiving the news, Thompson, Ann and Josh returned to their hotel and talked for several hours, sifting through their frayed emotions about what happened.

After the finishing touches were made to the press release, Josh left, and Thompson and Ann returned to their room. They put on their workout gear with the intention of going to their hotel's gym. They agreed a spin on the stationary bike would help soften the hard reality of Sullivan's murder. But, instead of heading to the gym, Thompson laid down on the bed— "just for five minutes." Now, he felt immobilized.

The oppressive thoughts filling Thompson's head swirled like the cigarette smoke that fogged the evening air outside the pub they had visited. His opponent in the Fall election, Sean Sullivan, was dead. Everything else seemed small and insignificant by comparison. Thompson had nothing to do with

Sullivan's murder, yet he felt truly remorseful. Oddly, he felt somehow he was ultimately responsible.

In a purely Machiavellian sense, he should be pleased his political challenger had been eliminated. Such reaction in himself might be producing the feeling of guilt, but that really wasn't it. In fact, Thompson felt somewhat disappointed there would be no competition in the fall—like an athlete learning the opposing team has forfeited an upcoming game.

Clearly, it wasn't schadenfreude, the German term for taking delight in the misfortune of others. He sincerely wished Sullivan was still alive. The source of Thompson's angst was much deeper.

As Thompson struggled to understand his own intense reaction to the murder of his political foe, his thoughts kept wandering to the moral dilemma he had been struggling with ever since he returned from Romania. Thompson had enough self-awareness to recognize that, while on the surface he was grappling with the death of his political rival, his darkest thoughts were about the taking of another life.

Once, and not that long ago, Thompson himself pulled the trigger of a gun that sent a man to his death. The incident haunted him since the moment he pulled the trigger. No day went by without him reliving that moment once or twice in his mind. He often stayed up late at night fearing the repetitive nightmares. Thompson relaxed ever so slightly as he embraced the realization his thoughts of guilt were less about the loss of Sean Sullivan and more about the life Thompson had personally taken. His solemn mood this morning was about his own life, not the death of his political opponent.

Dressed in her workout clothes, Ann walked to the bed and lay down at Thompson's side. Like her husband, she stared at the ceiling. She, too, felt grief about the murder of Sean Sullivan, but she was struggling to understand why her husband's reaction was so extreme. While the street murder of Sullivan was a sad commentary on life in general, they barely knew the man. Thompson's deep, brooding mood seemed to be wildly out of proportion to the entire situation.

Ann snuggled in closer to Thompson, rolled on her side and laid her head on his chest. She paused before breaking the silence, but then offered, "What's going on in that head of yours?"

Thompson continued to stare at the ceiling. With Ann's head on his chest, she could not see the pained look in his eyes. He always knew someday he would tell Ann about the horror that occurred in Romania and he struggled to determine if the time was now.

"I can't stand the silence, Richard," Ann continued, nearly pleading. "Something's up. I can tell. I need to know what's going on with you."

"I don't even know where to begin," he replied in a low voice.

Ann rubbed her hand down Thompson's side. "Any place," she said. "Start anywhere you want, baby. I just can't deal with the silence anymore."

Thompson took a deep breath. "This isn't about Sullivan," he said. "He was a good man. I actually liked the guy, personally. But there's more going on in my head than Sean Sullivan."

"I didn't think this was about the campaign." Ann's voice was tentative. Now that the conversation had started, she wasn't sure she wanted it to continue. Deep inside her soul, she knew this conversation, whatever it was about, was inevitable. There was no turning back now. "So what is it about, Richard? Something is causing you to react like this. What is it? You can tell me."

"Romania."

Ann stilled for a moment, her breath catching. Whenever anyone made reference to the tragic events that occurred during their trip to Romania several years earlier, Thompson conveniently changed the subject. It became clear to Ann that Romania and the Carpathian Mountains were strictly off limits for conversation. Now, with the death of Sean Sullivan fresh on their minds, Thompson suddenly brought up Romania.

Ann felt a shiver of dread lance down her spine and her whisper was barely audible. "I wondered when you'd finally be ready to tell me." Ann said, as goose bumps appeared on her arms. "What happened in

Romania?"

"The trip to the mountains," Thompson paused. He draped the wrist of his free arm across his forehead and his voice shook. "God, this isn't going to be easy."

"Wherever you want to start, that's the right place." Ann moved in tighter against Thompson. "Just tell me."

Thompson glanced down at his left arm hooked around his wife's shoulder. He was about to tell her a gut-wrenching secret that he kept from her for years. He needed contact with her body in order to say it out loud. In the back of his mind, he also feared that, once she knew the truth, he might have to hold her there to keep her from leaving.

Ann already knew the basics. Josh had been a member of Thompson's Congressional staff back then. While Josh had been in Romania observing their elections, he had been kidnapped by Communist rebels still resisting the transition to Western democracy. The rebels held Josh hostage in a remote part of the Carpathian Mountains. Thompson and Ann had gone to Romania to do whatever they could to assist the CIA in freeing Josh from his captors.

Ann also knew that, on one occasion, her husband went into the Carpathian Mountains along with the CIA to help look for Josh.

A deep breath seemed necessary for Thompson to begin. "We made it up into the mountains and found the cabin where they were holding Josh ... at least at the time we thought that's where they were holding Josh. They left with him just before we got there. The air was cold and damp. You could smell the smoke coming out of the chimney of the shack."

Thompson started to ramble a bit, but she didn't want to ask any questions that would interrupt him. He was finally talking to her about Romania, and that was all that mattered. "Go on," she encouraged.

"Jane Kline decided to go to the front door of the cabin and act like she was a campaign observer lost in the mountains," Thompson said. "That way, she could survey the situation and see if Josh was okay. Once she was inside, Shadow…"

"Who's Shadow?" Ann asked.

"Morrison," Thompson said. "Mark Morrison. Shadow was his CIA code name."

Ann fleetingly noticed Thompson referred to the young CIA agent in the past tense, but again she decided not to ask any questions. "Oh, I never knew he had a code name." The statement sounded trite, but Ann felt she had to say something to keep the conversation moving.

"Anyway, once Jane was in the cabin, Shadow was supposed to enter through the back window. I was hiding in the woods behind the cabin. They wanted me to stay behind. Then, when Shadow tried to crawl in the window, the frame collapsed … probably from dry rot. I knew the people inside had to have heard it."

246

Thompson's words transported him back in place and time. "Jane was inside with the rebels and Shadow just fell though the damn window. Things were not good and were rapidly deteriorating. I had to figure out what was going on inside. I had to do something." Thompson's voice broke. He stopped talking.

As Thompson suddenly went silent, Ann raised her head and looked at him. "So what did you do, Richard? It's okay. You can tell me anything."

Thompson snorted in disbelief before he could stop himself. He was not sure if his wife knew the extent of the "anything" he was about to tell her. His heart was racing and his voice strained to keep control. "I left my cover in the woods and snuck up to the side of the cabin. I tried to look inside a side window to see if I could figure out what was going on."

"And?" Ann asked. She started gently rubbing his chest as if trying to coax the words out of Thompson.

"It was bad," Thompson said. He shook his head and exhaled slowly as he remembered the desperate scene. "Real fucking bad. Kline was in a chair and some greasy looking guy was pointing a gun at her." He paused as his eyes wandered aimlessly around the ceiling while the events unfolded in his mind. "That's when I heard the gunshots."

"Gunshots?"

"Yeah. The leader of the rebels, some former Securiate general, heard Shadow fall through the window and went to check it out. Shadow was waiting for him. They exchanged gun fire. The general was killed and Shadow was wounded pretty badly."

An awkward silence once again filled the room. Ann waited breathlessly while Thompson gathered the courage to tell her what happened next. Jane Kline warned Thompson to never tell anyone the story, not even Ann. The secret had eaten at Thompson for too long. He had to share his burden. The time was right, and Thompson was determined to finish the story.

"So I looked through the window and saw Kline sitting there with a gun aimed at her head," Thompson said. "I reached into my waistband and grabbed my gun."

"Your gun?" Ann was trying to be silent, but Thompson saying he had a gun had startled her. Ann knew her husband did not feel comfortable around guns and that he never even kept as much as a hunting rifle in the house.

"Yeah," said Thompson. "Before he left me, Shadow gave me a handgun."

"Richard," Ann said softly, her voice a faint whisper. "What did you do?"

The silence was deafening.

"I shot him." Thompson's anguished reply was so simple, yet so hard to say. "He was standing there with his gun on Jane. He was going to kill her. There was nothing else for me to do."

Ann was stunned at his words, unable to believe what her husband just admitted.

"I shot the sonofabitch, Ann. I've replayed it a million times in my head, and there was nothing else I could have done. It was him or Jane."

"But…"

"But, as many times as I've justified it over and over in my head, I still can't get over the fact I did what only God should do, I took a man's life. There hasn't been a night that's gone by since Romania that I don't see his face in my dreams. I can still see his black eyes first looking surprised and then going blank."

Ann started to speak, but Thompson put his finger to her lips. "Don't," he said. "There's more."

Ann struggled to understand what "more" there could be in her husband's story. She was already numb from the revelation he had killed a man. Then, suddenly, it dawned on her. When Kline and Thompson returned to the American embassy, Morrison was not with them. They told everyone he had been called back to the United States. "Morrison," she stammered.

"Yeah," Thompson sighed. "Morrison. Shadow. He was wounded pretty badly and there was no way he was going to make it. Jane ended it for him."

Ann stiffened at the news. "Ended it? How?"

"While I held the gun on the one remaining rebel in the cabin, Jane shot Shadow."

"Jesus," Ann gasped. "Jane shot her own partner."

Thompson shifted nervously in the bed. "As bad as it sounds, it was a mercy killing. Shadow didn't have much time left."

"The other rebel, what happened to him?"

"Jane killed him before we left." Thompson shook his head slowly as he spoke. "Before we killed him, we needed to know what happened to Josh."

Ann dreaded what was coming next. "She tortured him," she said flatly.

"No," Thompson said deadly serious. "We tortured him."

"What did you do?"

"You don't want to know the details, Ann. I don't want you to know the details."

Ann had just listened as her husband had confessed to participating, to one extent or another, in the killing of three people. Ann struggled to understand what he could have done that was now beyond the bounds of discussion. Yet, she didn't press the point. "Why doesn't anyone know about any of this? There had to be evidence."

"No evidence," Thompson confessed. "We burned down the house when we left."

"Oh my God," the tone of judgment was clearly evident in her voice as she sat up in bed and put her head on top of her drawn up knees.

Thompson was not shocked by Ann's reaction, but he still felt the sting of her moral judgment. Whether it was Ann's response to him or the idea of the wrongs he had committed, Thompson became defensive. He jumped out of bed and walked to the window. The stiffness of his posture matched the stiffness of his reply. "It was the mountains, Ann. At that time and in that situation it's not like we could call for help. Jane and I did what we had to do. Then we covered our tracks and got the hell out of there."

Still struggling with the news, Ann slowly arose out of the bed and crossed the room to stand behind Thompson. She said quietly, "And you've lived with this since we came back."

"Yeah," replied Thompson. "I've lived with this ever since we got back. And, now you know my dirty secret."

What Ann did next relieved Thompson's deepest fear. After a very brief pause, she gently wrapped her arms around Thompson and laid her cheek on his back. She swallowed before she spoke. "As you've lived with mine, love. It won't be easy, but we'll get through this, too."

Thompson continued to gaze out the window, motionless. "Are you sure?" he asked. "I think murder falls outside the wedding vow promises."

"I said for better or worse, didn't I?" Ann's voice was soft and comforting.

"We both said it," replied Thompson. "You just seem to always be getting the 'worse' on your end."

Ann firmly turned Thompson around and looked into his eyes. "Let me ask you this. Would you kill again if it would save the lives of our children?"

Both their eyes were beginning to fill up. "Of course I would," Thompson replied.

Ann wiped the tear from her husband's eye. "Well, we always say Josh is like one of our kids. Richard, you saved his life. I don't know if I could have done what you did, but you saved Josh's life."

Thompson pulled Ann into a fierce embrace. He put his head on her shoulder. "God, I was so afraid that you'd ..." His voice trailed off.

"I'm not going anywhere," Ann comforted. "Better or worse, Richard ... let's start with that."

Although Thompson was barely able to utter the words, he never meant them more. "I love you," he said.

TWENTY-SEVEN

"Next up is Hip Number 156, a spirited two-year-old chestnut filly from the family of Devil's Bag," the voice came across the loud speaker.

Leo Argo eased into a cushioned seat in the back row of the Keeneland sales pavilion and carefully watched as a muscular horse was walked onto the main stage and paraded around before those assembled. People murmured to each other and marked notes in the catalogue of horses they were studying with a sharp eye. It was an odd sort of ballet Argo was observing, and he was not quite sure what it all meant.

Men in hunter green jackets with brass name tags were mulling around everywhere. Argo looked up at a booth above the stage on the back wall where a group of men keenly observed the crowd seated below them in the semi-circular theater. As the horse was led around on the stage, a man on a platform behind the stage began barking out numbers. He was talking fast and loud, but Argo was able pick out "$75,000."

Argo's attention shifted to the other men in green jackets standing in the aisles. Their eyes scanned back and forth across the crowd. Occasionally, one of them would point to a person in the audience and yell out "hup." The number being shouted by the man on the platform advanced to "$85,000." The "hups" continued at a rapid pace from other men in different aisles around the room, and the number rose higher and higher. In less than a minute, the auctioneer slammed a gavel and the horse was escorted from the stage.

"All right, what the hell just happened?" Argo whispered as he leaned over and asked The Fat Man about the first horse auction he had ever seen.

"That guy up on the platform, he's the auctioneer," The Fat Man responded. "He controls the price on the sale of each horse."

Argo pointed at the auctioneer. "Him?"

"Jesus, don't do that." The Fat Man slapped Argo's hand down in warning.

"What?" Argo looked nervously back and forth. "What the hell did I do?"

"Point," replied The Fat man. "Don't point."

"Why?" Argo shrugged.

"If one of those guys in the aisles takes it as a bid, points back and yells 'hup,' you may end up owning a horse."

Argo quickly placed his hands in his pockets. "Right." He shifted his body so his blue sport coat still covered the holstered service revolver and badge he revealed to security upon entering the pavilion.

The next horse was introduced and another auction began in earnest. "Okay," Argo started over.

"So I guess that means these guys in the aisles spot for the dude up on the main stage?"

"Precisely," said The Fat Man, scanning the crowd as he spoke.

"But I didn't see anyone in the crowd really do anything." Argo shifted in his seat and tried to follow The Fat Man's eyes.

"They don't have to do much," The Fat Man said. "The spotters are real pros. They can figure out who's interested in a horse pretty quickly when the auction starts. Sometimes all the buyer does is make a slight head nod. It doesn't take much. They know who's interested in the horse."

Argo looked up at an open room at the top of the back wall of the pavilion. "What about those guys up in that little room? What do they do?"

"Yeah, that's pretty interesting," The Fat Man replied. "There's a lot of action going on behind the pavilion stage. The high rollers like to stand back there to do their bidding. It's cool to watch the Arab families operate. They all dress down. You can't tell a Saudi prince from a farm hand back there. There's a lot of dough in their saddlebags and those guys up there in the skybox are tracking those bidders. We'll wander back there later when Finn's Lassie goes to auction."

The gavel sounded again and another horse was led off the stage.

"So what did they get for that last horse?" Argo asked nodding at the horse, but careful not to point.

"Two hundred and thirty large," replied The Fat Man.

Argo was astounded someone had just paid $230,000 for a horse. "No shit?"

"No shit."

"That's a lot of jack for four legs and a bunch of fur," Argo said.

"Hair," The Fat Man muttered distractedly while perusing his program and making notes.

"What?"

"Horses have hair," instructed The Fat Man. "They don't have fur."

Argo rolled his eyes and smiled. "Do you correct everyone?"

"Just my friends," said The Fat Man somewhat smugly.

"I'm surprised you still have any."

"Funny," said The Fat Man as he pushed himself up on the arm rests of his chair and led Argo to the hallway behind the seats. "You really need to see these horses up close and personal."

Argo looked through the large window in the hallway at the next horse being led to auction. "They are very noble," he said.

"When we get to the stalls, take a good look at a horse," The Fat Man instructed. "I love to look into their eyes. They look back at you like they know some deep dark secret they've been forbidden by God to reveal."

The brokers who sell horses spend a great deal of time getting a horse ready for its short time on Keeneland's main auction stage. Grooms will go so far as to buff wax a horse's hooves just before the sale. The Fat Man wanted to see if County Mayo Stables was doing anything unusual or unique with their horses. "Let's go back to the barns and see if they're getting Finn's Lassie ready for sale."

"Sure," replied Argo. He looked up and down the hallway for a restroom sign. "I need to hit the head first. I drank too damn much coffee at breakfast this morning."

"Sounds good," The Fat Man said as they both scurried down the hallway towards the restroom next to the cafe. "I could use a stop there, too."

After The Fat Man had finished using the facilities, he and Argo were standing at the sink washing their hands when Paddy Neal walked up and began using the sink located next to the pair. Clad in his blue jeans and flannel shirt, he may have appeared nondescript to most at Keeneland. When The Fat Man looked up, however, he noticed Neal's yellow hat with the words "County Mayo Stables" stitched across the front.

The Fat Man was instantly excited. "Excuse me," he said as he tossed his paper towel into a garbage can. "Are you from County Mayo Stables in Ireland?"

Neal glanced to his side. He did not recognize The Fat Man as a track acquaintance and immediately put up his guard. "Aye," he said tentatively.

"Wow, this is great," said The Fat Man as he extended his hand. "I'm Joe Bradley, an attorney from about an hour or so up north of here. I practice a bit of equine law here in Kentucky and I sometimes present at seminars on the topic. You guys have had a great couple of sales recently."

"Aye," Neal said as he warily shook The Fat Man's hand, "Paddy Neal." He shifted his eyes to Argo.

The Fat Man noticed his glance. "Excuse me. Where are my manners? This is my friend, Leo Argo. I convinced him to take a day off and come down here to see Kentucky at its best."

Argo stepped forward and offered his hand. "Pleased to meet you, Mr. Neal."

Neal glanced first at Argo and then The Fat Man before returning the hand shake. "The pleasure is all mine, to be sure," he said. As they shook hands, Neal caught a glimpse of Argo's holster. Neal's wariness bloomed into full-blown paranoia and he tried to slide along side the pair to exit the restroom. "If you'll excuse me lads, I have some business to attend to."

"Finn's Lassie?" asked The Fat Man excitedly.

Neal was nearly out the door when The Fat Man's words stopped him dead in his tracks.

"If she brings the kind of money you've been getting for your horses at the last couple of sales, you'll be the talk of the racing world." The Fat Man had been walking so closely behind Neal he nearly bumped into him when the Irishman stopped so abruptly.

Neal swung around and was startled to see how quickly and how closely The Fat Man had come up behind him. He stared at The Fat Man and then at Argo. Neal was not sure what was motivating the pair, but his gut was screaming it could not be anything good. He needed to end the conversation quickly. "Finn's Lassie ain't up today," said Neal abruptly as he backed out the door. "I've pulled her from the sale."

"Why?" asked The Fat Man as he continued his innocent pursuit. Totally oblivious, The Fat Man was unaware of Neal's discomfort. "I've been studying your sales. County Mayo has really gotten top dollar over the last couple of sales. I mean you've bred some good horses and all, but some of your stock have probably gone for more than what they're worth. It's really unbelievable. I'd like to know your secret."

"Aye, it's lucky we've been," Neal mumbled as he continued to walk away from the pair.

"Lucky? Are you kidding me? Lucky?" The Fat Man's voice was animated as he continued his dogged pursuit of Neal. "I've prepared a really interesting spread sheet showing how you've actually received the best prices based upon the performance of the horses."

Neal continued to walk. He was spooked and was trying to shake his new admirer and his silent and armed friend without being too obvious. "Sure and

I'd love to see it sometime, but I've got to …" he said in a hopeful effort to make The Fat Man go away.

Hearing only the offer, The Fat Man interrupted Neal and broke into a huge grin. "Great," he replied, obviously excited at the prospect of sitting down with Neal. He reached into his pants pocket, pulled out a rumpled business card and handed it to Neal. "I could show it to you while you're in town. And I'd love to learn more about County Mayo Stables and what makes you guys tick. I could include it in the materials for the seminar I am supposed to teach."

Neal looked at the card and shoved it into his shirt pocket. "Sorry boys. I'm leavin' town tonight. Maybe next time." No matter how much Neal quickened his pace, The Fat Man continued his talkative pursuit.

"Well, I go to Ireland once a year for vacation—holiday as you guys put it. Maybe after it's all done, I could come by and show it to you. I'd love to see what you're doing that's made your stable so darn successful."

"You're welcome at our barns anytime." Neal stopped and looked at The Fat Man and Argo. He decided he was not going to get rid of the odd, little man by being subtle. He decided to switch to a more frank approach. "But it's busy that I am now, lads. If I'm going to be taking my leave this afternoon, I really must attend to my business right now." Neal nodded towards Argo and The Fat Man. "Now, good day to ya."

260

"Nice to meet you, Mr. Neal," The Fat Man said as he finally stopped his pursuit and watched as Neal walked away. "Have a safe flight home." The Fat Man turned towards Argo, his exuberance overflowing. "Wow, how cool was that? I got to meet a guy from County Mayo Stable—one of the hottest stables in the horse business."

Argo scrunched up his nose. "He didn't seem real happy to meet you."

"Are you kidding me?" The Fat Man responded, unconsciously pumping his fists as he spoke. "He was just busy. It's sale time and he just had to pull his horse from the auction."

"I don't know, Joe," Argo countered. He looked over The Fat Man's shoulder as Neal disappeared around the corner of a barn. "Something didn't seem right. He seemed nervous about your interest in County Mayo Stables. I really don't think he wants to be your pal."

"You're just paranoid." The Fat Man was almost giddy and he certainly did not appreciate Argo's negativity. "You're with the Feds. The FBI thinks everyone is a crook."

"It's a living." Argo shrugged his shoulders. "Come on, your horse got pulled. Let's head back up the road." Argo slapped The Fat Man on the back.

"Whatever you say, Johnny Law."

Back behind the sales barn, Zafer was pacing furiously back and forth. Neal just delivered the news he was pulling Finn's Lassie from the sale. Zafer was wildly waving his arms as he stammered a string of curse words in a combination of English and what Neal could only assume was Arabic.

"Slow down now and shut the fuck up," Neal instructed. His tone was cool but it was clear he was becoming agitated by Zafer's extreme behavior. When Zafer continued, Neal grabbed Zafer by the arm and pulled him close. "You're attracting attention. Now is not the time and place to attract attention, don't ya know. Now shut up and listen."

"B-b-but we had a deal," stammered Zafer. His arms remained still, but his eyes were slitted and filled with rage.

"'Had' is the operative word here," Neal responded. He reached in his pocket and pulled out The Fat Man's business card. "We 'had' a deal until this Bradley fellow showed up."

"You are afraid of a lawyer?" asked Zafer.

"No," replied Neal. "'Twas his friend, it was, that made me nervous. He had a gun holstered under his arm. I went to the front gate and told security that I saw a man with a gun and described him. They told me not to worry. He had checked in and was FBI."

"Oh, shit," replied Zafer.

"Bloody hell right, oh shit," Neal replied. "Those two know something. I'm pulling the plug on the sale and getting out of here as quickly as I can get the plane and crew ready to fly."

"How do you know this Bradley showing up is not just a coincidence?" Zafer was indignant.

"I don't," Neal replied matter-of-factly.

"Then why are you doing this? This is our final one. The one we must have to complete our cause."

"Well, now, when it comes to spending the rest of me days in an American jail, I don't believe in coincidence or causes. It's deep shit that we're in and I'm pulling Finn's Lassie out of the sale. Done."

"But our buyers are expecting a delivery next week." Zafer replied angrily. "This is unacceptable."

"They be your buyers, to be sure. Their reaction tis your problem, not mine. I told you this was too risky in the beginning." Neal was firm in his resolve. "I'll be tellin' the groom to get her ready for a trip back home to Ireland," he paused. And with nothin' hidden in the straw."

As Neal turned to walk away, Zafer grabbed his arm. "There must be some accommodation. I cannot make a call like this to our … my buyers."

Neal looked at the hand Zafer placed on his arm and politely pulled it away. He looked coolly into Zafer's furious eyes. "The Lass and I are out of here as quick as I can get her across the street to the airport and on our plane. And if you've any sense, you'll get out of here, too."

Zafer thought for a moment and then slyly

grinned. "That is it, my friend."

"What is it?" Neal was in no mood for games.

"You get the filly back on the plane. I'll pick up the payload and meet you at the airport in an hour. I want to go back to Ireland with you."

"No way, boyo," Neal gritted his teeth and balled his fists as he spoke. "That's not gonna happen."

"Think of it, my friend." Zafer's brown eyes danced as he spoke. "The value of the payload just doubled."

"Not interested." Neal turned to walk away. Zafer grabbed Neal's arm again, but Neal snatched it from Zafer's grasp. "Back off."

"Do not be so quick to judge," Zafer advised. "What are we going to do with the parts? We cannot just leave them behind. They are already at the drop point. In fact, if your theory is correct, the FBI is watching them and us. If you are right, we cannot get out of the States, period." Zafer suddenly had Neal's attention. "On the other hand, if your encounter with the lawyer and his companion was purely coincidence, we can play that to our financial advantage."

Neal thought for a moment. Zafer's logic made some sense. When Zafer saw Neal's hesitation, he continued. "When we get to Ireland with the parts, I will call my partners in Dubai and tell them we encountered problems in the States. In order to make a final delivery, we'll need to drastically increase the price."

"What about Finn's Lassie?" Neal asked. "Is she still part of the deal."

"No," insisted Zafer. "We split the money and County Mayo gets to keep the filly. This is now a straight cash deal. Both of us shall profit."

Neal nodded as he silently contemplated Zafer's new plan.

"We can pack the parts on the plane with the horse," Zafer continued. "Call your boss when we are in the air. If he wants to continue the deal, we shall make this final delivery using County Mayo. If he does not want the deal, I will take full responsibility for further transport of the parts from Ireland to Iran and I will pay you personally for the transport across the Atlantic."

Neal pondered his options. If his instincts about the short, pudgy lawyer were correct, he may already be screwed. Agents would be waiting for them at the airport. On the other hand, if he was wrong about Bradley, Zafer had just doubled, maybe tripled, the value of the deal for his boss. Neal looked at his watch. "Go get the payload then and meet me and the horse at Bluegrass Field in an hour."

Zafer smiled. "You are doing the smart thing," he said confidently.

Neal glanced at his watch a second time. "Make it an hour and fifteen minutes. And pick up a bottle of Jameson on the way."

As he was leaving Keeneland, Zafer pulled out a disposable cell phone. "Are the parts in place?" he asked.

"They're right where you told me to put them," the man replied. "I've been watching the location for the past fifteen hours and there's been nothing out of the ordinary."

"You are sure," Zafer replied. He was clearly nervous about the pair of men Neal met at the sale. Zafer argued the meeting was coincidence, but was not confident in his position. "I must be sure."

"Absolutely," the man replied. "The place is clean."

"Good," said Zafer as he turned his car onto New Circle Road. "Stay in place until you see me pick up the goods and then follow me at a distance to the airport to make sure no one is following me."

"Got it."

"If you detect someone following me, I trust you to eliminate them."

"Not a problem," the man said. "I'm prepared."

"How goes the lawsuit?" Zafer changed subjects.

"Permanently dismissed," the man chuckled. "It seems the lawyer involved will not be taking on any new clients."

"Good," Zafer smiled. "So you have the hard drive also?"

"I don't have it yet."

"What?" Zafer was outraged. "That is unacceptable."

"Calm down," the man replied. "I'll get it. I just need a little more time."

"No hard drive, no money," Zafer said as he slammed his phone shut.

TWENTY-EIGHT

Jane Kline sat behind the desk in her office and leaned back in her leather chair. She used her cane to leverage the move and, once she was steady, she nervously tapped it on the floor. The data she possessed was mind boggling. More importantly, if what Zach MacKenzie had told her was true, it would rip at the very core of the agency. Still, it was hard for Kline to contemplate someone at the CIA itself was responsible for the assassination of Director Steele.

And, based on what she had now learned, that person was no less than Jimmy Day, the body guard for both Kline and the late-director.

Kline pushed herself up from her chair and hobbled around her spacious office. She peered out the window at the rain falling outside as she went over the facts one more time in her head.

According to MacKenzie, Director Steele was working with some foreign connection he had from his days in politics on a project involving very little internal CIA communication. The only people who knew about it were the contact, Steele and—because he was constantly at Steele's side—Jimmy Day. Apparently, Steele had been close to ordering action on the unknown project when Day went rogue and set up the hit on Steele at the entrance to CIA headquarters.

MacKenzie felt he was very close to discovering who flipped Day and why. The night before, MacKenzie went to Kline's house to tell her her own bodyguard was the prime suspect and he was pulling Day from her security detail. He felt he could keep a better eye on the situation with Day on desk duty. MacKenzie argued with Day involved in the assassination of Kline's predecessor, allowing him to have direct personal proximity to Kline was out of the question.

Kline overruled MacKenzie's order reassigning Day. She reasoned that if Day's normal routine were interrupted, he might become suspicious and run. The best chance for finding out who was behind Steele's death was to maintain a normal routine with Day.

Now, a few hours later, she was second-guessing herself.

As she thought back over the last few weeks, Kline realized Day had become overly friendly to her. She felt the change, but she did not attribute any significance to it. Maybe Day was trying to soften her up to get more information. She wanted to ask Day why he was not driving the day Steele was killed. But until MacKenzie finished his investigation, she would keep Day at her side and stay quiet.

Or, should she?

While Kline idly watched a man in the parking lot run through the rain to his car with a newspaper over his head, she remembered something a political consultant, Michael Griffith, told her.

Michael Griffith was one of the best political consultants in America. They met while she was on assignment in Romania. Griffith was known to advise candidates based upon what he thought the fictional Godfather Vito Corleone would say. He had told Kline that, as an agent, she should "keep her friends close and her enemies closer."

Kline took a deep breath and decided that was excellent advice.

TWENTY-NINE

Leo Argo came bounding off the elevator leading into The Fat Man's law offices, his loud laughter booming out into the lobby. He brushed his hands across the sides of his head as he spoke. "And so you stalked this guy and chased him down until you finally got his autograph for your macabre baseball collection."

"Stalking is an ugly term," said The Fat Man, pointing his index finger at Argo. "It carries with it an implication of mental illness."

"So you didn't get the autograph?" Argo asked with a broad grin.

The Fat Man hung his head and broke into a large, sheepish grin. "Yeah, I got his autograph."

"Now, tell me again, exactly who is Angel Bravo?" Argo snapped his fingers as he spoke as if the answer was just on the tip of his tongue.

The brunette receptionist sitting behind the cherry wood desk made eye contact with The Fat Man in an effort to quiet his revelry. She leaned forward in her chair and nodded her head to the side of the lobby where Tiana Sullivan sat in an overstuffed deep maroon leather chair.

"What the heck?" The Fat Man exclaimed as he stopped dead in his tracks. "Tiana. What are you doing here?" As soon as he uttered the words, he realized the tone of his question might have sounded unduly harsh when addressed to a young woman who just lost her father in a brutal murder. He quickly tried to recover by asking, "Are you okay?"

"I'm sorry, Mr. Bradley," the receptionist threw up her hands. "She's been here for more than two hours. I told her she could leave and you'd call her back." The receptionist looked back and forth between her boss and the young woman. "She insisted on waiting. I tried to call you. I figured you turned the ringer off at the sale and forgot to turn it back on."

As Tiana stood up and crossed the lobby towards The Fat Man, he noticed how the strain of her father's murder was showing on her face. Her athletic runner's frame stood tall and straight, but her eyes looked tired and her smile was forced and drawn as she spoke. "Hi, Mr. Bradley," she said.

The Fat Man only met Tiana once, but he felt true sympathy for her over the loss of her father, Sean Sullivan. In a profession where lawyers were so often stuffed shirts in a suit, The Fat Man and Sullivan were different. He had considered Sullivan a kindred spirit. He smiled warmly at Tiana and softened his tone. "I told you when we met at court with your dad, it's Joe."

"Thanks." Tiana returned a thin but sincere smile. She stuck out her hand. "Hi, Joe."

"That's better." The Fat Man returned the hand shake. "Hi, Tiana. How are you holding up?"

"I've been better." Tiana looked at the floor as she replied.

There was an uncomfortable pause as The Fat Man contemplated what to say to a young woman who just lost her father. Argo broke the silence by clearing his throat. "Oh, I'm sorry," The Fat Man said. "Have you met Leo Argo yet?"

"No," said Tiana. "We've not met."

Argo stepped forward and shook Tiana's hand while he sized her up. "Leo Argo," he said as they shook. "I'm with the FBI. I'm in town investigating your father's murder."

Tiana returned Argo's assessing gaze. "My grandpa told me you were in town. I wish I could say it's nice to meet you, but under the circumstances, it really isn't."

"I understand," said Argo.

The Fat Man jumped back into the conversation. "You don't look real good," he said. "I'm sorry. That didn't come out right. What I mean is…"

"It's okay, Joe." Tiana ran her fingers tiredly through her hair. "I know what you meant. I feel horrible and I probably look worse."

"I look horrible," said The Fat Man. "You look like a beautiful young woman under extreme stress."

"Thanks," Tiana replied, forcing a smile. "Daddy told me you were a nice guy. He liked you a lot. It's been a really horrific week."

"I can't even begin to imagine what you're going through," The Fat Man replied. "However, if I were going through something that traumatic, I probably wouldn't hang around for two hours waiting to see some lawyer unless it was really important. So, I'm wondering, what brings you here to my office today?"

"I know my father had a lot of cases hanging," Tiana said. "I went down to daddy's office at the laundromat to try and start getting his files in order. That's when I called you."

"I told you on the phone, we'd talk after everything settled down a bit."

"I know, I know," Tiana stammered. "But, I don't think I can wait on this one."

The Fat Man tilted his head. This young lady was going through something very difficult and The Fat Man felt the least he could do for Tiana was to give her some of his time. "Leo, you want to give us some space for a minute?"

"Sure," Argo replied and started to walk away.

"No," Tiana jumped in quickly. "I think he needs to stay. He needs to hear about this case Daddy was going to file."

The Fat Man nodded towards one of the conference rooms. "Hold all of my calls," he said to the receptionist. In reality, The Fat Man did not get all that many phone calls, but he liked the sound of the directive. "Let's go in here." After he followed

Argo and Tiana into the room, the three sat down.

"So what's the case?" The Fat Man wheeled his chair backwards to a credenza as he spoke. He pulled a legal pad out of a drawer and tossed it on the conference table. He scribbled the date at the top of the page and then looked over at Tiana. "Tell me about it."

"Daddy had this qui tam case he was looking to file in federal court next week." Tiana reached into her briefcase and pulled out a large file folder. She opened it and shuffled through some papers.

"Qui tam?" Argo directed the question to anyone who would answer.

"Pretty much a whistleblower case," The Fat Man replied. "A person brings a *qui tam* action when they believe their company is defrauding the federal government in some fashion. The person who brings the suit gets to share in the monetary recovery against the company."

"Daddy was real excited about it," Tiana said. She found the draft complaint and pushed the rest of the file across the table. "He didn't charge fees to most of the folks down in Covington, but every couple of years he'd land a big case. He lived off the fees from those types of cases. He was real wound up about this qui tam case. He said it was a lay down winner. He told me, when he decided to run for Congress, the fees from this case would take care of both of us for years."

"Catalano versus KLM Engines," The Fat Man read aloud from the draft complaint Sullivan had already prepared. He looked at Argo. "They make airplane engines. Their plant is about five miles from here." He flipped quickly through the draft. "It looks like it might be a pretty big case. The case says the company is preparing destruction certificates required by law for parts that aren't being destroyed." The Fat Man placed the complaint on the table. "Do you need me to try and get you a co-counsel? There's a lawyer over in Cincinnati named Heidrich who handles a bunch of these types of cases. I'm sure he'd take a look at this one."

"No, it's not that," Tiana replied. She tossed a yellow legal pad across the table at The Fat Man. It contained Sullivan's hand-written notes on the case. "I found Daddy's notes."

"And?" asked Argo. "What's in them?"

"Catalano was scared," Tiana said. She found a particular page in the legal pad. "At least that's what Daddy thought. He wrote that, after their last meeting, Catalano was considering dropping the case. He felt he was in danger."

"What did your dad think?" The Fat Man asked.

"Daddy wrote Catalano was being paranoid and getting cold feet about filing a case that implicated his co-workers." Tiana paused. "Daddy never saw danger anywhere."

"Fearless?" Argo took the paper from The Fat Man and scanned it.

"Daddy wasn't fearless," Tiana shook her head and her eyes began to well up as she thought of her father. "You never met him Mr. Argo, but my father was a remarkable man and an exceptional lawyer. He was different because he was motivated by his heart. He just looked for the best in every human being. He believed that, given enough time, he could pull good from the devil himself."

"I think Sean would have won that battle," The Fat Man interjected.

Tiana smiled at The Fat Man and then looked back at Argo. "Too fearless?" she queried. "No. Too trusting...well, that may be what got him killed." Tiana paused, focusing back on the qui tam case. "I would expect people to get nervous about filing a case implicating co-workers, but fearing for your life. That sounds a bit severe."

After the trio said their farewells and Tiana left, The Fat Man and Argo sat back down in the conference room. The Fat Man began tapping his cheap disposable ink pen on the table. Argo was staring at a painting on the wall of the storied thoroughbred, Alydar.

The Fat Man had been around Argo just enough to realize the conspiratorial wheels in his large melon were probably turning. He pointed his finger at Argo. "No," he declared. "You aren't even thinking about going there, are you?"

"What?" Argo threw up his hands, with feigned surprise in his voice. "I told you Antwone Mason doesn't feel right."

"Come on, Leo," The Fat Man replied. "It's a bit of a stretch. Anyway, sometime in the next day or two you're going to get the results from the DNA test."

Argo let the silence build. "Next day or two, huh?"

"Yeah."

"So then I've got plenty of time to go out and interview Dave Catalano."

The Fat Man closed his eyes and bit his lip as he realized the snare he had just stepped into. "You're good," he snorted.

"I try," replied Argo with a smug smile on his face.

THIRTY

The relief valve had finally been opened on the pressure cooker that Congressman Richard Thompson had become. His bedroom confession to Ann lifted a burden that weighed him down for a very long time. Since Ann had started her recovery in AA, she explained the 12 Step program to him. Over the years, she shared her journey through the steps on several occasions, but he never truly understood. When Thompson finally admitted the horrible acts he committed, he felt a deeper connection with Ann. He knew now that only through confession could true recovery begin.

The guilt Thompson felt for his actions in Romania had haunted him almost from the moment he had pulled the trigger. His admission freed his soul and made him understand he was powerless to change what happened in the past. He could neither change it nor make it disappear. His discussion with Ann was his first step to making it all manageable. He felt relieved. For the first time, he knew he was going to be able to overcome his very real anxiety about the possibility of eternal damnation.

In fact, to his surprise, Thompson felt almost light hearted. Ann was still confused and conflicted about what her husband had told her, but she did not question him when he told her they needed some time alone, away from the conference. He told her to pack an overnight bag, but did not announce their destination. They headed out. Every time Ann asked where they were headed, Thompson just smiled and told her to enjoy viewing the ruins dotting the Irish countryside.

What Thompson would not reveal to Ann was they were headed to Ashford Castle in County Mayo. Founded in 1228, Ashford Castle is located about an hour north of Galway on Lough Corrib. In the 19th Century, Ashford Castle became the family estate of Sir Benjamin Guinness. Later, when the castle was opened to the tourist trade as a hotel, it quickly became one of the top destinations in Ireland.

"Amazing," said Ann. She gazed out the window as Thompson eased the rental car slowly up the main drive winding its way through the rolling hills surrounding the hotel's golf course. "Simply amazing," she repeated before leaning over and kissing Thompson on the cheek.

"I thought you'd be surprised." Richard Thompson glanced over at his wife. The contented look on her face made him grin. He did not get much past Ann, but the destination of their overnight trip had truly surprised her. "Happy?"

"Oh, Richard," she exclaimed. "You can't even begin to imagine. I've seen shows about this place on the Travel Channel." Ann's eyes were darting quickly from side to side in an effort to take it all in. "But I never thought this would be where we headed today." When the massive castle appeared, she was speechless. She reached over and hugged Thompson.

Thompson was proud of himself for making Ann so excited. "Well, I just thought it would be a good way to break loose for a day." His eyes danced as he spoke.

The car slowly made its way over an old stone bridge across a tributary that led into the lough. As the doorman met them at their parking space to get their luggage, Thompson looked at his watch. "We need to check in and then, in about an hour, you've got a massage."

"You booked a massage for me?" Ann was impressed at the planning her husband put into the trip on such short notice. She grabbed his hand as they walked into the front entrance of the castle. "I love you. This is perfect."

"I figured you would like it." An attractive young brunette handed Thompson two keys to their room and went over the instructions about where and when tea would be served later in the afternoon.

As another young woman led them to their room, Ann asked, "What are you going to do while I get my massage?"

"I, my dear, am going to do what a gentleman does at a castle."

"Pillage the village?" Ann replied

"No, although that is a thought. I am going fly fishing out on the lough."

The young attendant opened the room and showed them around. Thompson then tried to tip the attendant, but she held up her hand. She explained to Thompson that employees at the castle refuse any gratuity and wished them a good stay.

Thompson walked to the window and looked down at the well manicured garden. An employee with a large leather glove on his hand was training a falcon. "Later tonight, we're going to go down to the village," Thompson said. "That's where John Wayne filmed *The Quiet Man*."

"Sounds like fun," Ann said as she clicked the bolt on the door. She walked up behind Thompson and put her arms around him. He turned and saw the fire in her eyes. He briefly felt relief to know that despite his confession, Ann still felt passionate about their relationship. Thompson grabbed Ann and kissed her hard. Once they had broken their kiss, Ann spoke. "You've saved enough time to initiate the hotel room, haven't you?"

"Absolutely," replied Thompson as he reached down and began unbuttoning Ann's blouse while she tugged at his belt buckle. "If nothing else, I believe in tradition."

Thompson stood in the small boat and cast his fishing line out towards the location where the guide indicated. "Right dere," whispered Tim Brewer. The old guide offered encouragement as he worked the oars of the craft against the lazy flow of the creek. With his red hair and pale skin, Brewer was an Irishman fresh out of central casting. "Be ready now."

Eyes fixed on the little white foam bobber, Thompson's thoughts wandered aimlessly. Thompson probably liked fishing so damn much because of moments just like this one. With a fishing rod in his hand, he could focus his mind on a single important thought or on absolutely nothing other than a little piece of floating foam. Either choice was acceptable. With what he had been through on this trip, nothing at all was a good topic of thought for the day. The bobber went down and Thompson yanked at the line. "Damn."

"Ya just missed him," Brewer said as he cranked back hard on the oars. When the boat was just above the spot where the fish had hit the fly, he nodded in that direction. "Try 'er again. Put 'er right in da same place."

Thompson could barely understand the wrinkled old man because of his heavy Irish brogue. "Aye, aye skipper." Thompson worked the line back and forth in the air before letting the fly settle down gently in the water just a few feet from where the last trout hit. Almost immediately, the bobber went underwater and

Thompson yanked hard on the line. The fish was hooked and the battle was on.

"You got 'em," declared Brewer as he reached around and tossed an anchor into the water to keep the boat in place. He reached for his net. "Look at how he's bending the rod. He's a big one, don't ya know."

Thompson tugged on the line to work the fish closer to the boat, but the fish was having none of it. He was not coming out of the water without putting up a good fight.

"Work 'em … work 'em," Brewer instructed. As the fish made a hard run at them, Brewer's voice seemed to rise in both pitch and intensity. "Tighten your line boy. Don't let 'em go under da boat." Thompson ran the line backwards as fast as he could. When the line was sufficiently taut, Thompson slowly led the fish towards Brewer. The old man reached into the water with his net and scooped the fish up and out. He unhooked the fly and held the 19 inch brown trout up in the air. "Yer first fish in Ireland, lad, and he's a big one now. Ya got yer camera with ya? We need a picture of dis one."

Brewer exchanged the fish with Thompson for the cell phone. After Brewer snapped a couple of pictures of Thompson proudly holding the fish, the cell phone began to ring. The sound made Brewer laugh at the thought of Americans who bring their cell phones fly fishing. He looked at the caller ID before trading the phone back again for the fish. "I guess dey have already heard about dis back in da States," he chuckled.

"Sorry about that," Thompson said, embarrassed by the timing of the call. He too looked at the caller ID. It was The Fat Man on the line. "Hey Joe. What's up?"

"Livin' large on my end," The Fat Man replied. "How's Ireland?"

"Good," Thompson replied. Then he thought of everything that transpired over the past 24 hours and added: "Strike that. Everything's great. I just caught a huge trout in the shadow of Ashford Castle. Life is great."

"I thought you were supposed to be in Dublin today." The Fat Man knew Thompson was going to travel around the country later in the week, and he was surprised Thompson was not still at the conference.

"We played hooky today," Thompson said as he gazed up at the castle and smiled. "Blew it off. Ann and I needed a day to ourselves."

"Atta boy," The Fat Man replied. He assumed the day off was simply Thompson's way of dealing with the angst produced by the death of Sean Sullivan. He brought up the web site for Ashford Castle on his computer as he spoke. "I didn't realize you were trying to unwind today, so I'll be quick. I need your permission to file a motion to have the writ of mandamus case dismissed."

Thompson was quick to respond. "Hell yes, you have my permission." He thought a minute. As much as he wanted the case out of his life, he knew there were still political implications to consider. After pausing, he back-tracked. "Run it past Griff first. He'll probably want to wait a week or so before we file anything. The motion will cause another news story. We don't want to seem too insensitive about what happened, and I should probably be around for press calls when we do it."

"Good idea." The Fat Man continued to surf pages on Ashford Castle's web site. "Hey, the place where you're fishing is in County Mayo."

"Yeah," Thompson replied as he watched Brewer gently place the brownie back into the cold water. "So what?"

The Fat Man moved the mouse on his computer around the map on the screen. "It looks like you're only about 15 minutes away from County Mayo Stables."

"Isn't that the horse farm you've been researching for your equine conference?" Thompson sat down in the boat, knowing Brewer was ready to pull up the anchor and move on to another spot.

"Yeah," replied The Fat Man. "You should drop by there and tour the place. I've heard it's beautiful."

"We're staying here tonight and we don't have anything on the schedule for tomorrow. We may just do that."

"Ask for Paddy Neal. I met him at the Keeneland sales. He told me I could drop by for a tour anytime. I'll give him a call and tell him you're a friend of mine. He'll love to give you a tour of the farm."

After Thompson said his goodbyes, he stuffed the cell phone back into his pants pocket. He looked at Brewer and shrugged his shoulders at getting a call in the middle of a fishing trip.

"Yanks," Brewer mumbled as he pulled the anchor back into the boat.

THIRTY-ONE

"In four tenths of a mile, turn left onto Amsterdam Road." Leo Argo looked at the GPS mounted on the dashboard in front of him and studied the small map on the screen. "In two hundred feet, turn left." Argo chuckled to himself at the slightly mocking tone of the soft female voice emanating from the small device. If only having a woman's voice in his life was as easy as selecting the correct button on a global positioning system.

As Argo made his way to the home of Dave Catalano, the plaintiff in Sean Sullivan's whistleblower lawsuit, the FBI agent was reminded of the currently off-again relationship he had with Jane Kline. Being with The Fat Man for a couple of days had taken Argo's mind off his failed lovelife. But the female voice telling him what to do brought it all back to the forefront of his thoughts. "I've got to change the voice on this damn thing," he mumbled to himself as he drove.

Argo dated a lot of women over the years, but he never found a companion who held his interest for more than a couple of months. Kline was different. Argo actually wanted the relationship to develop more. Early on, he begun to think maybe she was the woman he might actually settle down with someday.

He often wondered why Kline was different from all the others and had come to the conclusion it was because she was just as tough as he was mentally. Yet, at the same time, her rugged beauty was able to turn the heads of men half her age.

When Kline abruptly cut off their relationship, Argo was at first understanding. After all, she suffered a great trauma and damn nearly died. Naturally, she was hurt, confused and needed some space. Over time, Argo's thoughtful empathy was slowly replaced with anger. Now he was just pissed, wondering if it was time to just let it go and move on. But, damn it, he missed her.

"Arriving at destination on right."

"Fuck you," Argo muttered to the GPS as he looked up and saw the red brick house where Catalano lived. He pulled his credentials and notebook out of his briefcase on the passenger seat and headed up the steep slope of the driveway. He slid past a white Toyota pickup truck parked in the driveway and made his way to the front door.

Argo's first ring of the doorbell got no response. He leaned forward and squinted in an attempt to peer through the frosted pattern on the window in the door. He rang the door bell a second time and followed with a loud knock.

When no one answered the door, Argo scribbled a note on one of his business cards, asking Catalano to give him a call. He rang the doorbell one last time and then tucked the card into the tight space between the door frame and the door.

Argo turned to leave. When he got to the driveway, he let his hand brush against the front quarter-panel of the Toyota. Argo paused and put his hand on the top of the hood. It was hot. The truck had been driven recently. Someone had to be home and he wondered if the person he was looking for might be outside and unable to hear the doorbell. He headed around the side of the house to the backyard.

As Argo walked along the side of Catalano's house, a neighbor's dog yapped at him from the other side of a chain-link fence. "You got a big bark for a little white ball of fluff," Argo said. He paused, thought of Hoover, and then laughed, "I've got to stop talking to dogs." He shook his head and continued on around to the back of the house. No one was in the back yard. Argo looked through the small window of a security door leading out of the basement before heading up the steps to a deck jutting off the next level.

Once on the deck, Argo rapped on the sliding glass door. The sun was setting and casting a glare across the entrance. He placed his hand on the glass to block the sun and leaned in until his nose nearly touched the door. On the right side of the room, beside the breakfast bar that separated the kitchen and family room, Argo saw a man's shoe sticking out from behind the baseboard.

Argo grabbed the door handle with one hand and his service revolver with the other. The door was not locked. As he slowly entered the room, he shouted out a warning. "Mr. Catalano. Leo Argo. Federal Bureau of Investigation." He quickly spun to each side of the room, looking for any intruder before making his way to the kitchen. As he approached, the shoe became a leg and then a body lying face-down on the floor. Argo slowly leaned down and felt for a pulse. He found none.

Argo had just finished giving the address of the house to a 911 operator when he heard the dog next door begin to bark. "Shit," Argo grumbled. "The basement door." He looked out the kitchen window and saw a man running around the corner of the chain link fence. The man sprinted through the back yards of neighboring houses in the general direction of a wooded area that began about one hundred yards away.

As fast as he could run, Argo took off after the intruder. Kids were playing in their back yards and their parents were sitting on their decks. Argo did not dare to fire a shot. One parent saw Argo running with a gun and screamed. "FBI," Argo shouted in despair. "Get inside. Everyone get inside." The chorus of barking dogs grew.

Just before entering the woods, the intruder glanced back and saw Argo still in pursuit. The man ducked into the shadows of the thick underbrush. Argo was still too far away to get a good look at him.

Argo hit the woods running at full speed. Limbs of trees and branches of bushes slapped at his face, and he quickly found himself in a steep, slippery and confusing maze of underbrush, ivy and fallen trees. His pace slowed, and he could neither see nor hear the suspect. Nevertheless, Argo pressed deeper and deeper into the woods, hoping to catch a glimpse of the man. Eventually, as Argo crested the top of a hill, he was able to look down a couple of hundred feet into a parking lot of a small apartment complex. A dark sedan quickly backed up and laid rubber as it pulled out. He was too far away to get a look at the plates.

The routine interview had just turned into another murder investigation.

Neighbors gathered outside the barriers of the bright yellow tape surrounding the area as television crews scrambled to set up their cameras for a live remote from the crime scene. The flashing lights of police cars and first responders cut through the deep twilight. Tiana tried to steady her breathing as she approached an all too familiar scene in the passenger seat of The Fat Man's car.

Argo had called The Fat Man, told him what had happened, and asked him to swing by and pick up

Tiana as soon as possible. Per Argo's request, The Fat Man drove himself and Tiana straight to the scene.

"You don't look so good," The Fat Man said to Tiana as he parked the car about two houses away. "Are you sure you're ready for this?"

Tiana took a deep breath. "No, I'm not sure. But there's only one way to find out." She got out of the car and joined The Fat Man as they approached the house together.

"I'm sorry sir, but you can't come in here," a police officer in a crisp uniform informed the pair as they approached. "This is a crime scene." The young cop's tone was unnecessarily condescending.

"Really," replied The Fat Man sarcastically. "I thought all the yellow tape and police were to welcome Tony Orlando to the community." The Fat Man would not normally have been so flip to a police officer, but he was frustrated, concerned and eager to talk to Argo, who had—after all—summoned him. He was in no mood to take crap from a twenty-something rookie. He could see Argo from where he was standing.

Predictably, The Fat Man's remarks had not gone over well with the police officer. Indeed, he was already squaring his shoulders, puffing himself up, and reaching for his night stick. But before he could act, Argo intervened.

"It's okay, officer," came Argo's voice from the top of the driveway. "They're with me."

The Fat Man and Tiana ducked under the yellow tape. "I'm with him," The Fat Man said, pointing at Argo. The officer was not at all amused by The Fat Man's snarky tone.

As Argo came walking down the driveway to meet them, Tiana saw the scratches on his face. "Oh my God," she exclaimed. "What happened to you?"

"These?" Argo put his hand to his cheek. "These are just a few mementos I got tonight on my evening jog through the woods."

"How about in there?" The Fat Man pointed at the house.

Argo looked at Tiana. "I'm afraid the investigation of your father's murder just got more complicated."

Tiana's shoulders slumped. The Fat Man put his arm around her to offer moral and physical support. "Jesus," she whispered. "What the fuck is going on here?"

"Somebody was waiting for your Mr. Catalano when he got home tonight. And whoever it was, I just missed him. In fact, he was in the house at the same time as me. When I showed up he must have heard me at the front door and hid in the basement. He sneaked out the basement door while I was calling 911. I heard a dog bark, saw him run, and tried to follow. He had too much of a head start on me."

"Did you get a good look at him?" The Fat Man asked.

"No," Argo replied with a heavy sigh. "I saw his car from up on the hill, but I was too far away. Other than a rough estimate of height, he was a male Caucasian with dark hair. So basically, I got nothin'."

The Fat Man looked off into the distance. Argo could see the mental gears turning. "This can't be a coincidence," The Fat Man said.

"I agree," Argo nodded. "I don't believe in coincidence." He shifted his weight from one foot to the other before he continued. "I need both of you to help me figure out who Mr. Catalano might have been afraid of, and why."

Tiana suddenly realized what Argo and The Fat Man had already figured out—the intruder who killed Catalano was probably the same man who had killed her father. As she spoke, the rage was evident in her voice. "What do we do?"

"We don't do anything," replied Argo. "You can help me by going through all of your father's files, but that's it. And, until I catch this perp, I'm going to put a guard on you 24/7."

"That's bullshit," Tiana seethed. "I can …"

"Don't even think of finishing that sentence, Ms. Bolton," Argo said abruptly. "This is not up for discussion."

The Fat Man jumped in. "Stop and think about it, Tiana. The answers to who killed your dad are in his files." He put a restraining, yet gentle, hand on her arm. "I'll help you. We'll get some folks to deliver them to my office and we'll go through them together."

"I don't know." Tiana was hesitant.

"Please don't fight us on this," The Fat Man urged. "Sean would have wanted to make sure you were safe."

It took considerable effort on Tiana's part, but she fought back her rage. "Okay. Okay," she said. "Thank you." Now was not the time to argue.

THIRTY-TWO

"I don't want to leave," moaned Ann as Thompson made a left hand turn out of the gates of Ashford Castle. Ann looked longingly at the stone pillars as they drove past and blew a farewell kiss out the window before turning back to Thompson. "Can't we stay for the rest of the week?"

"After what we spent on dinner last night, I don't think so," replied Thompson. It had been an excellent, but pricey, one night excursion. Thompson had grown up in Ludlow, a small town in Kentucky, and he realized the cost of the previous night's meal probably exceeded his mom's entire food budget for a month.

"But wasn't that meal worth every penny?" Ann had totally enjoyed the stay at Ashford Castle and it was obvious in her voice. "My steak was the best I've ever had, and you gobbled down the lamb chops like you were a starving child."

"I only got them for the mint jelly," Thompson replied, not bothering to hold back his grin as he spoke.

"Right." She flicked her hand at him in disbelief. "I'm surprised you didn't pick up the bones and start gnawing on them."

"I actually considered it."

"Then let's go back for one more night."

"At those prices, I'm considering taking out a second mortgage just to pay for the appetizers."

"We can come up with the money," Ann pleaded. "We'll think of something."

"You'd have to prostitute yourself to raise that much money."

"Really?" said Ann jokingly. "Can I pick who? Because our waiter last night was really cute. And there was this gardener I saw out behind the castle cutting flowers …"

Thompson rolled his eyes. "That's enough."

Ann laughed and squeezed Thompson's arm before kissing him on the cheek. "I'm just kidding, honey. You're the only man I want to whore around with."

"I'm honored," said Thompson as they made their way slowly through the streets of Cong, a quaint village which Ann and Thompson had explored hand-in-hand the evening before. "Anyway, I have another surprise today. We're only about a half hour away from County Mayo Stables."

"A horse farm?" Ann asked excitedly. Since they moved from DC to Kentucky, Ann had come to love the sport of horse racing. She insisted they go to Keeneland at least once each session. "I've always been curious about the farms over here. The Irish horses always run so well on the turf at Keeneland."

"Yes, I know your rules," Thompson replied. Ann joined him laughing, "Always bet the Irish horse and if it's gray, double down."

"Well, anyway, Joe called me yesterday about the Sullivan lawsuit. While we were talking, I told him we ducked out of Dublin and were staying at Ashford Castle for the evening. He was happy we had gotten away by ourselves. It turns out he knows somebody at County Mayo Stables. He got up early back home and called them. He texted me at breakfast this morning to let me know he had set up a tour for us. The farm is only about a half an hour from Cong. I thought it would be a nice side trip on our way back to Dublin."

"Sounds great," Ann replied. "Let's go."

When traveling the roads of Ireland, what looks on a map like a quick jaunt often turns out to be a time consuming adventure. The country roads on the island are so narrow that two cars traveling in opposite directions nearly touch when passing. On most roads, the outside borders are lined on both sides by either tall hedgerows or stone walls. Sometimes, the hedgerows have stone walls behind them.

If that is not enough to intimidate most foreign drivers, older roads were laid out to avoid cutting down any Hawthorne trees. It is local lore that fairies live in those trees, as well as in several kinds of rock formations a driver will see along the roads of Ireland. The wee people will supposedly rain down bad luck down upon anyone who destroys their homes, so— as the story goes—the roads were laid out to swerve to-and-fro in order to avoid these fictional homesteads. The walls, bushes and curves make it very difficult for drivers to spot any oncoming traffic until a vehicle is almost on top of them. Toss in a roundabout every couple of miles, and an outsider soon understands traveling the country roads of Ireland is not for the faint of heart.

When Thompson and Ann pulled up to the security gate in front of County Mayo Stables, they were well past the time when The Fat Man told them to arrive. A slight drizzle was falling, but Ann already rolled down her window and was snapping photos of the horses lazily wandering through the lush green fields. Thompson rolled down his own window and stuck his hand out to wave at the man approaching the vehicle. "Hi, you must be Paddy Neal. I'm Congressman Richard Thompson from the States."

Paddy Neal had been nervous ever since he received the phone call that morning from the strange little man he met back in Kentucky at the horse sales only days earlier. There was plenty of reason to worry. After all, this Bradley fella had been in company of an FBI agent. Then again, Neal never asked to see the man's identification. He was told the man was law enforcement from a security guard. Moreover, when they had left the States, no one questioned Neal and Zafer's quick departure.

Initially, Neal even considered the two men might have been planted at the sale by Zafer himself. Neal did not trust Zafer, and he wondered if Zafer planned the encounter knowing it would cause Finn's Lassie to be pulled from the sale. Indeed, Zafer seemed quick to offer a solution that increased Zafer's own financial bounty. At the time, such a scenario certainly seemed plausible.

Today, when Bradley called Neal out of the blue and requested a farm tour for an alleged United States Congressman and his wife, it moved the focus of Neal's suspicions from Zafer to some other possible conspiracy. Neal agreed to the tour, but he also immediately took his concerns to the farm's owner, Rory Collins.

A short and wiry man with wrinkled skin and graying hair, Collins was the brains behind County Mayo Stables and all of its legitimate—and illegitimate—business dealings. Collins was far more than a simple farmer. Neal was sure he would know what to do.

When the Belfast Brigade of the Irish Republican Army began attacking forces of the Crown in the early 1920s, Rory Collins' grandfather, Brian, had been an officer in the First Division in West Belfast. Rory's father, Gerry, died in jail while serving time for his involvement in a 1983 IRA bombing in Manchester. The elder Collins men both instilled a strong sense of Irish nationalism in Rory. When Rory became a successful horse breeder and businessman, he also followed in the family tradition and quietly became involved in many political causes.

Initially, Rory Collins focused his financial influence on Irish causes such as funding the running of guns from American IRA sympathizers to the lads in Belfast. In more recent years, with things quieting down a bit in Belfast, he expanded his activities to include any cause du jour that happened to piss off the Throne.

With most of his activities, Collins had merely provided silent financial support. As hard as Scotland Yard tried to connect Collins to IRA activities, they always came up short. Collins successfully hid his activities through a shell game of complex foreign investments and bank accounts in countries with strict banking secrecy laws.

The partnership with Zafer was something new for Collins. The running of F-14 Tomcat parts to Iran was the first major, non-Irish operation in which Collins allowed himself to become more directly involved. America had sold the airplanes to Iran in the 70s. When the Shah of Iran, Mohammad Reza Pahlavi, was removed from power by the Islamic Revolution of 1979, he was replaced by the anti-American Ayatollah Khomeini. An arms embargo followed the taking of hostages at the United States Embassy, leaving the new Iranian government without direct access to replacement parts for the planes. At first, a few of the planes were cannibalized for replacement parts for other Tomcats in the fleet. Others were shot down in the Iran-Iraq War. Over time, the number of operational planes diminished.

Over the years, the government of Iran themselves began devising schemes to illegally import parts from the United States in order to get the planes back into the air. The partnership with Collins was one of those schemes. Collins was approached by former IRA leaders to meet with Zafer to discuss the possibility of using his regular private flights to and from the United States to smuggle parts out of the country.

In order to finance the scheme, Zafer arranged to have wealthy Dubai horsemen sympathetic to Iran drastically overpay for Irish horses offered for auction at the Keeneland horse sales. That put money into Collins' pocket which he could deploy in support of various political causes. As his part of the bargain, on the return flights from Kentucky, Collins would transport the airplane parts the Iranians so desperately needed.

The parts for horses scheme proved to be profitable for Collins and his causes, but it also increased the risks. Collins determined the most recent developments left him far too vulnerable to being exposed. He agreed with Neal's decision to pull Finn's Lassie from the Keeneland horse sale and determined this direct transfer of the illegal payload would be the end of his involvement. Collins hated the British government, but he was not willing to repeat his father's fate for his passion.

When Neal came to Collins about the visitors from America, Collins asked Zafer to join them in his office. An internet search confirmed someone named Richard Thompson was, in fact, a United States Congressman. The trio concluded the two men in Kentucky who approached Neal could not possibly be United States law enforcement personnel. The Federal Bureau of Investigation would never let Neal and Zafer leave the country with the illegal payload of parts. Collins concluded these people must have found out about the operation through Zafer's contacts and were going to try and extort money out of both sides. Such a view worked to confirm Collins' view of all American politicians as crooks who were not to be trusted.

At the end of the meeting Collins made his instructions clear, "Give 'em the tour and then do what ya have to do to put da fear of God in them. Let them know if they want to fuck with me, they better be ready to play rough."

Following the meeting, Collins pulled Neal aside. "Let Zafer go out by himself on this one," Collins instructed. "Give him a driver, but I don't want your fingerprints on it. If I'm wrong about this Thompson fella, we can eliminate Zafer and still continue the transaction. A dead Iranian in the Irish hillsides might be enough of a diversion for us to move the parts ourselves."

The fact the visitors missed their scheduled time seemed in Neal's mind to confirm Collins' conclusion. They probably figured out Collins' IRA connections, or Zafer's ties to Hamas, and thought twice about trying to extort money from such men of illicit influence. Neal was just about to leave the security shed at the front gate, when the car arrived. Neal called Zafer on a cell phone and told him the "tour" was about to begin and Zafer should stand ready to follow the couple to their next stop.

Later that morning, Ann reviewed the many pictures she had taken at the farm on her cell phone. "Oh my God, Richard," Ann said to Thompson, "that place was absolutely beautiful. It certainly is different from Kentucky farms. In fact, I think I like the stone walls dividing the fields as much, if not more, than the white fences on the farms back home."

"They certainly have enough rocks around here," said Thompson as he guided the car as close as he could to the stone wall bordering the road without nicking the silver paint. The drizzle falling earlier in the morning became a steady downpour. Sheets of cold rain were being whipped around by the strong wind. "Those walls looked good in the fields, but I'm not real fond of them right now."

Thompson plugged his iPhone into the radio before they left County Mayo Stables, and he dialed up a random mix of music. When *Thousands are Sailing* by the Pogues came on over the speakers, he worked the buttons on the steering wheel to increase the volume. "Damn these roads are tight," he said.

"You're just not used to driving on the wrong side of the road." Ann stopped her camera on a picture Neal had insisted she take. "That was a pretty filly Paddy made me take a picture of. What was her name again, Finn's Lassie? I've never seen a horse in a rain coat before."

"That was pretty funny looking," Thompson agreed. "I guess they get so much rain over here they need coats to keep the horses warm and somewhat dry." He momentarily took his eyes off the road and glanced at the cell phone. "Have you sent the picture to Joe yet?"

Ann was typing away on the cell phone's small keyboard. "I'm attaching the picture to an email to him right now."

Thompson leaned forward in his seat in an attempt to peer through the water being slopped around the car's windshield by the wipers. The hard-driving mandolin tune was reverberating through the speakers. Thompson looked in the rear-view mirror and noticed a white panel van coming up quickly from behind. He knew the Irish were used to these roads and driving conditions, but this van seemed to be approaching awfully fast. Thompson slowed down and got the car as close to the stone wall as possible. Tall weeds alongside the wall slapped at the side-view mirror.

When Thompson slowed down, the van purposely sped up and hit the car from behind. The initial impact slammed the car into the stone wall and Thompson struggled to keep the vehicle under control.

"Jesus, Richard," Ann shouted as the cell phone flew from her hands. "What are you doing?"

Thompson had no time to explain the situation as the panel van slammed into them a second time. This time, however, Thompson was unable to control the rental car on the wet pavement. The car went from side to side, bouncing off the stone walls like the chrome ball in a pinball machine. On the first impact, he hit his head against the side window so hard the window shattered. When the car finally came to a stop, Thompson's door was pinned against the stone wall.

"What the hell?" Ann shouted as the truck sped around them. Once it had passed, she looked at Thompson and saw that he was bleeding under his right eye. "Oh my God, you're bleeding."

Thompson was dazed and still trying to shake the cobwebs from his head.

"Richard. Talk to me," Ann grabbed Thompson's chin and looked closely at the cut under his eye. Blood was now running down his cheek. She could tell he was in a fog. "Are you all right? What the hell just happened?"

"Yeah," Thompson muttered slowly, still confused about what has transpired. "I think I'm okay." He wiped his hand across the cut on his cheek and looked at the blood on his fingers. He stared slowly around the car. "I'm not sure what just happened."

"We've been in an accident," Ann said.

"My head hurts," Thompson replied.

Ann looked up and saw the panel van turning around at a cattle gate. "That sonofabitch hit us," said Ann angrily. She opened up the passenger side door of the car and stepped out onto the road. Her rage at the people in the vehicle caused her to disregard the hard rain beating against her body. She put her hands on her hips and waited for the van.

Thompson was struggling to regain his senses. The sight of the van approaching his wife was all he needed. "Ann, don't," he shouted as he struggled with his seat belt. "Get back in the car."

Ann heard Thompson's shout and turned away from the approaching van. Over her shoulder, Thompson could see two men wearing hoods in the front seat. Panic shot through Thompson as he saw that one of the men had a gun. He was scrambling on all fours across the passenger seat to try to get to his wife. Adrenalin was screaming through his body, instantly clearing his fogginess. "Look out," he shouted.

Ann looked at Thompson with a puzzled expression.

"Get down," Thompson screamed repeatedly.

Ann turned back to face the van. Her eyes grew wide with shock and she froze at the sight of a man with a gun leveled at her head. Her brain told her to respond to her husband's command and drop to the ground. She found herself unable to move, frozen in time and place.

Thompson fell hard from the passenger door, his face on the wet pavement, when he heard the single shot. The van's tires sped just past, throwing rain and road grime into his bloody face as a final insult. Half in and half out of the car, he looked up to see Ann lying on the ground.

Not even aware he was screaming her name, Thompson crawled to Ann's side, and cradled her up into his arms as the rain washed her blood onto the highway.

THIRTY-THREE

There were a lot of former operatives littered around CIA headquarters and Jane Kline knew all of them from her time under Director Steele. Because of their bad experience, she had a higher level of respect for them. When she asked for their opinion or advice on certain matters, it was clear they held Kline in similar high regard. Kline traveled alone to the Jefferson Monument to meet privately with the Turk, one of those operatives turned policy analyst.

Baran Sancar was so nicknamed because of his Turkish ancestry. When a mole blew his cover in 1992, he was stationed in Moscow. Despite the daylight cast across his actual identity, the Turk had been able to escape through British channels. Once in the States, he was reassigned to CIA headquarters. He became one of the Company's most valuable policy analysts, working directly with operatives in the field. He was also an expert on internal investigations of leaks. Unfortunately, the years behind a desk had not been kind to the Turk's physique and he packed far more pounds than his short body should carry.

Kline wanted to meet the Turk away from headquarters, so they met on the National Mall. As they walked along the Tidal Basin, Kline stared out at the water. The Turk was reading the report MacKenzie prepared on Jimmy Day. "Well, Turk, what do you think?"

The Turk closed the file and tucked it under his arm. "We definitely have a mole," he replied. "And at a very high level."

"I was afraid of that," Kline replied. She stopped and placed her hands on the wall bordering the walkway. The wind off the Tidal Basin felt cool as it blew through Kline's hair. "So, do we move?" she asked.

The Turk looked back at the monument, avoiding eye contact with Kline. "You're definitely in danger," he replied.

"I've been there before," she said coldly.

"Never dressed like that," he turned and pointed to her dark blue pant suit. "And never with a bum leg."

"How long will it take you to figure out who's behind it and their end game?"

"We've got some people in the field who may be able to pick up some intelligence," the Turk responded. He shook his head back and forth contemplating a timeline. "At least a couple of days … maybe a week."

"Make it your top priority. I need to be certain."

THIRTY-FOUR

Josh and Wasfi left the conference in Dublin as soon as they had received word about the attack on Thompson and Ann. Navigating the unfamiliar roads of Ireland in the heavy downpour seemed like a daunting task to a shell-shocked Josh, but Wasfi seemed quite sure of his abilities as he drove them both to Castlebar. A simple explanation by Wasfi about how he became accustomed to driving in the rainy conditions of the British Isles led to a wider discussion about Wasfi's time as a pilot in the Royal Air Force. Wasfi carefully planned the conversation to take the young man's mind off the Congressman and his wife.

The RAF became more than a job for young Wasfi Al Ghazawi—it was the place that molded his political viewpoint. As a youth growing up in London, he had little time to think about his heritage as an expatriated Palestinian. His father seemed obsessed with it, but Wasfi was far too busy with soccer practice and girls to care.

When Wasfi began his training as a pilot, his outlook on life became more serious. While he trained for war, he began to question its causes. He became a voracious reader and began to study the philosophical differences which so often led to world conflicts.

The rescue mission in Bosnia that left Wasfi a wounded hero cemented his changed world view. The man who had fired the weapon was probably a Muslim. It took about a year for him to come to grips that he had nearly been killed by a child of Abraham—a brother as it were. It was this revelation that caused him to resign his commission in the RAF and establish a think tank aimed at peaceful resolutions of world conflicts by acknowledging similarities between faiths, rather than highlighting their differences.

As the pair approached their destination, Josh came to understand why his bosses at NATO had such respect for Wasfi and why they called on him so often to mediate in hot spots where trouble had broken out. Josh had told Thompson that Wasfi was naïve. He now understood he was, in fact, no different than Josh had been before Romania—a true believer. Josh longed to have that same depth of feeling again.

When Josh and Wasfi arrived at Mayo General Hospital in Castlebar, it was getting dark. After checking in at the front desk of the hospital, the pair made their way to the third floor where Ann had been admitted as a patient. Thompson was sitting in a chair when they entered the room. His face was bruised. There was a bandage on his temple and a row of stitches curved below his right eye.

As shocked as Josh was to see Thompson looking as if he had been on the losing side of a heavyweight prize fight, he was absolutely horrified when he saw Ann. It was not the fact she was lying in a bed with her left leg held up in a sling. Josh had already spoken to Thompson and learned the bullet wound Ann had endured was to her leg and was not life threatening. It was the look in Ann's eyes that stopped Josh in his tracks.

Ann Thompson looked scared. Her face was pale and her hair was disheveled. But her eyes revealed a fear Josh had never seen before. Ann was the one who was always helping Josh to stand tall, instilling confidence when he was unsure or afraid. Now, for the first time in his recollection, it was Ann who looked frightened. Josh saw through the thin smile Ann offered in his direction. Josh started to go over to Ann, but he stopped suddenly when he noticed a third person in the room.

"Hi, guys," Thompson said. "I appreciate your getting up here so quickly. This is Constable Mahoney. He's investigating what happened."

"Wade Mahoney," said the tall man as he stood up to shake hands with Josh and Wasfi. His sandy mustache sashayed back and forth as he spoke "Damn disgrace what happened here. The Parliament keeps passing laws to keep guns out of the hands of these damn hooligans. Shame we can't catch 'em and lock 'em all up."

"The guns or the hooligans?" asked Josh.

"Both," replied Mahoney. "There's more and more of this happenin' around the Isle. There was a bad shooting down around Limerick last year. A ganger killed a witness who testified in a trial. I guess it was just a matter of time until this kind of senseless violence made its way to the countryside."

"That's what you think happened here?" asked Josh. "Senseless violence?"

"Random act of violence by some gang of hooligans," Mahoney replied.

"Why do you think so?" Thompson interjected.

"Because there's no other real explanation for what happened," Mahoney opined. "There's nothing much out in that part of the county but horses and sheep."

Wasfi had been silent up to that point, quietly observing Mahoney as he offered his hypothesis to those assembled. "Any evidence to back up your theory?"

"Masks," said Mahoney with the confidence of a top detective. "The lads with the gun were wearing masks. Gangs try to hide their identity, ya know."

Wasfi was not buying the explanation Mahoney was offering, but did not let it show. "Anything else? Was there any evidence at the scene?"

"Just this," Mahoney said. He reached in his pocket and pulled out a shell casing in a plastic evidence bag. "Found it at the site of the shooting. No prints on it though."

Wasfi inspected the casing closely before handing it back to Mahoney.

"Well, if you would excuse me now, I've got to go back to the station to file a report." Mahoney looked at Ann and politely nodded in her direction. "They told me you'll be in here a couple of days. If I have any more questions, I'll know where to find ya."

Mahoney turned and shook Thompson's hand. "I'll try to keep your identity away from the news hounds for as long as I can, but that will only be a day or two. We don't have much activity like this in these parts. Word will get out pretty quickly. We've assigned a guard to keep the tabloids out of your room." Mahoney shook hands with Josh and Wasfi, and nodded as he turned for the door. "G'day, gents ... ma'am."

When Mahoney left the room, Josh immediately made his way to Ann's side. He grabbed her hand. "This will teach you to skip out on a conference." Josh knew he was failing miserably in his attempt to make Ann smile. Nevertheless, Ann appreciated the effort.

While Josh sat down on the edge of Ann's bed, Wasfi looked at Thompson and nodded his head towards the door. Thompson acknowledged the gesture and the pair stepped out into the hallway. Thompson already provided Wasfi with a detailed description of the incident over the phone. He could tell Wasfi had something more on his mind. And quite

316

frankly, was not sure if he was buying into the constable's explanation. "What's up?" Thompson asked.

"Tell me again what happened?"

Thompson leaned against the wall and closed his eyes. He had told the story so many times; it was starting to sound like a recording. "I looked in my rear view mirror ..."

"No, no, no," Wasfi cut Thompson off, waving his hands at his waist. "Skip over the part where your car got rammed. Tell me about the shooting. Tell me what happened as the shooter drove by you."

Thompson paused to fast forward the story in his mind. "Ann got out of the car after we crashed. I guess she was so pissed she wanted a piece of the driver's ass."

Wasfi chuckled. From the little he knew about Ann, she seemed like the type who would try to take down a hit and run driver.

"It all happened so quickly," Thompson continued. He rubbed lightly at the stitches under his eye. "I remember yelling at her to get back in the car. While she was looking back at me, I got a good look over her shoulder at the guy with the gun. He was pointing it right at Ann's head. Like I told the constable, they were wearing masks. I never saw their faces."

Wasfi nodded his head. "Next," he said. "Tell me what happened next."

"I didn't see it, but what happened next was just bizarre."

"Why?" Wasfi cocked his head.

"The shooter aimed the gun right at her head," Thompson replied. He pointed an imaginary gun at Wasfi. "Ann looked right down the barrel as he drove past. Then at the last minute, the sonofabitch lowered the gun and shot her in the leg."

"And where were you?" Wasfi asked.

Thompson hung his head. He was bitterly disappointed by the fact he had not been in a position to shield Ann from the attackers. His voice lowered. "My driver's side door had been pinned closed against a stone wall. I was climbing over the passenger seat trying to get out of the car."

"So exactly where were you when the shot was fired?" Wasfi repeated his query.

Thompson slowly thought back through the sequence of events. He looked up at the lights and shook his head. "I was on the ground. I stumbled trying to get out of the door and was lying on the fucking road. I tried to get to her, but I didn't make it in time."

"Don't worry about that now," Wasfi insisted. His pace of questioning quickened. "Those roads around there are awfully narrow. How did the van avoid hitting you?"

Thompson paused. He was not sure where Wasfi was heading with his questioning. "I don't know. Maybe they swerved."

"So, a couple of local hooligans driving through the countryside of County Mayo decide to ram a rental car and then selectively shoot one of the passengers in the leg." Wasfi scratched his head. "But they don't shoot the other passenger, and then, they swerve to avoid hitting him on the ground."

"What are you getting at, Wasfi?" Thompson decided to just ask. "Something has your mind working overtime."

"That shell casing Constable Mahoney showed us," Wasfi started. He made a motion with his thumb and index finger indicating the size.

"Yeah," Thompson replied.

"That was a shell casing from an FN Five-seveN," Wasfi said as he started to walk. He was looking upward and trying to think through the facts Thompson had recited.

"I don't even know what that means," Thompson replied while he followed along beside Wasfi.

"An FN Five-seveN is a very expensive hand gun," Wasfi replied. "It costs over $1,000 US. The ammo for the original design could pierce Kevlar, so the company agreed to widen the bullet. That is what makes the shell casing so distinctive." He stopped and shook his finger to make the point. "In fact, Ann is quite lucky the bullet caught the muscle in her leg instead of the bone. An inch or so over and it could have really caused some permanent damage."

"So what are you saying, Wasfi?" Thompson queried tentatively.

"The FN Five-seveN is not exactly the weapon of choice for a hooligan from Limerick."

"Okay." Thompson leaned back against the wall. "You have my attention. Who uses such a weapon?"

Wasfi thought for a moment. "It's made from polymers and it's very light weight. The low recoil makes it very easy to aim." He paused again. "Was the gun camouflaged or black?"

Thompson closed his eyes. He thought back to the moment when he saw the gun appear over Ann's shoulder. "It was camouflaged. But there's no military around here."

"I know," Wasfi responded. He put his hand on Thompson's shoulder. "This could be the work of a paid assassin."

"An assassin?" Thompson jerked his shoulder away from Wasfi's grasp in shock. "I was beginning to think the shooting wasn't random, but assassin is a bit dramatic, don't you think? Why would an assassin target us?"

"This country has banned guns for years," said Wasfi. "It doesn't mean there have not been guns around. A lot of weapons were smuggled in for the IRA decades ago. This gun does not fit that mold. There are not many newer, high tech guns around Ireland."

Thompson turned to face Wasfi. "Assasson," he mused, "I have a question."

"Go ahead."

"You think Ann was shot by an assassin."

"Yes, I do."

"Then why are we both still alive?"

"I have not figured that out yet."

It was after midnight when Wasfi hopped into his rental car dressed in black jeans and a black turtle neck. The questions he had regarding the shooting were nagging at him. He wanted to take a look at the farm for himself.

THIRTY-FIVE

"Gentlemen, it's game time," Colonel Arnie "Hawk" Simpson said as he chomped away on a freshly lit Cuban Churchill cigar. The lines in Simpson's bald head were a living testament to his twenty-five years of military experience. Despite his advancing age, he was fit and lean. His very presence commanded the respect of lower officers. Whenever he told his staff it was "game time," they knew it was time to go to work. When Hawk's eyes narrowed, frivolity ended.

The room was filled with twenty or more personnel, each with a particular role to play in the briefing. Front and center, sitting across from Pewther were two of his top veteran officers, James "Bizarre" Jakovenko and Steve "The Lion" Greiner. Both were experienced pilots who had been with Simpson for nearly seven years. The two subordinate officers quickly thumbed through the file folders in front of them before Lion spoke up. "What's up, Hawk?" He flipped a page, leaned back in his chair and looked at the briefing summary. "We goin' to Ireland?"

"Looks like it, Lion," Hawk replied. He flicked the ashes off the cigar and raised it to his mouth for a fresh puff. "You're going to be Flight Lead on this one. Bizarre you got the lead when we hit the ground."

Both men nodded acceptance of their roles.

The unit had been getting a lot of activity recently. These meetings were starting to have a certain pattern to them. "What's up this time?" Bizarre wrote notes on the file folder as he spoke.

Hawk looked over at one of the other officers sitting along the wall. "Charley," Hawk instructed, "you want to give them the intel?"

"Yes, sir." Charlie Rayburn, a veteran intelligence officer stepped forward. "We have a confirmed report our target possesses F-14 Tomcat parts," Rayburn said without expression. "We are working under the assumption they are trying to get them to Iran."

"Again?" The Lion interjected. He put his hands behind his head. "Jesus, didn't they just bust somebody back in the States trying to get parts to the royal rag head air force?"

"Yeah," Rayburn replied. "Busted and then went missing. We are assuming these are part of the same supply chain." Rayburn pulled out a piece of paper from his folder. "As usual, the Department of Commerce stumbled into the Miami situation by mistake. The guy they arrested claimed he was set up by some Indian company to buy junk parts and get them out of the US. The FBI got involved and arrested the guy. He got bail and disappeared. The CIA is still trying to find the Indian connection and the source of his money."

"Clowns-In-Action," Lion laughed, tapping his pen on the folder. "What do our people say?"

"Our boys located some shell corporations in India, but we couldn't figure out who was behind them," Rayburn replied.

Hawk inhaled his cigar and slowly blew a few smoke rings.

Bizarre wrote down more notes. "So we have a guy in Ireland with some F-14 parts. Is he connected to the guy back in the States?"

"We don't know yet," Rayburn replied leaning forward against the table. "And it really doesn't matter. All we know is the target has some specialized parts, drive trains, and a box of couplers which are unique to the F-14."

Both pilots knew their mission. Go in. Destroy the parts and get out with little or no bloodshed. Missions like this rarely involved local law enforcement or official government to government notification. Irish authorities cannot object to a raid they know nothing about. The target sure isn't about to complain his illegal cache of parts was destroyed. "So what's the plan Hawk?" Lion asked. Hawk was the Air Mission Commander and controlled all the details at this point.

"Quick in. Quick out. Of course, we're not going to alert local authorities unless one of you screws the pooch." Hawk looked at both men and rolled his cigar from side-to-side as he growled his next words.

"Neither of you are going to do so, are you?"

It was a purposefully inane question. Both answered "No, sir," in unison.

"Right answer," Hawk replied. "Houp," barked the Colonel. "Front and center. Give us the logistics."

Air Force Lt. Barry Houp powered up a computer that projected a satellite map onto the wall. He pulled a laser pointer from his front shirt pocket and aimed the red beam. "There is an open field about twenty-five miles north of the target."

"I am assuming our pathfinders are already on the ground?" Bizarre asked, referring to the unit of men who would set and activate radio devices in the field to mark the location. He looked intently at the screen to check the terrain of the surrounding area.

"Yes, sir," Houp replied. "They have indicated we have an eight second drop zone established. It's small, but should be able to handle everyone. Be ready for a small fog layer about 300 feet off the ground."

"Shit," mumbled Lion. "We going in CARP?"

"Possibly," said Houp, understanding the reference to using Computed Air Release Point when the actual drop zone is obscured. "You'll need to be on top of your game to keep from landing on one of the helicopters and damaging it."

"Fuck," said Bizarre. "What about one of them landing on us?"

"They're harder to replace," interjected Lion. A round of snickers filled the room.

"Knock it off, assholes." Hawk stood up, taking control of the briefing by clicking the computer to a photo of a MH-6M helicopter. "We're going to be dropping four Little Birds, two from each of the MC-130 cargo planes that will be going in first."

"Cool," Lion mumbled. He reached into his flight bag and pulled out an operator's manual for the MH-6Mcopter. "I love them Little Birds. They're so quiet. They'll never hear us coming."

"The third MC-130 will be carrying the assault force," Hawk continued, clicking another chart onto the screen listing assignments. "Once we have the Little Birds assembled, I want the actual force to be as light as possible. Each Little Bird will be carrying two men besides the pilot. There shouldn't be much to this raid, so I don't want a huge commitment of manpower. And I want as little noise as possible."

"Roger that." Bizarre shook his head in agreement. The mission sounded fairly benign.

Hawk was a man of few words. His meetings never lasted a moment longer than necessary. When he turned off the computer, the other two men knew the briefing was nearly concluded. "I'm going in with you. Houp and I will go over the rehearsal simulation with you on the MC-130, and I will answer any other questions you have on board."

The Lion smiled at the thought of having the old man on board with them. "You gonna drop with us, Hawk?"

Hawk rolled his eyes at the thought. "Are you kidding me? You're going in to blow up some metal poles and fancy plastic plugs. I've got important things on my plate, like counting the number of angels I can get to dance on the head of a pin."

"I thought you might enjoy it," the Lion responded sheepishly.

"That's what I have you two for," Hawk scowled, "so I don't have to jump on these bullshit missions."

Bizarre began placing his notes in his go bag. "What's the timing, Hawk?" he asked.

Hawk looked at his watch. "We needed to leave ten minutes ago."

THIRTY-SIX

The serving of breakfast at a small inn or B&B in Ireland is a major production. Innkeepers pride themselves on having their guests start a day filled with home-made breads, eggs cooked to order, blood pudding and thick-cut bacon. Like all meals eaten in Ireland, breakfast is served quickly and piping hot.

Josh reserved rooms for himself, Wasfi, and Thompson at a quaint inn just a few blocks from the hospital. The place had small, but comfortable rooms and a small bar off the lobby where an old, white haired gent named McNay served up Guinness. The garden along the street had small tables and chairs where guests could enjoy tea while watching for the occasional car passing along the quiet side street. Most importantly, the inn was within walking distance of the hospital where Ann was still being held for observation. She lost some blood as a result of the shooting and the doctors insisted on keeping her there for a day or so. Josh determined having sleeping quarters within walking distance of Ann was a necessity.

When Josh got up early and went downstairs, he discovered the breakfast provided by the inn was an added benefit to his earlier decision points. It was going to be a while before Wasfi and Thompson were to meet him for the feast, so he grabbed a cup of strong coffee and headed to the garden to contemplate the events of the previous couple of days.

Seeing Ann in the hospital had a surprisingly positive impact on Josh's mental attitude. When Wasfi and Thompson left the room the night before, Ann spoke softly to Josh about his own life and the direction he should be taking. The woman was still pale from a gunshot wound and she was more worried about his well being than her own. It may have been a simple point Ann was trying to make, but for Josh it marked a turning point. On the walk back to the hotel he determined it was time to get over Romania and move on with his life. Ann encouraged him to move back home to the US. Maybe she was right.

Josh was so deep in his own thoughts he did not hear Thompson come out into the garden and sit down in the chair beside him. When Josh did finally notice Thompson, he checked him out from head-to-toe. Josh clearly did not like what he was seeing. The eye where the stitches had been sewn was bruised around the socket and nearly swollen shut. A slight amount of blood soaked through the bandage on his temple. Thompson had not washed his hair. "You look like shit," Josh said.

"That's only because I feel like shit." Thompson took a sip from his coffee and placed it on the table between them. "The pain killers helped me sleep last night. But I was hoping to wake up this morning to find yesterday was all just a bad dream."

"No such luck, I guess," Josh replied. He knew Thompson felt physically and emotionally spent. Yet, he was not quite sure what to say to comfort his old boss. He paused and then decided to talk business. He handed Thompson the morning newspaper with a headline that read "Wife of US Official Shot."

"Fuck me," Thompson exhaled slowly while reading the headline. He tossed the paper on the table alongside his coffee without reading the story. He pulled a pair of sunglasses out of his pocket and placed them on his face gently, trying to avoid contact with the stitches. "Well that sure didn't take long."

"It's a small town, boss," Josh replied. "This is probably the most excitement they've ever seen here. I imagine it's hard to keep something like this a secret."

Thompson said nothing. His eyes followed a man riding past on a red scooter, chugging slowly along just outside the hedge bordering the garden.

Josh cleared his throat, trying to get Thompson's attention away from the street. "Don't worry—I'll handle the press when reporters start showing up at the hospital today. I've called my supervisor at NATO and I have clearance to stay here as long as you need me. I've also spoken to our embassy. They'll be coming up later today."

"I know I can count on you, Josh." Thompson reached across the table and patted Josh on his knee. He reclined back into the chair. "I wish to God I would have never left Dublin. Hell, I wish I would have never left the States."

"Come on," Josh said. "Let's go inside and grab some grub. The breakfast here looks phenomenal. After we eat, we'll walk over to the hospital and see Ann. Maybe they'll let her out today."

"I'm really not hungry," Thompson shook his head.

"You ought to eat something," Josh said as he turned to see Wasfi walk out of the building into the garden.

"Now, you're starting to sound like my wife." Thompson also noticed Wasfi as he approached, and he stood up to greet him. "Good morning, Wasfi."

"Top of the morning to ya'." Wasfi's attempt to mask his Middle Eastern accent with an Irish brogue made all three smile. "Anybody up for breakfast? The presentation of food in there is quite impressive."

Thompson again shook his head. "Not hungry."

"You have to eat," Wasfi insisted.

"You too?" replied Thompson, chuckling in Josh's direction. "I guess I have three wives now."

"What else are you going to do?" counseled Wasfi as the three started to walk from the garden to the house. "It appears the only thing on your schedule today is to walk over to the hospital and sit around waiting for your wife to be released. She will absolutely insist you eat. So you can either have hospital food or a good made-to-order breakfast."

Thompson opened the door for Josh and Wasfi. "I'll eat later. Right now, I need your car keys."

Wasfi narrowed his eyes. "What for?"

"Before you head back to Dublin, I want to head back out to where the shooting occurred to retrace our steps. The whole thing is such a blur. If I go out there, maybe something useful will come to mind."

"It's too dangerous." Wasfi shook his head.

"Look Wasfi, I know your background in the military teaches you to see conspiracies everywhere. Truthfully, I don't know what to think right now. Something out there may just jog my memory for a clue."

Wasfi looked closely at his watch, worried about the timing of Thompson's request. "I just can't let you go out there," said Wasfi as he put his arm around Thompson. "I'll get my work done today and come back tomorrow. Then we'll go out together."

"Okay," said Thompson.

"But it's all contingent on eating breakfast this morning first," Wasfi concluded.

Thompson struggled with a smile. "You drive a hard bargain."

The wind rustled softly through the trees as Thompson walked along the outside wall of the curve in the road where he and Ann had been attacked. Broken glass and other debris from the accident still littered the blacktop. Thompson ran his hand along the porous stones in the wall where paint from the wrecked car had left its mark. He reached down and picked up the car's side-view mirror. After contemplating the shattered mirror for a moment, he tossed it back to the ground.

Thompson had ignored Wasfi's instructions to stay away from the scene of the shooting. As soon as they finished breakfast and Wasfi had left, Thompson had walked to the garage where his rental car had been towed. The owner of the garage jumped at Thompson's offer to borrow his car for a couple of hours in return for a hundred euro. If only for mental relief, he needed to be by himself as he walked back and forth along the twenty or so yards of pavement. The fresh morning air smelled clean as the light wind blew across the wet fields. Thompson closed his eyes and thought of home.

As he walked the length of road where the incident happened, Thompson replayed the accident over and over again in his head. Nothing new came to mind. All he could think about was how helpless he felt as he saw the van approaching Ann and the sick feeling as he heard the single gunshot.

No cars were coming, so Thompson walked to the center of the road. Although the hard rain from the previous afternoon washed Ann's blood from the pavement, Thompson felt its presence. He took off his sun glasses, knelt down to touch the ground and closed his eyes to fight back tears.

When Thompson heard the rumble of an approaching vehicle, he put the sun glasses back on and moved to the side of the road. A flash of panic streaked through his body as the vehicle appeared around the curve in the stone wall. It was a white panel van with two men in the front seats. This time there were no masks, and Thompson could clearly make out their faces. A momentary impulse to flee quickly left his head. Blocked on either side by a stone wall, Thompson had no where to run.

The van screeched to a halt on the road, and an Arab man in the front seat pointed a gun at Thompson.

"You just will not give up, will you?"

Wasfi felt uncomfortable leaving Thompson and Josh alone back at the B&B, but Wasfi needed to be at the horse farm. A drive past the entrance to County Mayo Stables revealed nothing more than the simple lay of the land. Wasfi drove a mile or so past the farm and turned around. On his way back along the same road, he turned up a lane that climbed one of the gently rolling hills bordering the farm to its east. Once Wasfi reached the peak of the hill, he pulled the car as close to the stone wall as he could and popped open the trunk. In the trunk, he reached into a gap between the quarter panel and spare tire and fumbled around. Soon he found the package left there for him—a small black duffel bag. He smiled when he pulled it out before closing the trunk. He laid the bag on top of the trunk lid and unzipped it to reveal a handgun, two knives, and a small pair of long range binoculars.

Once Wasfi had removed the Barska zoom binoculars from the bag, he wedged himself sideways between the rear quarter-panel of the car and the wall. Placing his heel on the rear tire he raised himself up, placed his elbows on the stone wall and brought the binoculars to his eyes. The farm seemed peaceful enough. Horses roamed the lush green fields devoid of any human interaction.

As serene as the fields appeared, there was a flurry of activity at a barn near the main house. Men were stacking boxes of what appeared to be Irish whiskey. Several long tubes and three unmarked boxes sat next to those with liquor labels on them.

Wasfi looked at his watch. He was just about to climb down from his perch to go to another location, when a flash of white caught his eye. A white panel van, similar to the one Thompson had described as being involved in the shooting the day before, was entering the farm's grounds through the front gate followed by a car. Wasfi readjusted the binoculars and followed the van to the barn. It stopped next to where the men were stacking the boxes. When the men opened the back doors of the van, Wasfi was shocked to see the payload they dumped to the ground. It was

Congressman Richard Thompson.

"Son of a bitch," Wasfi muttered. "I should have known you would come back. This has just gotten very complicated."

THIRTY-SEVEN

"We've got a problem," Paddy Neal said as he stormed into the farm house office of Rory Collins to tell him Zafer captured Congressman Richard Thompson walking along the road near the farm. Without Neal's knowledge, Zafer and a farm hand took it upon themselves to apprehend the man and bring him to the farm. He was being held in one of the stables.

"Tell me about it." Collins flipped the newspaper onto his desk in front of Neal. "This is not good."

"What's this?" said Neal, reaching for the paper.

"'Tis' the morning news," Collins replied as he ran his fingers through his hair. "I assume the story on the front page is the problem we're about to discuss."

Neal picked up the newspaper and quickly read the story about the wife of a United States Congressman being shot in County Mayo. "Oh, fuck me then," he mumbled as his face went pale.

"I told the ignorant bastard to scare him," Collins screamed, "not shoot his fuckin' wife. The man is a menace. Now what has he done?"

Neal quickly explained to Collins that Zafer encountered the American lurking on the road near the farm. According to Zafer's own account, he grabbed Thompson and forced him into the van. Neal slapped at the newspaper in disgust.

A knock at the office door was followed by a muffled shout from Zafer announcing his arrival. Collins put his fingers to his lips indicating they should not speak freely in front of Zafer. "Come on in then," Collins replied.

Zafer quickly entered the room, holding a wallet in front of him and smiling. He was so excited he stuttered as he spoke. "He is a Congressman," Zafer said proudly. Zafer opened the wallet and pulled out Thompson's Congressional identification card from the wallet. He handed it to Neal, who looked at it and then passed it to Collins.

The two Irishmen looked at each other. They were shocked by Zafer's joy. "We know he's a Congressman. He's all over the news, for the love of Christ." They shared the same thought. They had a really big problem on their hands. "And you're happy about it?" Neal asked, hesitantly.

Zafer nodded. "We have captured an American elected official," he bragged. "This is a man who votes for the weapons that have been killing my people for decades. If you think we can get a lot of money for some airplane parts, just wait until they find out we have a war criminal to hand over to them. Men like this Congressman have bounties on their heads."

Neal started to voice an objection, but Collins shot him a look indicating he should remain silent.

Neal bit his lip as Zafer continued his rant about the captive American.

"This man is a pig," Zafer snarled. "He is a descendent of the men who laughed while my father died in poverty. His hands are stained with the blood of the martyrs, and I shall deliver him to a slow and painful death."

Zafer was oblivious to the shocked looks on the faces of Neal and Collins. They had never before seen this side of Zafer, who paced frantically and waved his arms wildly as he spoke. "I shall be remembered as the man who delivered an agent of Satan to the Council. Long after this man is dead, my father's name shall live on as a prophet."

Collins rubbed his chin as he thought for a moment. "Fine, Zafer," Collins replied. "We shall give revenge to your family name." Zafer smiled in appreciation before Collins continued. "But we'll be needin' to step up our schedule and move out quicker than anticipated. Get the couplers loaded into the whiskey boxes and attach the rods to the bottom of the van."

"Why?" Zafer asked. "Why move in daylight?"

Collins remained calm as he spoke. "Someone will be missing this American bugger soon, and we need to get him out of County Mayo as quickly as possible."

"Good idea." Zafer's eyes were set as he nodded and made his way to the door. "This shall make us immortal," he declared. "We shall make a great deal of money and have the added bonus of killing an American in the process."

Once the door was closed, Neal looked at Collins. "You can't be serious, are ya?" he asked incredulously. "The man is a lunatic."

"I'm not," Collins replied, shaking his head. "Zafer has gone too far this time. He thinks the American is an asset. He doesn't realize that he—Zafer—is as big of a liability as the Congressman."

Collins stood up and paced to the window. He looked out at several horses grazing leisurely in a field close to the office. He took a deep breath, and then he spoke with little emotion. "Put the American and the airplane parts into the lorry. Have Zafer ride along with you. Head out like nothing is amiss. Before you hit the main road to Dublin," he paused, "kill them both. Keep the bodies in the truck overnight. Then meet me tomorrow at Brogan's in Ennis. From there, you and I will go and personally dispose of the bodies and airplane parts. We'll have to make sure there is never a trace of any of them."

"Got it," Neal replied.

Collins turned and looked at Neal. "Our involvement with the Iranian government has just come to an end."

THIRTY-EIGHT

The Fat Man's love of horses was evident in the décor and feel of his law offices. The walls rising from the egg-shell white marble floors were adorned with paintings and prints of famous horses bred at farms from Kentucky to London to Dubai. The receptionist for the office normally sat behind a rich wood reception counter that had the firm's name displayed on it in raised gold lettering. It was after hours and the reception counter sat empty.

Many law firms name their conference rooms after deceased and retired lawyers from their ranks. The Fat Man ensured the conference rooms off his firm's lobby bore brass plaques with the names of great race horses like Genuine Risk, Whirlaway, and the greatest horse of all time, Secretariat. Pictures of each particular horse hung in the conference room with a brass plate out front bearing the horse's name.

The look of the lobby might have caused a stranger walking in off the street to think they somehow wandered into the clubhouse at Keeneland rather than a law firm, with the attendant at the front desk being a maitre d' instead of a receptionist.

Tiana liked The Fat Man's law office from the moment she first walked into it. The warmth of the equine décor reached out to her at a time when she needed such superficial comfort. After Catalano was murdered, The Fat Man insisted Tiana spend her working hours in a spare office at his firm in order to allow him and Leo Argo to keep an eye on her. Her father's files were placed in a conference room just off the main lobby, where Tiana and The Fat Man currently sat trying to create a system for organizing the mass of random paper and files.

It was clear Tiana was agitated, but The Fat Man did not know exactly why. Obviously, her life had taken some horrific turns recently. The stress seemed almost manic today. He took the direct approach. "What's wrong, Tiana?"

Tiana didn't look up for the box of files she was reviewing. "What do you mean?"

"Something is clearly bothering you," The Fat Man replied. "If I said something to make you angry, I'm sorry."

Tiana looked up at The Fat Man. "It isn't you, Joe. You didn't say anything."

"Then what is it?"

"I've burdened you enough already," Tiana said, shaking her head.

The Fat Man put down his pen. "Burden me a little more."

Tiana leaned her elbows down on top of the file box she had been working on. "I've had a hard time figuring out my emotions over the last couple of days," she said.

"That's understandable," The Fat Man replied. "It's been a rough time in your life."

Tiana nodded. "They say everyone is supposed to have time to grieve, and I've just figured out my chance to do that has been stolen from me by some guy who's still out there killing people."

"I'm sorry," The Fat Man replied. "I really am."

"It's not your fault, Joe." Tiana shrugged off his condolences. "I guess I just figured out that, on top of everything else, I'm really, really pissed."

"You're entitled to whatever emotions you want to feel right now," The Fat Man replied.

Tiana started to pace. "I lost my daddy," she said, "and instead of sitting around his favorite pub listening to all of his friends tell stories, I'm in FBI lock down."

"It's for your own safety, you know," The Fat Man said.

"Don't think I don't appreciate it, Joe," Tiana replied. "I do. I know this is for my own protection, but I'm angry." Tiana crossed her arms and stared at The Fat Man. "I want my time to mourn." She paused for a long second and then pounded her fist on the conference table. "I deserve that right."

The Fat Man wasn't shocked by Tiana's outburst; after all she was Sean Sullivan's daughter. He waited a moment and then smiled slowly. If she wanted stories about her dad, he'd give her stories. "The first time I went to court," he said, "your dad was on the other side."

"Really?" Tiana's eyes lit up.

"Yeah," The Fat Man reminisced. "It was a piddly little collection case before a jury."

Tiana sat down at the table. "What happened?"

The Fat Man laughed. "I was so nervous I forgot to lay the foundation for putting the payment record into evidence."

"You? No way?"

"Your dad asked for a sidebar to explain his objection to the judge. Afterwards, out in the hallway, I asked him why he did it that way."

"What did he say?"

"He said he didn't want to embarrass me in front of my client."

Tiana leaned back in her chair. "That was Daddy," she said. She took a deep breath and let it out slowly. "Thanks, Joe. Got any other stories about my dad?"

The Fat Man smiled. "It's your turn. Why don't you tell me one?"

Tiana thought for a second and then started laughing. "This one time, when I was ten years old, Daddy took me to the …"

The Fat Man and Tiana were so engrossed in telling stories about Sean Sullivan they never heard the man as he entered the third floor suite through the fire exit.

A shadowy figure peeked around the dimly lit corner of the hallway and peered into the glass walled conference room. He smiled to himself. "A twofer," he whispered to himself. "I can get the hard drive and get Zafer off my ass." He winced slightly as he pulled the gun from his waist band. The stitches he had sewn into his stomach were still sore.

"This is too fuckin' easy," he said as he stepped out of the shadows into the hallway. He raised his gun and stepped into the doorway of the conference room.

Tiana and The Fat Man jumped when he walked through the door and asked "Now just what are you kids doing working on the weekend?"

THIRTY-NINE

The Turk was sitting at his desk when his secure phone rang. "This is the Turk," he replied, picking up a pen. He flipped a legal pad to a clean page. "Who is this?"

"It is Tots."

"Intercept is on its way," the Turk replied as he put down the pen. He looked at the clock. "I got you a Special Ops Unit out of Germany. They should already be at the drop zone. The intercept will be within the hour."

"Listen to me closely," Tots instructed. His voice was deadly serious. "I may not have time to tell you twice."

"What's going on, Tots?" the Turk asked. He had known Tots for decades. Tots did not panic easily. "What's wrong? Has something happened?"

"The mission has changed," Tots replied. "I need a package extracted."

The Turk rose up from his chair. "We're not equipped for an extraction. I can't make that call."

"Then call the Director immediately. The life of a high ranking American official is in jeopardy. Tell her it is a Congressman, her friend from Romania."

"Shit," the Turk mumbled as he wrote notes on the pad. Several of the operatives had been briefed on what happened in Romania when Shadow had been dispatched. He also knew of the involvement of Congressman Thompson. "I'll call her immediately."

Tots continued. "I need a change in mission. I am depending on you."

FORTY

Leo Argo flipped through the pages of *Blood-Horse* magazine as he sat on the toilet. "Damn," he mumbled to himself, "the sonofabitch even has horse magazines in the can." He tossed the periodical on the floor of the restroom stall and pulled a smart phone out of his pocket. Once he was done with the latest stories on the *Daily Caller* (and with his business), he washed his hands. As he splashed water on his face in an effort to stay fresh, he looked into the mirror and wondered to himself what Kline was up to.

"You, boy, are no spring chicken," he said, as he pointed at his reflection. He made a decision maybe it was time to move on. "Finish your career and move back to Miami. That's what you need to do. Find love in retirement. That's the only way you're going to enjoy it anyway." He wasn't sure if he convinced himself or not, but it was good enough for the time being. He ran a paper towel across his face and threw open the men's room door. "Who's up for some pizza?" he shouted.

The response was not what Argo had expected. There was a man standing in the doorway of the conference room holding a gun on Tiana and The Fat Man. He turned and swung the barrel of his gun in Argo's direction. Argo's adrenaline kick-started his training instincts. In one smooth motion, Argo pulled his gun from his shoulder holster, dropped to the floor, and rolled to his right.

The rage building up inside of Tiana burst out of her like molten lava from a volcano. The man standing before her took her father from her. He even deprived her of the private wake she was having in the conference room. She heard nothing being said around her. Her heart pounded. She snarled something inaudible as he waved the gun at them.

When Argo startled him, the man turned and took aim at the rolling FBI agent. It was then Tiana let out a primal scream and took off running at the man.

"Tiana, no," The Fat Man shouted.

Tiana was beyond listening. Just as the man took a shot at Argo, Tiana's small but firm body hit the man at full stride. Tackling him from the side, she hit him with all the power she could muster. The pair went sprawling onto the floor.

Argo heard the gunshot fired by the man ricochet off the marble floor near his left ear and he watched as Tiana and the man bounced off the floor. The man's hand hit the floor and a second shot fired wildly up the hallway. As the pair slid across the marble floor, Argo saw the gun fall out of the man's hand.

Tiana also saw the gun fall. She rolled off the man and immediately made a move for it. Argo was up and rushing towards the pair when Tiana jumped up holding the man's gun.

"Stay on the floor," Argo shouted at the man who was up to one knee. The intruder saw the gun trained on him and froze.

"Are you okay?" Argo asked Tiana.

Tiana did not even hear the question. She was panting heavily. Her eyes were wild and glassed over.

Argo knew what she was thinking. "Put the gun down, Tiana."

The Fat Man emerged from the conference room. "Don't do it, Tiana," he pleaded. "Your dad wouldn't want it this way."

"My daddy is dead." Tiana waved the gun in the man's face. "And this fucker killed him. Now, I'm going to do to him what he did to my daddy."

The Fat Man moved closer to her. "Remember those stories I told you in there?" He gestured back to the conference room. "Sean was a lawyer. He believed in justice."

Tiana's gaze went sharp and her voice harsh. "This is justice," she replied. "Eye for a fuckin' eye."

"No," The Fat Man pleaded softly. "Let a judge deliver justice. That's what Sean would have wanted."

Tiana closed her eyes. She knew The Fat Man was right. She sighed and slowly lowered the gun.

The Fat Man and Argo both looked at each other in relief. Argo let his weapon drop to his side as he reached for a pair of hand cuffs. The intruder saw what he thought was an opening. He reached quickly to his ankle and pulled a small pistol. Before he could raise the gun, a shot rang out. Argo swung his gun up and around while The Fat Man made a dive for Tiana. The intruder crumpled down to the floor.

"Motherfucker," Tiana snarled. "That's for my daddy."

Argo purposely waited before calling for back-up from the local police. Once he was sure Tiana had her self-defense cover story straight, he turned his attention to the body on the floor. Argo wanted to do a quick investigation of his own before he made a call to the locals. It was going to get very hectic, very quickly and Argo wanted to make sure he had what he needed before a swarm of police and press engulfed the building.

Blood stopped pouring from the wound in the intruder's back onto the marble floor of the law office. Argo walked around the body, careful not to step in the pool of crimson liquid. He knelt down onto one knee and pushed the man's head aside so The Fat Man and Tiana could see his face. "Either of you recognize this guy?" Argo asked.

"No, not me," Tiana said. She placed her hands in the back pockets of her black denim jeans to try to keep them from shaking so badly.

"Me neither," said The Fat Man. Curiosity had replaced his fear. He lowered his head to see from another angle. "Not a clue."

"I didn't think it would be that easy," Argo replied. He stood up and walked around the body again. Argo had only seen him from a distance, but he was sure it was the same guy he chased from Catalano's house. Argo could see the bulge of a wallet in the man's back pants pocket, so he reached down and carefully removed it. He opened it up and pulled out a driver's license. "He's a local guy," Argo said.

The Fat Man gestured the trio back to his office, sat down behind his desk, and jostled his mouse to get his computer out of sleep mode. "What's his name?" he asked.

Argo squinted at the driver's license. "Donald Patrick," he said. When Argo said the name, Tiana thought hard for a minute. Something about the name sounded familiar. She headed back down the hallway to the conference room where the boxes of her father's files were stacked against the walls. She didn't stop to glance at the body on the floor. She started digging through the boxes, one after another.

In The Fat Man's office, Argo paced as he dialed the number for FBI headquarters and waited for the operator to answer. "Agent Leo Argo here," he said to the operator. "Patch me through to records. I have a 911 for an immediate identification search."

As Argo spoke, The Fat Man began typing furiously, while squinting closely at the computer screen.

"I need some information on a dead perp," Argo said. "Donald Andrew Patrick. Kentucky driver's license, birthday is 14 January, 1962."

The Fat Man mouthed the birthday, confirming what he had on the screen conformed with the date Argo had just uttered. "He's a two-tour Navy Veteran," The Fat Man interjected, continuing to stare at his monitor.

Argo pulled his cell phone away from his ear and looked at The Fat Man. "What?" he asked.

The Fat Man never looked away from the computer screen and continued to type. "His mother's name is Grace."

Argo cocked his head and stared at The Fat Man. "What the hell are you talking about, Joey?"

"Patrick," The Fat Man leaned back in his chair and finally looked at Argo. "He's a veteran and his mom's name is Grace. His dad died eight years ago. His name was Robert."

"What are you looking at?" Argo asked.

"Ancestry.com," The Fat Man replied, pointing at the computer screen.

The voice came back on the line. Argo shook his head in disbelief as he directed his attention back to the cell phone. "Yeah, yeah," he repeated into the phone before reciting the information he was being given out loud. Argo looked at The Fat Man quizzically. "Navy Vet with eight years of service," The Fat Man shrugged his shoulders and smiled at Argo.

"What's his mom's name?" Argo asked.

The Fat Man repeated the name as Argo said it out loud, "Grace."

"Anything else?" The Fat Man said in a whisper as he raised his arms in triumph.

Argo frowned at The Fat Man before turning his attention back to the phone. "Encrypt it and send it to my laptop," he instructed before clicking off the phone and placing it in his shirt pocket. He replied to The Fat Man's question. "Yeah. I got something else. Does your website tell us why this guy likes to kill people?"

Before The Fat Man could answer, Tiana walked back into his office carrying a file folder. "Donald Patrick," Tiana announced. "I knew that name sounded familiar." She handed the file folder to The Fat Man, but kept the legal pad in her hand. "This guy was going to testify as a witness in Daddy's qui tam case."

"The whistleblower one?" The Fat Man asked. He took the file and opened it.

"Yes. I've got his interview notes right here." Tiana sat down in a chair across from The Fat Man and drew her legs up underneath her before starting to read. She winced as she flipped through the pages of the legal pad all covered with her dad's handwriting.

The Fat Man handed the file folder over to Argo and turned back to the computer to search further on Ancestry.com. "He worked at the engine factory,"

Tiana said as she read. "He was Mr. Catalano's supervisor and Catalano told him what he had found and about the lawsuit. This Donald Patrick guy agreed to testify in support of Catalano's claim. Damn. He killed one of his own workers."

"What did Patrick do at the plant?" Argo asked as he started to thumb through the rest of the file.

Tiana flipped the interview notes back to one of the first pages and read, "Director of Staged Supplies."

"Inventory clerk," mumbled The Fat Man. "What about the hard drive Patrick asked us about in there before all hell broke loose?"

Tiana again thumbed through the hand written pages. "Daddy's notes say Catalano removed a hard drive from a computer at the factory that had information on it to prove his claims."

"Go see if it's in any of the boxes," The Fat Man instructed. He leaned forward and looked intently at the screen. He clicked his mouse to read the next screen and froze. "Hey Leo, you better come and take a look at this," he said.

"What?" Argo walked over to where The Fat Man was sitting and peered over his shoulder at the computer screen.

"Your pal out in the lobby has a cousin who works in Washington. Does this name look familiar?"

Argo stared intently at the screen. "Sonofabitch."

FORTY-ONE

The damp smell of impending rain filled the air as Wasfi wiped the condensation from the lenses of his high powered binoculars before leaning his elbows back on the wall to view the scene in the valley before him. He had been there for more than an hour, and men continued to rummage around the white panel van at the horse farm.

Sweat poured from Wasfi's brow. With a swipe from the cuff of his shirt, he tried to clear the moisture off his forehead. He was trying to take in all of the activity occurring over several hundred yards, so he moved his binoculars back and forth in slow but precise measures. He watched as Thompson was led into a barn about thirty yards from the van immediately after his arrival, but Thompson never reappeared. A few men wandered in and out of the farm house about a hundred yards to the other side of the barns. The white panel van continued to be the center of all visible human activity.

A dark skinned man appeared from the small house and made his way to the barn area. Shortly after entering the main barn, he re-appeared leading Thompson by one arm. Wasfi zeroed the binoculars in on the two men. Thompson's hands appeared to be duct taped behind his back and there was tape over his mouth as well. The man walked Thompson to the white van and shoved him roughly through its back doors. After slamming the doors shut, the man got behind the wheel and started the engine. A few moments later, a second man appeared from the house and got into the van on its passenger side.

Brushing his hair back with his hands, Wasfi contemplated his options. This was moving more quickly than he anticipated. He worriedly looked at his watch. He could not wait. He had to act.

Wasfi threw his gear into the car and whipped it around on the tight lane. As soon as he reached the main road, he took a quick left and drove a few hundred yards. On a very tight, blind curve Wasfi braced himself and then spun the car into the stone wall lining the road. When the car came to a stop, he inched the vehicle forward at an angle so it was now blocking three-quarters of the road. With walls on both sides there was no way to get around the dented car.

Wasfi took one of his knives and looked into the rear view mirror. He put a slight cut near his hairline so that a thin stream of blood ran down his face. He took the butt end of the knife and smashed it against the windshield, causing it to crack from a central point just in front of the steering wheel. The wreck in place, Wasfi placed his gun inside his jacket, exited the car, and took a minute or so to make his final preparations.

Final preparations made, Wasfi could see the white van approaching from the distance. As it got closer, Wasfi walked to the center of the road and began to wave his hands furiously. The van started to slow down.

When Paddy Neal exited Collins' office, he had a Walther P99 semi-automatic pistol tucked confidently in the pocket of his farm jacket. Collins handed it to Neal with specific instructions to kill both Zafer and Thompson as soon as the van reached the first stop sign, about ten kilometers down the road from the farm. Neal did not like the idea, but he agreed with Collins they were in far too deep at this point to do anything else.

When Neal got into the van, he began to visualize the killing scene in his mind. At the stop sign, when Zafer would look away for traffic, Neal would put a bullet in his ear. The Congressman could be killed at the same location, a minute or so later. Neal's Irish politeness came through in an odd way as he mused it would not be proper to make an innocent man suffer the anticipation of his own death for too long.

Not much was said between Neal and Zafer as the van turned from the farm drive onto the main highway. Neal studied Zafer's face. If Zafer suspected anything was amiss, he was not showing it. As they drove, Neal tried to steady his breathing in order to prepare for the task he was about to complete. They were about two kilometers from the stop sign and Neal was gathering up his courage, when Zafer began to slow down for a man standing in the road, waving his hands for the vehicle to stop.

Neal was not sure what was happening. Knowing his instructions from Collins, he did not want to stop. "Drive on by, boy-o," he instructed. "Drive on by."

Zafer waved his hand in the direction of the man with the bloody face. "I cannot get around him," Zafer replied.

"We can't stop," Neal replied in angrily.

"I cannot get around him, Paddy," Zafer responded testily. "I am sure all he needs is for us to call someone on his behalf. I have to stop."

"No, God damn it," Neal shouted. "There'll be no fuckin' stoppin.'"

Zafer was surprised at Neal's agitation, so he reached over and patted his leg. "Do not worry, my friend." Zafer pointed at the hanging cloth separating the front seat from the back storage area of the van. "He cannot see in the back."

Neal clutched the gun in his jacket pocket. Ever so briefly, he contemplated killing Zafer, the Congressman, and this new man right on the spot. But another dead body would not make things any easier for him and Collins. Still nervous, he pulled the gun to his side while Zafer was distracted by the man on the road.

When Zafer stopped the van and unrolled his window. The two men greeted each other with a nod. "Where are you from?" Wasfi asked, appearing to be shaken up from the accident.

"Iran," Zafer replied. "You?"

"I am Palestinian," Wasfi stated. "Thank you for stopping, my friend," Wasfi switched to Persian so the other man in the van could not follow the conversation. "I am afraid I have wrecked my car on these narrow roads."

In the back of the van, Thompson recognized Wasfi's voice, but did not understand the language being spoken. He struggled against the duct tape binding his wrists.

Zafer chuckled at his new friend's dilemma. "Do not worry," he said. "It is easy to do on these roads. There is a farm a few kilometers back down the road. I will call them and have someone come up to assist you. Until then, could you move your vehicle a bit so my friend and I may continue upon our way?"

"Thank you," Wasfi replied. He started to reach out to shake Zafer's hand through the window of the car, but pulled it back. He wiped it low across his jacket first. "I am sorry, but my hand is bloody from my accident."

Wasfi wiped his hand back-and-forth across his jacket once more as he stepped in closer to the van. When he wiped his hand across his jacket a third time, he pulled his Springfield 1911 from his waist band.

He leveled it at Zafer and fired. The single shot hit Zafer directly between his surprised eyes. His head whipped backwards, hit the headrest, and then bounced forward.

Blood and brain matter filled the interior windows of the van and splattered across Neal's face. Neal's hand had been gripping his own gun when Zafer was hit. He quickly raised his gun and fired three wild shots. The third shot caught Wasfi in the left shoulder—he spun around and fell to the pavement.

When Neal saw Wasfi fall, he ducked down through the curtain covering the entry to the back portion of the van. This was not turning out the way Neal anticipated. Neal ripped the duct tape from Thompson's mouth and grabbed him by the hair. He shoved the gun up under his chin. "Who the fuck is out there?"

"I have no idea," Thompson lied. "But I think he's about to kill you."

Neal shoved Thompson's head down on the floor of the van. It was decision time and Neal was about to make one, every man for himself. Fuck Collins and the rest of the crew, Neal needed to get his arse out of there, and the car on the side of the road was probably his only ticket.

Wasfi crouched with his back against the grill of the van. The pain in his shoulder was not nearly as bad as when he had taken shrapnel as a pilot. He touched his jacket and looked at the blood on his hand. As he pointed the gun at the ground, he thought about his options. He determined his best option was waiting. Suddenly, Wasfi heard a voice shout out.

"I have what you're looking for, boy-o." Neal shouted loudly, his gun aimed at Thompson's head.

Wasfi was glad to hear the man wanted to start a negotiation. "Hurt him and you are a dead man," Wasfi replied. He recognized the man's Irish brogue and decided to play on his heritage. "If his blood is spilled, I can assure you you will never see another Irish sunrise."

"Tis' a bit of a standoff we have, then," Neal replied. He looked at Thompson and narrowed his eyes. "I want to get da' fuck out of here, and you want dis' piece of shit alive."

"And thus is our dilemma," Wasfi responded. He wanted the man in the van thinking he was in complete control. "What do you suggest?"

Neal needed the car. "I'm thinkin' you wrecked your own car, but it's still operational," he shouted.

"Oh, you are the clever one," Wasfi said sarcastically. He did not want his foe to think escape was going to be too easy.

"Shut up and go start the car," Neal instructed. When he heard the engine fire up, he continued. "Now you're to be layin' your gun behind the car in a place where I can see it."

Wasfi laid the gun down in a portion of the road where Neal could see it. "It is done," he shouted back.

Neal could see through the front windshield the instructions had been followed. The back door of the van opened slightly and Neal emerged from the back of the van. He had Thompson by the hair, and he had his gun placed firmly at the back of the Congressman's head. Neal saw the gun on the pavement by the back of the car.

When Neal instructed Wasfi to lie down on the ground, he complied. Neal reached Wasfi's gun, grabbed it, and tossed it over the stone wall. Neal smiled to himself at the thought he was in the clear. It was his time to make a clean escape.

Thinking of no one but himself, Neal shoved Thompson to the ground before literally jumping into the driver's seat of Wasfi's banged-up car.

The blood curdling scream cut through the thick dampness of the Irish air. Before exiting the car, Wasfi had wedged one of his knives directly under the driver's seat. When Neal jumped into the seat, the serrated blade plunged directly into his groin. Blood shot from the sensitive place where Neal had impaled himself on about three inches of the sharp double-sided knife. As Neal shot backwards from the extreme pain in his groin, the second knife Wasfi had wedged into the rip he made in the leather back of the driver's seat cut into Neal's back just above his kidney.

The combined pain in Neal's groin and back were so intense his pistol slid through his fingertips and fell to the ground next to the car. Wasfi moved to the side of the car and easily picked up the fallen weapon. He watched as Neal whimpered in the driver's seat. When Wasfi aimed the gun in Neal's face, Neal offered no resistance. "Do it," Neal instructed.

The bullet Wasfi put in Neal's head could have been considered a mercy killing, to put the Irishman out of his bloody, throbbing misery.

Wasfi walked back over to where Thompson lay on the ground and knelt down. He bit a tear in the duct tape on Thompson's wrists before ripping it all off.

"Come on," Wasfi instructed as he helped Thompson to his feet. He looked at his watch. "We have to move fast. You are about to see a lot of friendly faces. We need to get over this wall so we can catch a ride out of here."

Thompson rubbed his wrists. He heard the thump-thump-thump of approaching helicopters and looked directly at Wasfi. "Sure," he replied. "I just have one question."

"What is that my friend?"

"Who the fuck *are* you?"

FORTY-TWO

When Wasfi and Thompson walked down the hallway towards Ann's hospital suite, Josh was pacing nervously outside the room. The pair had been gone all day with no word from either of them. When Josh spotted the pair approaching, he met them halfway. Thompson smiled. His shirt was torn, but he looked amazingly calm. Wasfi's shoulder had been field treated and was in a make-shift sling.

"What the hell have you guys been..." Josh said as he hurried over to them, unable to complete the initial thought. "I've been going out of my mind here."

"What a mouth." Wasfi shook his finger at Josh mockingly. He looked at Thompson and laughed. "You need to talk to this young man about his deplorable language."

Thompson nodded his head at Wasfi in agreement. "Josh, do you kiss your grandma with that mouth?" he added in jest.

Josh looked at both of them in disbelief. Blood soaked through Wasfi's shirt and made a crusty stain. He did not know what to say to them.

"Do not worry," Wasfi smiled. "This will not go onto your permanent record at NATO."

"Cut the crap, guys." Josh shook his head. "Thank God Ann has been taking meds that have kept her sleeping this whole time. I had no idea what to say to her. What the hell have you guys been doing?"

Thompson looked at Wasfi who returned the gaze. Both simultaneously burst into laughter. "Just a little drive in the country, Josh," Thompson laughed. "I'm always up for a little drive in the country."

After Thompson and Wasfi were extracted from the Irish countryside by Lion, things happened fast at County Mayo Stables.

Rory Collins was used to the quiet of country living, and it took a minute for him to understand the significance of what he was hearing. First, he heard shouting from his men near the barns. The shouting was followed by a couple of shots from the ground. A louder burst of repetitive fire from the air ended all of the noise at ground level.

County Mayo Stables was under attack.

Collins looked out the window of the farm house and saw four small, six-bladed unmarked helicopters. Three were hovering over the farm and another was landing in a field a little farther up the road. Several farm hands were lying on the ground dead or dying, their weapons at their sides. Those not hit by the spray of bullets were also prone on the grass. A loud speaker from one of the helicopters was telling them to place their hands behind their heads. Those still alive were compliant.

The alternatives Collins faced were few and dire and none of them involved him walking away alive. Surrender was not an option as Collins had sworn he would never go to jail like his father. Waving a white flag would mean spending the rest of his life in prison.

Collins walked to his gun cabinet and looked at his small but lethal arsenal of weapons. He began stacking the rifles on the right side of his desk and ammunition for them on the left.

"If I'm going out," Collins mumbled as he kneeled behind the desk, "it'll be in a blaze of fuckin' glory." He took aim at the door.

When Hawk received word his crew was now extracting a United States Congressman from the target, he decided to go ahead and drop with the others. Bizarre was still the ground lead, but Hawk knew as mission commander, the safety of the Congressman was on his shoulders. He watched as Bizarre took full command of the situation.

Hawk surveyed the barns and farm house with a pair of infrared binoculars. The barns were clear, but there was someone in the farm house. The figure was kneeling in a weapons ready position, and his infrared image made him look like a glowing version of a green plastic toy army man a kid would buy at a five and dime store. He handed the binoculars to Bizarre. "Don't fire until we know the Congressman is extracted."

Hawk and Bizarre waited until they heard Lion in their ear piece. "I've got the package to be extracted. He is safe and unharmed. I repeat, safe and unharmed. Our other package has been shot, but not seriously wounded."

"Roger that," Hawk replied. "Get the wound field dressed and transport them both to the transfer site, ASAP. We'll find someone to de-brief the Congressman later."

"Roger that," Lion replied. "All parts have been collected and gift wrapped for delivery home."

Knowing the extraction was successful, Hawk turned to Bizarre. "Get the shit and finish the mission."

Several of the men on the ground located the F-14 parts and loaded them onto the lead Little Bird. They gave Bizarre a thumbs-up to signify their actions were complete.

"What about this joker?" Bizarre pointed towards the house where Rory Collins was hiding.

Hawk grabbed the mouthpiece to the helicopter speaker system, while keeping a watch on the house with his binoculars. "To the person there in the house," he shouted in the microphone. "You have one chance, and one chance only, to come out before we come in."

In his office, Collins reinforced his attack position and steadied his aim at the door. "Come on in then," he muttered to himself.

Hawk looked at Bizarre, who was kneeling to his side. "Time to end it," he instructed.

Bizarre smiled, stood up and pulled a large carrying case from the back hatch of the Little Bird. He flipped the case open and pulled out a Light Anti-Tank Assault Weapon. Before placing it on his shoulder, a 34 inch rocket was loaded. Bizarre awaited the command.

"Fire at will," Hawk instructed.

"Firing at will," Bizarre repeated, moments before pulling the trigger. "Knock, knock, motherfucker," was all Bizarre said as the farm house exploded in a magnificent ball of orange and red flames.

FORTY-THREE

"Not a bad ride," Josh said as he looked around the interior of the small jet NATO provided to return Congressman Thompson and Ann back to the United States. "I do like traveling in style."

Thompson looked at the headline on the local tabloid that read "Congressman and Wounded Wife Headed Back to the States." He folded the paper and handed it to Josh. "You did a good job on the press for us," Thompson said. "I really appreciate it."

"Thanks," Josh replied as he looked again at the article. "It was nice to be working for you again." Josh looked at a headline under the main article, "Gas Explosion at County Mayo Stables Leaves Owner Dead." He chose not to ask any questions about what connection Thompson and Wasfi may have had to the story.

Thompson and Ann held hands and smiled at one another. They were glad to put Ireland behind them. Ann was elated Josh had agreed to head back with them.

Ann sipped a cup of coffee and looked at Josh. "You've made the right decision," she said.

"Yeah," Josh replied. "It's time."

The young military officer assigned to act as Thompson's assistant on the flight approached.

"Congressman, we've established the conference line you requested," he said, handing Thompson a small speaker phone to place on the table separating the trio. "Here you go, sir. Everyone is on the line. You can start the conference by pushing the red button."

Thompson followed the instructions and hit the button. "Joe, are you there?"

"Right here." The Fat Man's voice sounded remarkably clear over the transoceanic connection. Britt Rodgers sat in the chair in front of The Fat Man's desk, taking notes of the call. "The team is assembled on my end."

Griffith jumped in quickly. "I'm here, too," he interjected. He was joining the call from his office in Northern Virginia. "How are you doing, Annie? Do you feel alright?"

Ann looked down and touched the bandages wrapping her leg. She appreciated Griffith's concern, but was honestly worried about the scars that would remain—mental and physical. But now was not the time to discuss them. "I'm good, Griff," she replied. "Thanks for asking. Although this was not exactly the vacation I envisioned."

Thompson squeezed his wife's hand for moral support. "Thanks for getting together today guys. We've got a few things to cover."

"Not a problem," The Fat Man replied. "Just tell us what you want us to do."

"Here's the deal," Thompson said as he leaned in to the speaker phone. "We're flying into a military base and then taking a chopper to Ft. Campbell. Ann's sister is bringing the kids down, and then we're headed over to Kentucky Lake. We're going to decompress and go sailing for a few days."

Griffith had a lot of issues he wanted to discuss with Thompson, but he knew now was not the time. "Good," he replied. "You've earned it."

"Thanks," Thompson nodded. "We need to spend a few days together as a family before we face the press. But, Griff, I want to be ready for their questions when we come home."

"Good idea," Griffith replied. "Try not to wait too long. I've got reporters crawling up my ass already looking for an interview."

"Don't worry," Ann interjected. "Richard will be giving them plenty to write about."

Thompson pulled a legal pad from his brief case and put it on the table. The pad contained the to-do list Thompson and Ann had drafted the night before. "Joe, are you ready to do some work on the lawsuit?" Thompson asked.

"Yeah," The Fat Man replied. He had anticipated the question and had been preparing various documents for filing. Rodgers handed him the drafts. "I've got the motion to dismiss ready to go. I've convinced Sullivan's daughter you're a good guy after all. She's agreed to join us in the motion. All you have to do is give me the go ahead to file it."

Thompson looked at Ann, then Josh. A conspiratorial smile flitted across his face. It was time to right some wrongs. "We're not going to file a motion to dismiss."

The Fat Man's eyes shot across to Rodgers, who shrugged her shoulders in silent reply. He was truly confused. "We're not going to dismiss. Why? What are we going to do?"

"We're going to confess a judgment," Thompson instructed as he placed a check mark next to the top item on his list.

"What?" The Fat Man's voice shot up.

"You heard me," Thompson said. "I want to confess a judgment against myself. Sullivan was right about what I'm doing here. I ran as the voice against pork projects and earmark spending. Now I'm bringing it home. I've thought long and hard about it. I need to be true to myself."

The Fat Man was not surprised at the rationale behind Thompson's decision. "Good man," he said as he smiled and nodded at Rodgers.

"Good man?" Griffith fired back over the phone. "What the hell are you saying? You're admitting you're wrong."

"I am wrong, Griff," Thompson said. "You know it and I know it. Now, I'm going to let the voters know it."

"Don't get all self-righteous on me, Richard." Griffith's frustration was coming loud and clear through the phone line. "An admission like that is political suicide. It won't hurt us now. They can't come up with anyone to run against us in the fall. But the next election will be different. The next election they will use it against you. They'll beat you up so badly they'll need dental records to identify your body. You know they will."

Thompson took a deep breath before making the next statement. "There won't be a next election, Griff."

The statement Thompson was calling it quits almost shocked Griffith into silence. "No," he pleaded. "You can't be saying what I think I just heard."

"I'm done." Thompson reinforced his previous statement. He was relieved he had said it and rubbed his forehead. "This is my last election, pal."

"You can't possibly be serious," Griffith exclaimed. "You're at the top, man. They can't beat you."

"The top," Thompson repeated and shook his head. "Maybe that's why I need to get out. The top changes people, Griff. We talked about it for years, sitting around watching our heroes being changed by power and influence."

Thompson looked at Ann, who was reinforcing his commitment with mere eye contact. "I've given up a lot over the years for politics. This time I almost lost what was most important to me. This time, Griff, it just wasn't worth it. I'm done."

Griffith tried another angle. "Don't announce it yet," he begged. "Give yourself time to reconsider."

"No reconsidering, man." Thompson shook his head. "Get the statement ready."

"Ann?" Griffith tried to appeal to a higher authority.

Ann expected Griffith would ask her to try to change her husband's mind. "I had nothing to do with it, Griff," Ann responded. "In fact, I tried to talk him out of it last night. But you know what he's like when he makes up his mind."

"I'm done, guys," Thompson reiterated. "Get used to it. This is my last race." He looked at the pad of paper and checked off the second item. "Anyway, Griff, I've got a new client for you."

"Who?" A disgruntled Griffith asked.

Thompson looked over at a freshly shaven Josh, who was blushing. Thompson checked the third and final item on the list as he spoke. "I've convinced Josh to leave NATO and move to Kentucky. I'm thinking he has a future in this business. He's going to need someone to help him build a political base."

As upset as Griffith was about Thompson quitting, he was begrudgingly excited about Josh coming home to set up a possible Congressional run. "Is that right, Josh? Are you moving to Kentucky?"

"Yeah," Josh smiled. "The Congressman and Ann have convinced me it's time to come home."

Griffith rolled his eyes. "So Annie's behind this?" he laughed. "I should have known."

"Maybe," Ann said slyly. "Anyway, I'm looking forward to playing a little match maker here. Joe, what's the name of Sullivan's daughter?"

"Tiana," Joe said. He paused.

"Tiana Sullivan-Barkman," Ann replied. "That has a nice ring to it, don't ya think, Joe?"

Josh looked up. "Whoa, hold on you two, let me at least find a place to live before you book the reception hall."

As the laughter subsided, The Fat Man continued. "On a more serious note, you won't even begin to believe what's been going on back here …"

FORTY-FOUR

Jane Kline sat stoically behind her large desk, arms crossed and her jaw set. There was little, if any, emotion in her expression. Her cane leaned against the side of the desk, and a single manila file rested in the center of her otherwise unencumbered red leather desk blotter.

Kline took a deep remorseful breath as she reached across her desk for her telephone and punched in a couple of numbers. "Zach, please bring Jimmy Day into my office."

Kline did not stand when Day and MacKenzie entered the plush office. Day looked nervous as he entered the room. "Have a seat, Day," Kline instructed in a firm voice. MacKenzie walked behind Kline's desk and stood just to the side of the Director.

Once both were seated, Kline started the meeting. She leaned forward and placed her arms on her desk. "Jimmy, do you have any idea why you're here today?" she asked.

Day's eyes shot over to MacKenzie. He shook his head. "No, Madame Director. I have no idea."

Kline could tell Day was lying. Her focus shifted to MacKenzie to see if he was picking up anything.

"Director Steele was assassinated," Kline continued. She slowly rubbed her chin, contemplating her next words. "It's become clear he was set up by someone at the Company. It was an inside job and we know who did it."

MacKenzie struggled to keep his face impassive as Kline spoke. He was enjoying the sight of Day squirming in his chair. Kline pushed her chair back and put her hands down on the desk to stand up. MacKenzie moved quickly to grab the director's cane and handed it to her.

As Kline began to walk around to the front of her desk, Day's eyes shifted wildly around the room. "What?" he asked. "You don't think it's me, do you? You don't think I killed Director Steele?"

For dramatic effect, Kline took her time moving to the front of her desk. She leaned her backside against the edge and faced Day. "Who else could it be, Jimmy?"

Day tried to stammer a reply, but Kline cut him off. "Whoever set up Steele had to be in daily contact with the Director ... someone who knew his schedule right down to the minute by minute detail ... someone who could extract information from the Director and then make sure it was never passed along to proper channels." Kline paused, but never broke eye contact. "Why did you take that day off?"

"Director," Day's voice was desperate as he leaned forward, "I had that day scheduled to be off for weeks. I went over all of this with our team following the explosion."

"Precisely," replied Kline. "You had asked for the day off weeks in advance. That gave you plenty of time to plan and execute the hit."

MacKenzie, arms crossed, fixed a laser-like gaze on Day. Kline was conducting the interrogation just as MacKenzie had prepared it. Day was going down. MacKenzie could feel it.

Day shook his head. "No," he said, rubbing his forehead. "No. I didn't do it."

"You had more access than anyone," Kline continued. She moved from her perch on the edge of her desk and walked across the office to the window. "I kept trying to figure out why you did it." She turned sharply. "Why did you set up Director Steele?"

Day turned his head and started to speak. "Shut up, Agent Day," Kline barked. "Shut up and listen." Day lowered his head and stared at the carpet while MacKenzie smirked.

"Now, where was I? Oh yes, I remember, I was discussing your motive." Kline pointed to her desk. "See that file?"

Day looked up and nodded. "Yes, ma'am."

"That file was prepared by Deputy Director MacKenzie especially for me. It sets forth, in detail, all the facts that point directly to you, Agent Day. Do you know the implications? Do you realize what my second-in-command has put in my hands?"

"No, ma'am," Day said miserable, cradling his head in his hands.

"Well, I have a certain reputation at the Company," Kline responded. "I'm a stone-cold bitch. So, normally, I'd read that file and Jimmy Day would simply disappear. I have no time for people who cross the Company. I've had too many of my colleagues die because of moles, and people who know me understand I would have no problem with dispatching you. Hell, most people around here understand I'd take pleasure in doing it myself. The file, Agent Day, is your death warrant."

Day sat transfixed on Kline.

"Enter FBI Agent Leo Argo. A couple of nights ago, someone tried to kill him and two of his friends."

MacKenzie's head snapped up in surprise. This was not part of what he and Kline had rehearsed. Suddenly all eyes in the room were focused on MacKenzie.

"What?" MacKenzie cleared his throat. "Madame Director, let's stay on point, and …"

"Your cousin is dead," interrupted Kline. She looked directly at MacKenzie for a reaction. "Would you like to see the crime scene pictures?"

"What cousin?" MacKenzie coolly returned, shrugging his shoulders. "What the hell are you talking about?"

"Come on, Zach," Kline said, her face as cold as her tone. "Don't be coy with me. You know God damn well which cousin. The one that has been stashing cash for you the last several months. And the little dance you set up here—trying to implicate Agent Day. From the start, it was just too damn perfect. It all fit too easily into place."

MacKenzie stiffened his back and raised his chin defiantly. "Director, I'm not sure where you're going with all of this, or what load of shit this FBI agent has fed to you, but I can assure you…"

"Cut the bullshit, you fucking coward." Kline cut MacKenzie off mid-reply. "I'm in no mood to be messed with today. My leg hurts, you know, the one I lost because of you."

"Jane, come on …," MacKenzie said nervously. His chin dropped slightly, his insistence suddenly a little less convincing.

"Steele was a political appointee," Kline continued. "When he got a tip about the illegal transport of F-14 parts from one of his colleagues overseas, he wouldn't know what to do with the information. Who would he go to … his driver? Or, would he give it to the policy analyst closest to him?"

"Day was with him constantly," MacKenzie insisted. "He heard everything Steele was working on. It had to be him."

"What on earth made you think you could play me?" Kline replied. "Because I'm a woman?"

"I'm not playing you." MacKenzie's eyes shot nervously to the two doors out of the office and took a small step forward.

"There's no where to run, sir," Day instructed, glad he didn't have to act any longer. He badly wanted to kill MacKenzie for trying to set him up for the murder of Director Steele. "It's over, asshole."

Kline could tell Day was getting angry. "That's all, Agent Day. Mr. MacKenzie won't be leaving. Thank you for your time and service on this. You're dismissed." Kline purposefully omitted MacKenzie's title.

"Yes, ma'am." Day's eyes shot daggers at MacKenzie as he left the room.

Once Day was out of the room, Kline looked at MacKenzie. "There's a funny thing about bank secrecy laws, Mr. MacKenzie," she said shaking her head. "In reality, those accounts aren't really secret. Once we looked closely at the hard drive you and your cousin were trying to get hold of, it didn't take us too long to figure out there were some wire transfers to Belize. Do you like Belize, Mr. MacKenzie?" When MacKenzie failed to reply. "Well, you must, because you have, or should I say had, a shitload of money in an account down there."

MacKenzie raised his chin in defiance, all pretense of innocence aside. "What now?" he asked belligerently.

"Open the top left drawer on my desk," Kline instructed. When MacKenzie hesitated, she encouraged his action, pointing to her desk. "Go ahead. Open the drawer."

MacKenzie stepped over to the desk and slowly opened the drawer. He looked up at Kline.

"You have a choice," Kline snapped.

"Choice?" MacKenzie snorted. "You mean like a 'right' or 'wrong' kind of choice? What the fuck do you know about right and wrong? You dispatched so many people in your career you can't tell the difference anymore."

"Maybe." Kline ignored the slur. "But your choice is how you die. You can do the honorable thing and do it yourself."

"Or..."

"Or, I can do it for you," Kline said coldly.

"I'm dead either way," MacKenzie replied. "What's the difference?"

"Me," Kline snapped. "I don't get the satisfaction of causing you as much pain as humanly possible before putting a bullet in your brain, you lousy motherfucker."

At Kline's pronouncement, Mackenzie bravado evaporated. "Jane, my family, will you guarantee..."

"Don't talk to me of guarantees," Kline said savagely. "You killed Steele for money you greedy bastard."

"But ..."

"The doctors guaranteed I'd never walk again without pain," Kline snarled. "They guaranteed my hearing in one ear is gone forever."

MacKenzie stared down at the drawer. "Promise me my family will never know."

"When you're carried out of here," Kline said, "I destroy all evidence of your involvement. Your wife gets your pension and your kids remain proud of their daddy's years of patriotic service."

MacKenzie reached into the drawer, pulled out a single pill, and placed it in his mouth. Within seconds his eyes rolled back into his head and he crumpled to the floor.

Kline exited the room, closed the door and headed down the hallway. She passed the Turk and another man. The other man was carrying a folded body bag under his arm. The Turk already planned the announcement that MacKenzie died of an apparent heart attack. But, before he released the news, Kline had one more item of business to wrap up.

"What's up, Tots?" Kline asked as she entered a conference room where a lone operative sat waiting.

Wasfi Al Ghazawi stood up to greet Kline. "You know I really hate the code name TOTS," Wasfi replied.

"You're the one who wanted to be known as The Orange Tufted Sunbird," said Kline, ruefully shaking her head. "I told you years ago the Company would make it into an acronym."

"You were right," he replied. "I should have just gone with Sunbird, but I was trying to capture the whole Palestinian national bird thing." Wasfi's smile faltered. "No matter what you say to the contrary, I know this situation has been difficult for you."

Kline waved away Wasfi's comments. "It's done and the Company is protected. Frankly, I would feel a lot better right now if I could have shot the bastard myself. But all in all, it's better this way."

"As you please, Director," Wasfi replied.

"I'm just glad we had you on site in Ireland, or I might have a dead Congressman on my hands—a Congressman I am quite fond of." Kline shook her head and laughed. "I can't believe you went to that horse farm at night by yourself. You realize we're getting a bit old for covert."

Wasfi laughed at Kline's comment. "I know, I know," Wasfi said. "But something did not fit about the shooting of Thompson's wife. I wanted to see the farm for myself. That's when I found the couplers. The engineers who designed the F-14 made the couplers unique. They wanted to make sure they could not just be bought off the shelf from some other manufacturer."

"Just like the $800 hammers a few years back," Kline replied, referring to the Congressional investigations into the custom manufacturing of specialty hammers for large amounts of money, when the same basic hammer could have been purchased at a hardware store for under $10.

"Precisely," Wasfi replied. "As soon as I saw them, I knew what they were and could pretty well assume where they were headed."

"Lot of chatter about Iran these days," Kline replied. "Thanks again. You kept my ass out of the ringer."

"Not a problem." Wasfi paused before tentatively asking. "Well, what do you think?"

Kline didn't pretend not to know what Wasfi was asking about. She knew he was asking about his cover. "I really can't tell."

"Give me your best guess, then," Wasfi replied. "Do you think the mole sold me out?"

"The fact you called the Turk directly may have kept you in the clear," Kline responded. "I already built a wall around MacKenzie by that point. I don't think he ever knew of your transmission. The Turk contacted me directly for authorization. I was suspicious of MacKenzie from the moment he came to visit me at my house. Anyway, my best guess is you're still in the shadows, but I can't be sure."

"Then I want to go back," Wasfi said immediately

"It's too dangerous right now," Kline replied. "It might be time to shut down Abraham's Olive Tree."

"I must continue," he pleaded.

"It's against my better judgment," Kline countered. Her gut reaction about field operations was usually pretty good. She was wavering a bit now, but she decided to stand firm. "It's time to pull out."

Wasfi sat down in one of the chairs opposite Kline. He leaned forward and spoke softly. "Director … Jane … I realize this all started as a cover, but the mission of Abraham's Olive Tree needs to continue. I was taught to believe that Moses, Muhammad and Jesus Christ were all direct descendents of Abraham. Maybe it is a myth. Or, maybe it is a historical fact. I cannot say. But I do know that Jews, Muslims, and Christians all have more in common than we want to admit."

Wasfi pointed to Kline's cane. "You and I walk with a limp for our convictions. I do not intend to make mine be an impediment to what I can accomplish for the remainder of my life."

"So you're quitting the Company?" Kline queried.

"No," Wasfi replied. "I need the Company to accomplish my mission. Jane. I understand how every mole sets the Company back decades. Just imagine what one Iranian F-14 Tomcat attack on Israel would have done to peace efforts in the Middle East. I need the Company as much as it needs me."

Kline smiled and reconsidered. "Okay, then," she nodded. "You can stay, but I'd like for you to move your operation to Ramallah. We can keep better contact with you there."

"Thank you, Madame Director." Wasfi stood up. Kline stuck out her hand. Instead of shaking Kline's hand, Wasfi bowed and kissed it. "Good day, Director

Kline." Before leaving, Wasfi paused, turned to Kline and smiled.

"What?" she returned his smile.

"I've known you for many years, Jane," Wasfi said. "I've made a life for myself outside of the Company. You're a suit now. You're not in the field. You're entitled to a life. You've earned it."

Kline felt uncomfortable at her old colleague's directness. "I have a life," was all Kline could muster.

"Very well, my friend." Wasfi shook his head, started to walk out and then paused. "I heard there is a man from the FBI who has shown great interest in you. What was his name … Argo?"

"Take a hike, Tots," Kline snarled laughingly as Wasfi walked out the door. "I can still change my mind you know."

There wasn't much said that evening as Jimmy Day drove Jane Kline home to her Alexandria residence. As the car turned down Duke Street, she dialed a number on her cell phone.

"Hey, Leo," Kline greeted.

"Jane …" Argo responded somewhat stiltedly. "How are you?"

"Hoover misses you," Kline replied. There was no initial response from Argo. "Leo, are you still there?"

"Yeah, I'm here," Argo replied. "How about you, Jane? Do you miss me?"

"Damn it, I miss you, too," Kline paused and then went out on a limb. "Why don't you come over tonight for dinner?"

"I'd like that." There was a sound of relief in Argo's voice.

Kline thought about her next words. "And Leo."

"Yeah."

"Bring your tooth brush."

Epilogue

The Fat Man walked down Main Street in Covington to the building where Sean Sullivan's laundromat once operated. The washing machines and dryers had been moved out months earlier. There was a fresh coat of paint on the outside. The neon sign had been removed from over the front doorway and replaced by a sign painted on the windows announcing SULLIVAN & SULLIVAN—Attorneys at Law. A birth and death date were below Sean Sullivan's name.

When The Fat Man opened the door, the bell gave a jingle. "Is this the world corporate headquarters of Sullivan & Sullivan?" he asked out loud.

Shirley Sullivan sat at a receptionist desk in the front of the storefront. "Why, yes it is, Mr. Bradley. Please come on in."

"I think these will look good on your desk," The Fat Man said as he handed a vase of red roses to Shirley.

Shirley was absolutely thrilled to receive them. "They are lovely," she exclaimed as she placed them on her desk. "I suspect you're here to see Lawyer Sullivan."

"Why, yes I am," The Fat Man replied. "That is, if she's not too busy to see an old colleague."

"I'll see if I can fit you in," Shirley smiled. She appreciated what The Fat Man had done for her daughter and was grateful he had already sent a couple of clients her way. A young man stood next to a table by the wall filing papers. "Antwone."

Antwone Mason turned around. "Yes, ma'am?"

"Will you please go tell Tiana she has a visitor?"

"Yes, ma'am." Mason walked towards the back room of the office.

"He's going to get his GED next month," Shirley nodded proudly. "Then we're going to help him go to the community college."

"That's great," The Fat Man said. He knew the kid's background with Sean Sullivan. "Let me know if I can help. I bet I can get the Congressman to help him find some grant money for college."

"No wonder Sean liked you so much," Shirley replied. "You're a good man, Mr. Bradley."

When Tiana walked from the back office she was beaming. "Hey, Joe." She gave The Fat Man a big hug and kiss.

"What's up, kiddo?"

"I have my first jury trial next week," Tiana said.

"I know," The Fat Man replied. "I brought you a little good luck gift." He handed her a bag with tissue sticking out of the top.

When Tiana removed the tissue and peeked inside, she was speechless. Then she started to laugh as she pulled out a pair of pink fuzzy slippers.

Acknowledgments

As book number four goes to print, I have come to understand more than ever that completing a manuscript is a team effort. "Team Thompson" is a great accumulation of sample readers, family, publishers, editors, publicists, friends, book store buyers and, this time, even a movie producer.

My sample readers do serious heavy lifting. Jim and Kathy Brewer, Eric Haas, Debbie Streitelmeier, State Sen. Damon Thayer, Jeff Eger, Mark Morris, and Dennis Hetzel all deserve a boat load of thanks. Aref Bsisu and Mark Oschenbein not only read the manuscript several times, but also helped with research.

The success of my last book, *Manifest Destiny*, was due in large part to the efforts of the folks at Paradies Shops who placed it in their airport stores nationwide. Thanks to Shelley Trotter, Pat Wallace, Greg Paradies and all the great Paradies employees who rolled out the red carpet for me over the past year. See ya again soon.

Authors Jack "JA" Kerley, Rod Pennington, Steve Lyons and JT Elliston always seem to be there for me when I have stupid questions. Tucker Carlson and Peter Tucci allow me to ramble about politics in the *Daily Caller* whenever the mood hits me. Tommy

Krysand with Pelican Sports Radio in Baton Rouge allows me on his radio show once a week to talk baseball. Thanks to all.

When *Manifest Destiny* was named the Best Indie Book of 2010 (thanks Bruce and Deb Haring), it got a lot of media attention. Shout out to Fred Anderson for noticing and hooking me up with producer Peter RJ Deyell, who now owns the movie rights. Fred's a darn fine proof-reader, too.

Thanks to Bob Elliston from Turfway Park for taking me to the spring sale (and for having a crash condo in Miami). Thanks to Frank Kling for taking me on a backside tour of the track. Located just steps from the paddock, Keeneland CEO Nick Nicholson has the greatest office in all of sports. Thanks for giving me free run of the most storied barns in the world.

Ultimate Jet Charter keeps me in the air and always on time. Rick Pawlak, Eddie Moneypenney and Barb Rohr make sure their jets are the only way to fly.

I will forever be appreciative of Sean Hannity and his crew for giving me my first national television appearance.

If you are getting tired of seeing my mug around town, blame my drastically underpaid publicist, Debbie McKinney. Thanks for 30+ years of friendship. I could not write these books without the critical editing of Jeff Landen. You're a great editor, but a better friend.

Kevin Kelly and Sherri Besso came up with another great cover.

Cathy Teets and all the folks at Headline Books sometimes believe in me and my books more than I do. No wonder Headline was the Indie Publisher of the Year for 2010.

My kids Josh, Zach and MacKenzie continue to be the inspiration for my writing.

There is nothing like having your wife tell you that a chapter really sucks. Fortunately my wife reads enough that when she makes such a declaration, I listen. These books are as much hers as mine. I don't say I love you often enough, so here it is in writing.

About the Author

Writ of Mandamus was named Grand Prize Winner at the London Book Festival January 2012 and Rick Robinson carried off honors as International Independent Author of the Year.

Writ of Mandamus has also won the following awards:

WINNER Indie Book Awards
   Best Mystery/thriller
Finalist Indie Book Awards
   Best General Fiction (over 80,000) Words
International Book Awards Finalist
   Best Mystery/Suspense

Best selling author P.J. O'Rourke says that Rick Robinson "may be the only person on Earth who both understands the civics book chapter on 'How a Bill Becomes a Law' and knows how to get good seats at the Kentucky Derby."

Robinson's previous novel, *Manifest Destiny*, was named 2010 Independent Book of the Year and he was awarded 2010 Independent Author of the Year. *Manifest Destiny* was also a Winner at the Paris and New York Book Festivals along with Finalist Awards in the USA News Best Book Awards for Best Thriller/ Adventure, Best Fiction Indie Book Awards, Best Thriller Indie Excellence Book Awards, Best Thriller International Book Awards, and Honorable Mentions at the San Francisco, Hollywood, London, and Beach Book Festivals. This title has also been optioned by film producer, Peter Dyell, and is headed for the big screen in the future.

Rick's first book, *The Maximum Contribution*, was named Award Winning Finalist in the 2008 Next Generation Indie Books Awards in the genré of political fiction. It also won an Honorable Mention at the 2008 Hollywood Book Festival. His second novel, *Sniper Bid*, was released on Election Day 2009 and opened on Amazon's Top 100 Best Seller list at #46 for political fiction. *Sniper Bid* has earned 5 national awards: Finalist USA Book News Best Books of 2009; Finalist Best Indie Novel Next Generation Indie Books Awards; Runner-up at the 2009 Nashville Book Festival; Honorable Mentions at the 2008 New

England Book Festival and the 2009 Hollywood Book Festival.

Rick Robinson has thirty years experience in politics and law, including a stint on Capitol Hill as Legislative Director/Chief Counsel to then-Congressman Jim Bunning (R-KY). He has been active in all levels of politics, from advising candidates on the national level to walking door-to-door in city council races. He ran for the United States Congress in 1998.

Other Books by Rick Robinson

Novels
The Maximum Contribution
Sniper Bid
Manifest Destiny

Non-Fiction
Strange Bedfellow